Red City on the Ocean

by Max Sprin

Montreal, 2023

Version 1

Dedicated to my daughter

Alina Spring

Ebook ISBN: 978-1-7380244-1-4

Paperback ISBN: 978-1-7380244-0-7

Book Design and Setting © Max Sprin 2023

Table of Contents

Introduction

The Reconquista – the centuries–old process of expelling Arab conquerors from the Iberian Peninsula – was coming to an end. The south of the peninsula was now scorched earth, abundantly watered with tears and blood.

The religious tolerance of the Iberian monarchs was also ending. The Spaniards and Portuguese expelled the Jews and the Muslims, who had taken root in their lands long before. The espoused monarchs, Isabella I of Castile and Ferdinand II of Aragon, were preparing to establish Catholicism as the singular religion of their now united kingdoms and end tolerance of all non-Catholics.

The Inquisition would formally be established in Castile beginning in 1478, which persecuted suspected heretics including "false Christians," Marranos and Moriscos, people who converted to Christianity from Judaism and Islam to avoid persecution. The Inquisition would spread across the entire territory that would become Spain and beyond even those borders.

The expulsion of the infidels was accompanied by the confiscation of their property, despite the fact that they often made large donations to the Reconquista. As they were driven out of the Iberian Peninsula, the financial systems of states, intellectual fields of activity, and refined crafts began to decline.

The kingdoms of Portugal and England had entered into an alliance that gave the Portuguese great advantages over their rival neighbors, the Castilians, as well as other naval powers of the Mediterranean. Portugal would soon enter the Golden Age of its history, an era when it would become the prevailing leader among the European maritime powers. However, Portugal's coming Age of Discovery still lay in the future, promising glory for the monarchies of the Iberian Peninsula. After all, taxes and trade, especially with overseas countries, remained a predominant means of revenue.

In 1481, King Afonso V of Portugal died of the plague. His exploration and widespread conquests in North Africa early in his reign earned him his nickname "The African." Along with his accomplishments in Africa, Afonso V also had eyes on Castile. He even once claimed the throne of Castile and sought the hand of the princess, the future Queen Isabella, but it never came to fruition. His son, Joao II, officially inherited the throne upon his father's passing.

In Portugal, there was an assembly that represented the estates of the nobility, clergy, and bourgeoisie called the Cortes, a precursor of a parliament, but at that time they were not yet a major political force and could not seriously influence the decisions of the king, who could summon and dissolve the Cortes at will. As a rule, Portuguese kings convened the Cortes only in exceptional cases such as when they were going to introduce new taxes or change the basic laws of the kingdom. These issues were often coordinated with as many subjects as possible. The Cortes delegates not only considered the king's proposals but could also submit their own petitions to the royal council.

Having ascended to the throne, Joao II began to revise many of the charters of Afonso V and previous monarchs. Many of the affected nobles were in the Cortes, and this caused sharp discontent among the nobles and great opposition to the throne. Some even started secret negotiations with Queen Isabella of Castile.

Joao II understood what the implications of his actions would be. Therefore, he decided to get ahead of his enemies, to strike first at the most powerful factions in the kingdom. The most prominent was represented by the country's largest landowner, Fernando II, Duke de Braganza. Fernando II was highly esteemed by the late Afonso V, and he and the duke maintained a strong friendship throughout the monarch's life and reign.

Some historians believe that Duke de Braganza counted on the support of not only the aristocrats but also the other members of the Cortes in his endeavors to curtail the powers of the king. However, apart from the wealthy aristocracy, few actually shared his political views. Much of Portugal was aligned with the monarch and hoped for expanded trade that would add both wealth and new territories to the kingdom from unknown lands across the sea. This conflict between the king and his wealthiest subjects would come to a head in May of 1483, causing a widespread crisis across Portugal.

The navigator Vasco da Gama's journey to India around Africa still lay ahead. He would accomplish the task of the century for Portugal – finding a sea route to India, and gaining access to their riches: spices, silks, and other valuable goods. Da Gama's predecessors had already established a small number of trading posts in West Africa, and Portuguese explorers had just reached the equator. Trips further south remained voyages into the unknown. In those years, no one knew how far they would have to go to explore the coast of Africa, and Portuguese navigators were captivated by the challenge of finding an alternative sea route to India. Some suggested sailing to the west to reach India, and although Portuguese sailors were quite capable of such trips, they may not be affordable for the king. After all, without knowing the distance, it was impossible to estimate the cost of a voyage. The captains had to persuade the monarchs to take great risks in order to get the coveted riches of India.

The existence of other continents in addition to Europe, Asia, and Africa, and even inhabited by people, was still unknown to the enlightened powers.

Chapter 1. Arrival

It was the earliest hours of the morning, and a full moon shone over the calm, almost motionless sea. If someone had looked out to sea from the shore, he would have seen two boats approaching the shore along the luminescent path. It was so bright that even from afar you could see men aboard them. The silhouettes of these people were complemented by feathered headdresses adorning their heads.

The first boat came to the shore and a half-naked man jumped out of it. He wore a scarlet loincloth, and a huge headdress towered on his head. A necklace of many strands of precious stones and gold covered his shoulders and chest with a wide stripe.

Other half-naked people began to disembark behind him. The first man was Coatl, the leader of the foreigners. His clothes and jewelry were far more exquisite and rich, distinguishing him from the others. His companion, who jumped ashore after him, was Ocotlan. He was a man of enormous stature with imposing muscles.

Tupac landed third — the commander of the ten warriors who followed him ashore. Moonlight glittered on bracelets, chains, and precious stones set in gold, which adorned the figures of these people, who otherwise wore only loincloths and capes made of squares of painted leather that covered and protected their shoulders. The chest of each was decorated with tattoos and a necklace of gleaming gems and sharp fangs. All the warriors wore fancy helmets that resembled the heads of jaguars or eagles except Tupac. Their faces were painted half blue, and half red or yellow.

Coatl fell to his knees and touched the ground. Under his hand was a smooth flat stone that still retained the warmth of the day. Ocotlan did the same, "This land is made of stone!" he said, looking at Coatl.

Coatl did not answer. Feeling the ground, he raised his head. Where the shore ended the smooth ascent, there was a high sheer cliff of black stone about four times the height of a man. "The coast here is not at all like ours," Ocotlan continued, "This is an inhospitable land."

"The land of Huitzilopochtli must be hidden behind this wall," Coatl said. "The wall guards his world."

Meanwhile, the stars, whose solid carpet stretched over the heads of the wanderers, began to disappear. The sky above the wall was brightening, and the moon – Coatl looked around – was also beginning to lose its dazzling brilliance. "Huitzilopochtli is coming out now," Coatl whispered reverently, "Maybe we can get around this wall somewhere." He looked around. In the distance, the wall began to descend. "Follow me!" Coatl commanded and began to walk along the stone bank wall; the other foreigners followed.

Coatl was accompanied by an elite group of people from Aztlan, their homeland. They were the finest, bravest, most invincible warriors. They walked with a springy gait that may appear odd to others. The rubber used in the thick soles of their shoes was virtually unknown to the rest of the world. The rubber was made from extracts that were expertly worked by the masters of Tenochtitlan. These rubber soles not only protected their feet and made their gait noiseless, but also allowed them to make huge jumps. As they reached the end of the descending wall, Coatl climbed up and found himself on the edge of a cliff, under which a black expanse of cooled lava stretched out to the sea. Coatl's twelve companions jumped up before they reached the end of the wall so that all were standing on the edge of the cliff.

The first rays of the sun were already bursting over the horizon. An unknown land stretched out before their eyes. Even from afar, it was clear that intelligent beings were cultivating this land. Here and there it was covered with rectangular plots of different colors, just like in their homeland, where different crops were grown next to one another. In areas where the land was not cultivated, it was lined with winding paths. However, the smells of this land, its crops, and its forest, darkening in the distance, were completely different from the aroma of their native shores.

Was Huitzilopochtli himself reigning somewhere nearby?

Coatl suddenly felt the weight of the golden plate hanging on his chest. The plate depicted a pyramid protruding from the water. The edges of the plate were decorated with multicolored gems, between which there were images of bizarre half-humans, half-animals in human poses. Coatl put his hand under the plate and began to rub his chest. Despite the freshness of the morning, he felt stuffy.

"Where is Huitzilopochtli?" Tupac whispered behind his back, eagerly peering into the darkness of the forest.

"Huitzilopochtli doesn't have to come to us right away," Coatl replied. "Before he descends to us himself, he may send his servants first."

As if to confirm Coatl's words, two figures emerged from the morning haze. They were moving along the road leading to the sea from the fields and woods. "Here they are!" Coatl exclaimed, and all the men, in one simultaneous movement, fell to their knees.

The two horsemen rode along the road. Some locals would have recognized them as soldiers from the Leiria castle, their faces and figures not yet disfigured by years of military service or peasant work. The soldiers were tipsy; having recently been escorted out of some roadside tavern that had closed for the night. Their armor, greaves, breastplates, and battle helmets were covered with dew.

One of them was just saying to the other, "Yes, Cristiano, that guy really hit you hard. Next time he sees you, though, you are going to really get it. He is never going to forgive you for what you did."

His other man remained silent. With his left hand, he supported his right. A huge bloodstain spread out on his sleeve. Suddenly he shouted, "Jose! Look!"

On the edge of the cliff in front of the riders stood a group of strange half-naked people. On the head of the one standing in front of everyone was a huge headdress made of colorful feathers, resembling the tiara of the pope depicted in the stained-glass window in the garrison church. The man's face was covered with jewelry made of turquoise and emeralds, hung wherever possible – on his nose, chin, and ears. The man standing next to him was distinguishable from the others by his tall stature and massive frame. His headdress was also strange, although not as big. The shoulders and chest of the giant were covered with a cape made of pieces of thick leather and decorated with feathers of unknown colorful birds.

All of the foreigners were on their knees and stretched out their hands to the riders as if wanting to embrace them. Their dark faces expressed confusion, even horror. Their hands were shaking; they were trembling with fear. They had never seen horses before, but the images of their teteo represented exactly such combinations of human and animal bodies. They believed in those depictions as much as anything they saw in ordinary life. But this appeared as if those paintings were actually coming to life!

One of the strangers, the man in the ornate headdress, was in front of everyone kneeling on only one knee. On his chest, in addition to the necklace, there was a large plate richly decorated with multicolored stones. The rays of the rising sun, bursting out from behind the soldiers, forced the ornate disc to reflect and even enhance the sunlight.

There was a deathly silence. It seemed that even the horses ceased to understand what kind of world they were in. Jose was the first to come to his senses. "Cristiano," he muttered. "Damn me, they have gold around their necks. I swear it's gold!" Turning back to the strangers, he yelled "Hey! Who are you? Cristiano, they probably don't even understand our language."

Cristiano, who continued to support his bloody right hand with his left hand, said, "They don't look like good Christians. Are they fleeing from the Castilians? Probably Marranos. Or maybe Moriscos?"

"How do I know!?" Jose exclaimed. The hops were beginning to fade from his head, giving way to a dull hangover. "I only know that if we pull their necklaces off their necks, we can feast for the rest of our lives. Think about it, friend. What do you say?"

Cristiano was silent.

Jose was only a couple of years older than Cristiano. But during this time, he managed to fight in many places and behead more than one enemy with his sword, whether it was enemy soldiers or Marranos or Moriscos who were attempting to avoid slavery. He looked at the newcomers attentively but could not figure out if they had any weapons. "Hey, you," Jose shouted, putting his hand on the hilt of his sword. "If you want to wander around our land, you should pay for the hospitality. Is that clear?"

The warriors continued to look at the riders in silence and horror. They thought the voices of the teteo should sound different. And yet these two-headed four-legged creatures could not be human either.

Jose, a brave fighter, was already figuring out which of the strangers would likely rush at them first. He had already identified their leader and noted the group of ten standing behind the three leaders comprised two separate groups. The upper arms of the five were tied with yellow ribbons, and their torsos were covered with jaguar skins. On the heads of these five were helmets in the form of jaguar heads with bared fangs. The other five, whose bodies were not covered with animal skins, wore crowns on their heads, from which eagle feathers scattered in different directions. In the middle, above the forehead, these headdresses were decorated with open eagle beaks, and scarlet ribbons were visible on their upper arms. The giant and another man standing next to the leader were clearly his confidants or assistants.

"We have come to meet Huitzilopochtli," said Coatl. "We implore Huitzilopochtli to let the world pass into the next Xuihpohualli and not let the fifth Sun fall on the people of Aztlan on the next New Fire ceremony. We no longer offer up gifts of those who celebrate our festivals with us, as the Nahui Ollin commanded us twenty-eight tonalpohualli ago. However, we bravely fight and are merciless to those who do not acknowledge Teotl, offering up their hearts, blood, and flesh in honor of Huitzilopochtli and other creators of everything natural around us!"

Jose stared at Coatl and silently tried to repeat the few syllables of his speech that he could make out.

Coatl looked closely at the riders and saw the blood on Cristiano's sleeve. He got up from his knee, lowered his hands, turned to his warriors, and said, "Stand up." The men slowly stood up. The silence that followed was broken by Tupac's whisper, "These creatures have two heads and four legs. Their magnitude is immeasurable."

"They must be incredibly rich," Ocotlan replied. "There is no metal in our land that is equivalent to that from which their macuahuitl and ichkahuipilli are made. It must be very strong. Have you seen how the sun plays on the tip of his macuahuitl? The end shimmers with a rainbow. The sun can only play this way on very sharp and hardened edges."

"And do you think these creatures are made of this metal themselves?" Tupac asked, squinting at Ocotlan.

Jose continued to look at the strangers' adornments with a grin, and it seemed to Coatl that he was beginning to understand the appraising looks of the creatures. Could it be that the gold from which their jewelry was made was considered an expensive metal in this land? After all, there was no gold on their bodies.

Jose got down from his horse. The foreigners shuddered as, before their eyes, a man seemingly took off his own head and, as if there were nothing unusual, put it next to him. The soldier approached the foreigners, and they leaned back. Fear continued to grip their souls. Jose was befuddled, but he could also see from the faces of the strangers how confused they were as well.

Jose pointed at the Nahui Ollin necklace adorning Tupac's neck. The latter looked over at Coatl with fright. "Does he really know what Nahui Ollin is?!" Coatl said with an astonished face, "Or maybe it was him who sent the great dream of Moctezuma at the last New Fire ceremony at the last Xuihpohualli? Tupac, give it to him."

Tupac took off the necklace and handed it to the soldier. Jose grabbed it, turned it over in his hands, and then threw it to his companion, who still sat on his horse. "Cristiano!" he said, "I do not know from what sideshow these curiosities escaped, but their jewelry is definitely enough to buy the whole damn tavern where that guy wanted to kill you. And also buy your own palace in Lisbon and hire a steward to look after it. With this gold, we will eat bountifully and sleep in comfort for the rest of our days. Did you fall asleep, Cristiano? What do you think?"

Cristiano, meanwhile, was speechless, looking at the piece of jewelry that he held in his hands. He had never seen such wealth, even on noble ladies in the church of Leiria during Mass. It was a large medallion hanging on a gold chain, a golden emblem in the shape of a butterfly with an image of a half-closed human eye in the middle. The edges were decorated with elaborately cut crimson, green, and transparent, precious stones.

"He has probably recognized it," Tupac whispered.

Jose raised his sword and, flashing the blade, drew an arc in front of Tupac in one fell swoop. The foreigners backed away again. "The teteo never demanded such paltry offerings from humans," Ocotlan declared.

"You're right. These are not Huitzilopochtli's messengers," said Tupac. "These are not spirits or their servants. If they are not friends of the creators, then they are no friends of ours either."

Ocotlan bent his right arm at the elbow, which immediately became tense with muscles, and raised his palm up with fingers splayed, the scarlet ribbon hanging from his arm. Immediately behind Ocotlan, the five warriors wearing eagle helmets and scarlet ribbons lined up in an even line. Ocotlan raised his left arm, marked with a yellow ribbon, and the warriors wearing jaguar helmets and yellow ribbons lined up behind the first.

Jose backed up to his horse and, without looking, grabbed her reins. There were no clear thoughts in his head yet, but something prompted him to worry. He expertly, without looking at the horse, jumped up into the saddle.

Cristiano tried to take up his sword but immediately groaned. The pain that flashed through his body made his right arm fall limp at his side. He took ahold of the crossbow strapped to his saddle with his left hand, pulled the bowstring at the ready, and aimed at Tupac, who was standing closest to him. Tupac looked at the crossbow in surprise.

"Show me the way to Huitzilopochtli, or he will meet you at the estli ahkopechtli," Coatl said, glaring angrily at Jose.

Ocotlan got down on one knee and rested his left fist on the ground. The warriors behind Ocotlan repeated his pose. They did it so smoothly that the soldiers no longer had any doubts about their intentions: they were going to attack!

Terrified, Cristiano pulled the trigger of the crossbow. The bolt whistled into Tupac's arm, rending the scarlet ribbon. The warrior clutched at the wound; the scarlet ribbon fell to the ground. The morning breeze picked it up and carried it off the cliff and out to sea.

Ocotlan jerked his right hand up. At this command, the jaguars crouched even lower, and suddenly leaping from their place, covering a dozen steps at once, jumped in different directions. Once on the ground, they encircled their enemies in a ring. The soldiers began to panic and look around at one jaguar, then at another. Although the strangers' faces were completely alien to them, the riders understood their expressions all too well. Nothing good would come of this. At the same time, the eagles got behind the jaguars in a combat stance.

Ropes flew and looped around the necks of the riders. Cristiano dropped the crossbow and grabbed his throat with his uninjured hand, trying in vain to free himself from the noose. In his other hand, he still clutched the Nahui Ollin necklace, but as the alien warrior tightened the noose around his neck, it fell from his hand. The warrior crouched down and began to pull the rope toward himself. Cristiano wheezed and fell off his horse. There was a crunch, the fall exacerbated by the soldier's heavy armor, his neck was broken.

Jose's gaze clouded; his eyes began to roll in opposite directions. He swayed in the saddle and fell off the horse. Luckily, he did not break anything in the fall but hit his shoulder hard. The soldier's horse neighed loudly. His hands reached out and grasped the necklace that Cristiano had dropped.

"What luck! Our first captive on Uehkatlan as we prepare for the Festival of Tezcatlipoca!" Coatl shouted, pointing at Jose, whose pupils were moving from side to side. "Tomorrow we will celebrate the first day of Toxcatl with dignity!"

Patli, the oldest of the warriors, who had been requested to join the warrior party personally by Ocotlan, walked up to Jose, who was lying on the ground. At the end of the year, he would be thirty years old, his face disfigured by war, his nasolabial folds leading to the ever-drooping corners of his mouth. He was the most experienced but at the same time a gloomy warrior. He always foresaw the worst course of events and was almost always right. He produced bundles of water-soaked vines from under his cape. A moment later, Jose's hands were wrapped in a knot of a strong vine, which Huitzilopochtli himself could not untangle. Patli lifted Jose by the collar and gave him a good kick. Smiles appeared on the faces of the warriors for the first time since landing on the shore.

Tupac caught Jose, who was awkwardly jogging to keep up, with his healthy hand, and snatched the necklace from the soldier's fingers, which he had continued to squeeze with some kind of childish faith in the legality of the property that once turned out to be in his hands. Tupac put the necklace back on his neck and looked around.

Ocotlan came up to the injured warrior. "Close your eyes," he said. Tupac squeezed his eyes shut. Ocotlan took hold of the bolt still sticking out of Tupac's upper arm and pushed it forward. From the other side of the shoulder, along with the flow of blood, the tip came out. Tupac growled softly. "Be a real warrior and endure," Ocotlan said. He felt the metal tip of the bolt and was surprised. It was amazing how the exact shape had been molded by the blacksmith who forged this tiny point from an unknown solid metal. Ocotlan broke off the tip and, grabbing the bolt by the shaft, pulled it towards himself. Tupac screamed in pain.

"That's it, Tupac," Ocotlan said, showing the warrior the tip and shaft of the bolt. "Take a sip of octli and the pain will pass. Tomorrow you will celebrate Toxcatl with everyone. Hey, who's got a piece of maguey cloth? Bind this wound on his arm!" Patli picked up a drop of blood from Tupac's hand with his finger and put a red dot on his shoulder, just above where the ribbon had been tied.

"Congratulations, Patli," Coatl said to the old warrior. "Your captive will be a special gift for Tezcatlipoca. This is a wonderful gift from Uehkatlan to the Toxcatl festival. This has never happened before!" The loud victorious cry of the warrior resounded over the black stones of the inhospitable shore.

A Moment from the Past - Little Estela

In the center of a Portuguese town, houses on both sides of the streets stood so close to each other that neighbors could shake hands over the pavement without leaving their homes. There was always little light here, but these two girls knew a place where the sun shone brightly all day. It was there, at the intersection of two narrow streets, under the canopy of a spreading sycamore tree, that they were sitting. One of them was saying something and rocking a rag doll in her arms. The other girl also had a doll in her hands, making it walk along the ground. Each toy was made of the same fabric from which its owner's dresses were sewn. One, multicolored, was sewn from small pieces of fine foreign-made fabric. The other, a dingy drab gray, was made from a piece of unbleached wool. The first doll was always clean because dirt simply did not cling to it. The second kept traces of all the tumbles onto the ground and into puddles.

A tall, burly woman came around the corner, a basket hanging from her half-bent arm. Passing by the girls, she broke into a smile. "Good afternoon, Senhorita Marisa," she said. The woman took out a pie from the basket, golden brown, lush, with streaks of jam, already hardened on the underside. She handed it to the girl in the brightly colored dress and, smiling once more, went on.

"Say hello to your mother!" she shouted as a farewell.

The girl brought the pie up to her mouth but changed her mind. She broke it in two and handed the smaller half to her friend. They both began to eat heartily.

A little later, another woman appeared on the otherwise deserted street. She also carried a basket, but her burden was much heavier than a basket of pies. It was obvious from the face and gait of this young woman that she was very tired, and it was still early; the sun had not even reached its zenith. The girl in the gray dress jumped up and rushed to meet her. "Mom! Mom!" she grabbed the handle of the basket and pulled it towards her.

"Don't take it, dear," the mother said. "You can't carry it; It's heavy."

"Mom, why was Marisa given a pie and I wasn't?" the girl asked, sincerely puzzled.

"Because Marisa's father is a lieutenant general," her mother replied with barely noticeable sadness, "and Marisa is also wearing a beautiful dress. Your dad is a simple captain and is far across the sea in Africa. However, if he returns victorious, he will be promoted, and you will no longer be the daughter of a simple captain." The mother smiled and kissed the girl. "In the meantime, come along, Estela, you can help me do the laundry."

The girl sighed and, looking back at her friend, waved her hand. Mother and daughter walked side by side. "Do you really need a beautiful and expensive dress to be fed with sweet pies?" the girl thought with resentment.

"Mom, will you make me a new dress?" she asked.

"Of course!" the mother immediately replied. "If your dad defeats his enemies, the king will reward him handsomely. Then Dad will buy us as many beautiful fabrics as he wants, and I'll make new dresses for both of us." She shifted the laundry basket to her other arm and, unnoticed by her daughter, wiped her tears.

Chapter 2. The Scarlet Ribbon

On the afternoon of May 20, 1483, Leandro hosted guests at his Sinta estate. Sometimes it happened that the table in the dining room of his house was full of fried pheasants and partridges, jugs of wine and cider, pates, and dishes with pieces of roast beef, lamb, and stewed vegetables. A huge farm with fields, orchards, vineyards, and homes of peasants who regularly paid rent or worked on the estate, provided everything that the owner and his family needed, but lavish feasts in the manor house rarely happened. As a rule, they only occurred on those days when Leandro's guests were not those closest to him.

Today, the usual family dinner was being held at Leandro's house, and apart from the household, there was only Estela, daughter of the castellan of the fortress of Leiria, and Senhor Bianco, the new assistant to the Venetian envoy. Senhor Bianco said he specifically wanted to visit Don Leandro at his estate so he could expand his knowledge of Portugal in a relaxed atmosphere.

Contrary to the custom at large feasts, women did not occupy a separate part of the table but sat mixed with men. Estela was sitting next to Leandro's son, Nuno. Nuno could only see the girl's dazzling beauty in profile. It was pleasant because Estela's face had one flaw — a deep wrinkle that ran through her forehead. In Nuno's imagination, this wrinkle never appeared, but every time he looked at Estela's face, the slight imperfection surprised him as if he were seeing it for the first time. From this angle, he couldn't see this blemish.

Nuno and Estela were the same age – both were seventeen. Many years ago, a jousting tournament was held in the fortress of Leiria, which gathered all the surrounding nobility including Leandro and his family. After the tournament, Daniel, Estela's father, the castellan of the fortress, invited his wealthy neighbor, the landowner Don Leandro, to a feast. Manuella, Nuno's mother, and Carmina, Estela's mother, met at this gathering, and having children of the same age, found they had much in common to talk about. Moreover, their children immediately started chatting with each other as if they had been friends for many years.

Neither the destiny of Estela nor Nuno had yet been truly decided, and these destinies were developing quite strangely.

The other children born to Daniel and Carmina had all died one after the other. Estela was the only child who survived, and her parents loved her unceasingly. Estela, as a child, would often play with the toys of her deceased brothers and sisters, weathered tops and worn dolls - she adored them all the same. Daniel had no choice; he needed an heir, so he raised Estela like a boy. He carried her on his saddle, took her hunting, and put her next to him at feasts. The strange mark on Estela's forehead was a mystery to her mother, but Daniel remembered well. In just one evening, Estela's character had changed forever. It happened after he ordered her to slaughter a wounded baby deer. In the morning Estela woke up with this wrinkle and a look completely unfamiliar to her father.

After Daniel's distinguished fighting in the battle of Asilah, Morocco, in 1471, the king awarded him by making him castellan of the fortress of Leiria and its environs. The fortress, which stood only a day's gallop from Lisbon, guarded one of the central districts of Portugal. In the twelve years following, he spared no expense for teachers and tutors for his daughter, and Estela grew up an intelligent, inquisitive girl with a strong character. Eventually, Estela, with the help of the king, became the first Portuguese woman to attend university. At the university, she inevitably turned out to be the most resourceful in academic debates, the most knowledgeable book reader, and the most astute natural scientist.

Leandro treated Estela with a level of respect that a woman of that century was rarely afforded by men, and not just because she was Daniel's daughter. He and Don Leandro were not friends, and although Leandro still had a little respect for the famous soldier, he disliked his constant readiness to fulfill any order of the king. However, Estela was a completely different and internally independent human being.

In Leandro's spacious house, which Estela visited from time to time, there was even a special room for her, and on the occasions when she came to his estate, sometimes with her mother, sometimes with servants, and in recent years alone, he was always amazed to see how she flourished. And each time he was surprised and delighted by the growth and strength of her character.

One day, Estela, who was about twelve years old at the time, came with her mother to visit Leandro's family. The owner himself had left for Lisbon for business. Nuno and Estela went for a walk around the estate, and the girl noticed that the foresters had left harvested logs, intended for the construction of a new forge, right on the ground. Estela knew that the forge was to be built the next season. She ran and caught up with the foresters' wagon train and forced them to go back and stack the logs properly — on the baseboards, and so that their ends were facing the wind, which typically blew from the direction of the field. If the logs were left lying on the ground, they would quickly begin to rot. Such attention to detail was unusually astute for a twelve-year-old girl. Leandro greatly appreciated Estela's quick action, and from that time, he always heeded what Estela brought to his attention when she came to visit his estate.

As for the son of Leandro, his world was vastly different. He also grew up a favorite of his parents. However, they were completely different from Estela's father and mother. Nuno was allowed to bask in bed in the morning, and water was warmed for the whole house in the mornings just for him alone. His life was spent in dovecotes, fields, and groves, where he and Luis, his childhood mentor, studied the habits of various forest and field creatures. On rainy days, Nuno usually played dice and other games with Luis, listened to his stories, or sat reading a book from his parents' rich library. Nuno had a clear gift for painting; he was especially adept at depictions of animals. His father, finding his son's sketches in the margins of books, sighed, vexed, but at the same time he admired them. No matter what Nuno grew up to be, it was already clear that he would be good at everything. It was just the waiting, perhaps another year, no more. His parents believed firmly that childhood should be lived to the fullest. In the meantime, let him read books about giants and monsters, about travel and adventures – no one has ever gotten worse from reading books.

However, it cannot be said that Nuno plunged into his boyish amusements and books too deeply and irrevocably. He would also spend hours hanging around the blacksmiths, carpenters, or craftsmen who worked around the estate, helping them, finding some work for himself, or even replacing the occasional novice worker. He was good at crafts and in all the occupations that required skilled hands.

Sometimes peasants and artisans invited Nuno to lunch, and he ate lentil soup from a common bowl hungrily and broke off pieces of bread from a single large loaf. For this, he was repeatedly reprimanded by his mother. She did not trust the cleanliness of the peasants. Besides, after such meals, Nuno ate little at family dinners, which also upset her. Nuno grew up a kind boy, maybe too kind. Manuella, his mother even once had a nightmare that Nuno became a monk, after which she kept checking on Nino's adventures with suspicion in regard to his future.

On this afternoon, Manuella was sitting at the table directly opposite Nuno and, as usual, trying to imagine the fate of her son. From time to time Estela said something to Nuno and pressed her lips to her cup. Manuella noticed that Estela carefully examined a piece of cheese in the dish in front of her and crumpled it with her fingers. Manuella was not at all surprised by this, and even more so she was not offended by Estela's attitude to the treat. She was well aware of the young lady's upbringing, and this attentiveness to quality made her so different from Nuno. Leandro behaved exactly the same as Estela since he knew well the value of the dishes that were on his table.

The house musician, who was sitting in the corner of the dining room and leisurely plucking a lute, suddenly left the strings alone and coughed. Leandro's voice became clearly audible. He told Senhor Bianco, "You see, mio caro, our country is in many ways similar to the Republic of St. Mark. The Doge of Venice has enormous powers, and yet he is not omnipotent. The Doge takes into account the opinion of the Grand Council. Everyone remembers that Doge Marino Faliero paid with his life when he went against the elected statesmen. Our king, may the Lord grant him many summers, is very similar in his ways." After drinking wine, the usually stern Leandro began to relax and did not notice that his voice was getting louder. "The Cortes is the name of our assembly of representatives from the nobility, clergy, and citizens," Leandro continued. "They can submit proposals, requests, or complaints to the king. Sometimes the Cortes even hands a paper directly to the king with a ready-made decree he can read and sign. Here, the right of the king remains exclusive; he may, by his sole decision, accept the decree or reject it, and then the Cortes may have to ease their proposal so that the king approves it."

Leandro kept silent about the fact that the current king had ceased to reckon with the Cortes.

"The government of your kingdom has employed the best features and policies of the republics of antiquity, Don Leandro," Bianco said. He arrived in Portugal quite recently but already spoke Portuguese well. "But what about nobles? Do the aristocrats find a common language with merchants and act together?"

"Tell it straight, Leandro," Manuella said. "We are not some Arabian army on a campaign circling around in the desert. In our country, as in Venice, among not only nobles but also merchants and priests, there are people who can directly petition the king about the needs of their estates."

"That's right!" Leandro slammed his fist on the table emphatically. "The support of the king is primarily given to the military, merchants, peasants, and clergy. The nobles, who, as is commonly believed, owe everything to the royal throne, are more likely to be in opposition to the king, but all of the estates make up the Cortes."

"Don Leandro is part of the Cortes," Manuella continued, looking at Bianco with a smile. "He is a representative of the nobles, although the nobles consider him first a friend of the people, and only then a servant of the king." Leandro nodded grimly. Even his wife had little idea to what extent the new king was neglecting the old way of government in the country. The King did not want to hear the voice of the people, believing that he knew their needs better than the Cortes. He just spat on them, sawing off the branch on which he was sitting!

Nuno did not participate at all in this conversation or any of the like. He cared little about state affairs. Sometimes he wanted to ask his father to stop worrying so much and consider that he himself might be wrong. The king couldn't have acted so rashly if so many were on his side. But of course, Nuno couldn't afford to say that out loud. Suddenly, he felt Duarte's cold nose nuzzling his knee. The big dog, who faithfully accompanied Nuno outside the house, was lying under the table and clearly bored. Nuno lowered his hand, and his palm was immediately moistened by the dog's warm tongue.

The huge, gate-like entrance doors creaked. Francisco, the steward of the house and estate, entered the hall. After making a slight bow to the assembled guests, he walked over to Leandro and, bending his head, said something quietly.

"What?" Leandro cut him off mid-sentence. "Speak your report aloud."

"Yes, Don Leandro," Francisco obeyed. "News just arrived from the settlement by the sea. A dead man was found there, right on the seashore."

"Oh, my!" Manuella exclaimed.

"A peasant? From the fortress? A sailor?" Leandro asked with surprise but remained calm.

"So far no one has recognized him. They only said that he was young and simply dressed. He looks like a soldier, although he did not have a weapon with him."

Estela raised her cup to her lips, took a sip, and calmly asked Nuno, "Well, shall we examine the find? You seem to know all the local dogs and boys, don't you?"

"Won't you be scared?" Nuno asked apprehensively. "I must admit, I don't like dead people."

"It's time to get used to it," Estela said. "Times are restless these days." She turned her attention to Leandro, "Don Leandro! You won't mind if Nuno and I go, will you? We can inspect everything and report back to you when we return."

"Go ahead," Leandro agreed. "Just take someone with you; take Luis."

* * *

Estela and Nuno were approaching the stable. There, Francisco's son, Raul, together with Luis, were already saddling horses. In one hand, Nuno held a bow, and with the other, he adjusted the strap on which hung a quiver with arrows. Duarte wagged his tail and romped in circles around his owner. Luis gave Nuno the reins of the bay horse, and the boy jumped into the saddle in one fell swoop and looked at Estela. She put her foot in the stirrup and pushed away Raul's hand as he was trying to help her. The moment Estela jumped up on the horse, her beautiful blue dress outlined, for a brief moment, the shape of a girl's body in all its hidden beauty. Nuno's breath caught in his throat.

"You can spot good horse owners right away," Estela said, stroking the head of her white mare. "No iron in the bridle."

A minute later, Luis led the horse he had saddled for himself out of the stable, and the riders started off. Estela's shock of luxurious flaxen hair trembled in time with the light trot of her mare. Luis brought up the rear.

The road began to descend, and Estela looked back at the house they had just left. It was a solid two-story pink house. Perhaps it could even be called a palace since it included several buildings adjacent to each other. The huge windows, with jagged borders on the edge of the roofs, seemed to resemble fortress walls. The house, surrounded by a variety of trees and bushes, stood on a raised platform, which was surrounded by a high border of rough stone that also resembled a part of a fortress.

However, inside everything was quite peaceful. The rich decoration—starting with the spacious, carpeted staircase leading to the second floor—was often the subject of Leandro's obsessive worries. He had suffered much since his youth as his parent's house fell into disrepair following the death of his mother. Estela thought of her own childhood home with sadness and distaste. Life within a fortress can also leave a military imprint on the dwelling of the Castellan, which Estela's mother tried to manage. There were damp walls, dusty carpets, a disgusting smell from the street where both horses and soldiers defecated with equal ease, and the inescapable smell of dinner cooked for two hundred people at once. Of course, when her father became a castellan, they moved to a house outside the walls of the fortress. But even that house was a doghouse compared to Don Leandro's mansion, and to her kennel, she would have to return.

***

Nuno and Estela rode along the forest road – each on a different side of the tracks left by the wheels of peasant carts and manor carriages. From time to time, they had to bend down to avoid a branch of a spreading oak.

The two-and-a-half leagues separating the estate from the seashore were already coming to an end, but the forest through which they were traveling was still quite dense.

Life triumphed in its depths. Birds were singing with might and main, the hubbub drowned out by Duarte's barking now and then. The flowering branches had already shed their white, carmine, and yellow petals, and in some places, pistils could be distinguished on them. The forest consisted primarily of thickets of cork oak with almost no undergrowth. In some places, among the oaks, one could see lonely juniper bushes, from a distance looking like travelers wrapped in cloaks, frozen. Among the customs of the local peasants was the rule: collect the stones of eaten plums, oranges, apples, olives, and other fruits, and then scatter them in suitable places. Therefore, fruit trees also found places for themselves among the oaks, and by how often they were seen, travelers could judge how close they were to human habitation.

Suddenly the way of the riders was crossed by a red flash of a fox rushing at full speed. Duarte followed her out from under the canopy of the forest. A moment later, the dog disappeared into the thickets on the right side of the road in pursuit. Duarte, spoiled today with leftovers from the master's table, was not in a hurry. He didn't even have enough desire to hunt or bark. From the thickets came only a lazy, low-voiced growl that echoed deep into the forest. It seemed that the appearance of the fox offended Duarte more than it humored him.

Estela, assessing the situation, asked casually, "Why aren't you hunting, Nuno? You have a bow and arrows."

Nuno looked at Estela's beautiful, sculpted face and shrugged. He had a hunch about where this conversation was going. "I don't really like hunting."

"Then why do you need a bow?"

"My father says that sooner or later I will need it, that I should master the art of war," Nuno mused, and then continued in a more joking tone, "Besides, we're not going on a holiday. In the forest, you know, it's not always peaceful. Estela, you seem to have lost your sense of it while in Lisbon."

"And what art of war have you already mastered?"

"With a sling," Nuno said.

Nuno really had learned how to throw stones with a sling. He had already hit the target at a hundred or more paces. The skill came naturally. He just had to throw stones as often as possible and, at the same time, keep in mind the feat of David, who struck the giant Goliath.

"They say you hit yourself last week, Nuno? Is it true?" Estela smiled.

Nuno laughed abashedly. He knew who would have told Estela about this.

"Yes. The stone fell out of the sling and hit me in the leg."

"Did it hurt?"

"Not really. No more painful than a hammer blow on a finger in the workshop," Nuno continued to laugh.

"And that's why you decided to change your sling for a bow and arrows?"

"No, my father says that I will need to master this weapon as well, and I want to learn to do it on my own. Here, look…" Nuno took an arrow from his quiver, nocked it on the bowstring, pulled back, and shot at the remains of a huge, bark-less oak tree that could be seen in the depths of the forest. The arrow pierced right into the middle of the trunk at the height of a man. Luis rode unhurriedly to the oak tree to retrieve the arrow.

"Bravo," Estela said calmly. "But you know, if you're going to command a regiment of archers, you probably won't need this skill. Don't you want to learn how to command? Or build fortresses? Or both? My father could help you master those arts."

"I don't want to," Nuno muttered, "And in general, I like the peaceful life on the estate. Not war." It wasn't that he didn't like studying, it was just that Nuno was interested in completely different things in his studies, and as for the art of war, he did not want to be a soldier at all. Shooting a bow at a tree is one thing, but shooting an arrow at a person, or even an animal, is quite another. A quiet life, where there was no need to even think about such things, suited him perfectly.

"And I don't like the countryside," Estela said. However, she immediately secretly admitted to herself that Nuno's estate was different, and she really liked staying there. She stood up in the stirrups and straightened the folds of her dress. "I am interested in studying and learning. Do you understand? And you can only study at a university in Lisbon. I enjoy talking to smart people. Village life makes people stupid. Even the smart ones."

"And what do they say in Lisbon?"

"Our navigators have returned from a long voyage to Africa. Many hope that soon merchants will begin to carry black slaves and gold from there. Perhaps some of the new slaves will soon be working in your fields." Estela looked ahead. Nuno gazed at her as she spoke, she had the visage of the marble Aphrodite standing in the hallway at his father's house. Alluring lines reached from the outer corners of her blue eyes almost to her temples.

"And what do smart people say at the university?"

"They say that an arrow that flies, at the same time, stands still. It wouldn't have occurred to me before, but now a new logician and mathematician, a Greek from Constantinople, came to lecture us, and he explained it all. Achilles will never catch up with a tortoise; If you break off half of a stick it will never end, because it must reach half before it reaches the end. And all this can be proven, you know?"

"Are you really interested in all this, Estela?"

"Something else surprises me, Nuno. Why aren't you interested in this? You're so smart! So talented! You draw beautifully, shoot accurately… You have no equal in chess."

He just laughed. "Well, you beat me twice" He was glad to end the conversation as they approached the seaside. "It seems we're getting to the place." From afar, the muffled roar of the surf could be heard.

"There's a cliff already visible," Luis interrupted their conversation, pointing forward with an arrow he grasped in the middle.

"What do you think happened there?" Nuno asked him.

"A drunken fight; it must have been," Luis shrugged, giving the arrow to Nuno. "Maybe over some girl; maybe they fought over a debt. Sometimes they fight without any reason, out of boredom."

* * *

As soon as the riders left the forest, a salty sea wind hit their faces. At the top of the coastal cliff, they saw a crowd of people. Even from this distance, it was clear it was the locals – peasants and fishermen from the nearest village. Grimly, without looking into the faces of the riders, people began to move to allow Nuno, Estela, and Luis space to pass through. Along the road that ran near the shore, lonely merchants drove their donkeys and nags. They rode around the crowd of dirty peasants, trying not to look at them.

Just off the road, a dead man lay face down, partially obscured by the crowd of villagers. Two saddled horses stood nearby, grazing as if nothing had happened, the grass surprisingly thick and lush for a rocky peak. Nuno and Estela rode up to the crowd where it had parted, and the riders dismounted.

"Turn him over," Estela ordered imperiously. The dead man was turned over.

Looking into the mirrors that decorated the manor house in Sinta, one could not see oneself well. The quality of even the most famous and well-made Venetian mirrors was too low at that time, and yet Nuno was familiar enough with his own reflection. He realized that the dead man looked much like him, with the same boyish face, the same youthful figure, and slightly above-average height. Even the clothes were the same – a dark leather sleeveless top over a white shirt and black pants tucked into dark boots. There was a spot of dried blood on the dead man's right sleeve. His unnaturally twisted neck was surrounded by a dark blue bruise.

Nuno had never thought about death before. The concept itself seemed far away from him, but as he now contemplated, here it was, death, right in front of his face. This young man could easily have been himself, and no one would have asked him if he was ready to die. The realization of this scared him the most.

"Has he been identified?" Estela asked and once again examined the villagers around her with her sharp gaze. The crowd was silent. The men looked at Estela from under their brows, her beautiful dress and white face. Hardly any of them had seen such a beauty before. Villages were not rich with beautiful women and by the age of Estela, beauty would have already faded, their faces dark from the sun, lined with worry and the boorishness of their husbands.

"Can anyone tell me what kind of person this could be?" Estela raised her voice. "Are these his horses? Why are there two of them? Where is the second rider?"

The crowd pushed a strange little man in a torn shirt with the sleeves rolled up to Estela and Nuno. There was a smile on his face, either drunk or insane. "Maybe he knows," someone in the crowd said. "Come on, Augustine, say something."

"It seems like there were two of them, Your Grace," the peasant said in a raspy voice. "I've seen them both on horseback. They rode along the coast. Then, they came up here, but then I didn't really look."

"Where did the second one go?" Estela asked. "Maybe someone in the village or on the road saw a stranger?"

The crowd was silent. The village fool, Augustine, was still grinning with a toothless mouth.

"Luis," Nuno called. "Have you seen this man before?"

"I won't say so directly what I saw or didn't see," said Luis. "I don't look at faces, they all lie. But his shoes seem familiar to me. One craftsman makes such boots in the fortress in Leiria. He stitches along the sole with a red thread with just such a special design, it requires a special talent. It is red, and not faded yet. I am not mistaken; I used to wear boots like this myself once. That cobbler made these boots; they are from there; that's for sure."

"Cristiano!" Nuno suddenly exclaimed. He stepped closer to the body of the deceased and shouted again as if he wanted to wake a sleeper: "Cristiano!" Duarte, who finally came running out of the forest, raised his muzzle to the sky and howled. "I remember him! This is Cristiano. God, how he's grown!"

"Who's Cristiano?" Estela asked.

"I knew him as a child," continued Nuno. "He taught me to sail a boat against the wind near Villa De Porto. How could I have forgotten him? Five years have passed! But he was already a real sailor then! And the son of a sailor, it must be!"

Nuno couldn't believe how suddenly death could overtake someone he knew. Once upon a time, he and this man chatted and laughed carelessly together. How could something so terrible happen to someone so young? It seemed unnatural. Estela was silent. Luis shrugged and sighed. There was nothing they could do. Or could they?

"Luis, go to the village and bring someone from the undertaker," Nuno said, recovering from the shock. Luis picked up the reins of his horse but then dropped them, waved his hand, and began to descend to the plain.

"I really need to wash my face," Estela said, tired of the road and the weight of what was happening. "Let's go down to the sea."

Nuno didn't mind. He needed to quell his anxiety. Fortunately, the shore was quiet and completely deserted. The lava, once cooled, was piled up here in a solid wall, as if skilled masons created even layers of the same thickness. Where the lava gave way to the sea, the shore was intricately drawn into squares. The gaps between these black squares, some regular, some slightly oval, were covered with light sand, and therefore the shore below the cliff resembled the back of a giant turtle.

Estela filled her palms with water, splashed it on her face, sighed, and looked at the sun, and then at Nuno. Something in her face changed when she looked at him. Her flaxen hair reflected the rays of light, and her blue eyes were thoughtful. It seemed as if the edge of this shore of inexpressible beauty, the sea wind, and some sense of freedom were calling her somewhere. Unexpectedly, even for herself, Estela said everything she had wanted to say for a long time, "Nuno, your eyes reflect the sea and the sky. Over the years, they will become this color;" Estela pointed to a block of dark blue basalt that emerged from the black lava, "Like your father. And your beard will grow the same as well, like Don Leandro or the Assyrian king. Your shoulders are already as wide now. Do you know what wise women say about people like you? People like you always have beautiful children. What would you call your son, Nuno?"

Nuno looked at Estela with surprise, even with fright. He had not expected such a conversation at all. They both looked at each other in silence. Estela's gaze was full of tenderness and love. It was as if she was waiting for something from Nuno, but he was no longer paying attention to her, peering at something behind her. "What is that? Look!"

Estela turned around to look where Nuno pointed. Something was waving from a huge, half-submerged snag. On one of its appendages hung a surprisingly bright scarlet ribbon. Estela waded out to the snag, took off the ribbon, and examined it. "Nuno, look… What is it?" Nuno looked at the ribbon with interest. Estela squeezed the material between her fingers and rubbed it. "I've never held such a cloth in my hands before, Nuno. This is not usual fabric, maybe from overseas… Look!" Estela stretched the ribbon and held it in front of Nuno.

The entire length of the ribbon was embroidered with images of human figures with animal heads in bizarre poses. Estela turned the band over and showed it to Nuno again. There were also strange signs on the reverse side, one line and four dots. He had never seen anything like it before. Overseas merchants sometimes passed through their parts, but not recently. Nuno shrugged thoughtfully and looked around. "I don't understand either. People rarely come here. Perhaps the poor man up on the cliff dropped it?"

Estelle said nothing. She tucked the ribbon into the sleeve of her dress and looked around. Neither she nor Nuno noticed anything unusual on the shore – only clumps of algae and half-submerged, water-blackened fragments of a tree. The young pair went back up to the plain. There they saw that Luis and a gloomy-looking man, who was pulling a small handcart, were already approaching the edge of the cliff. Together they carried the deceased to the cart, and the undertaker, glancing at Nuno and Estela with a gloomy look, pulled the cart back toward the village. Nuno and Estela followed them in silence.

* * *

The villagers knew Nuno well as he was the son of the owner of the local lands. In addition, curiosity and passion for mastering crafts repeatedly brought the young man to their homes and workshops. Even as a very young boy, Nuno wandered into many of these places every now and then.

Questioning these people did not clarify much. Apart from Augustine, no one else saw the riders, one of whom was found dead. The most recent of the peasants questioned by Nuno and Estela said that the poor man must have served in the fortress of Leiria, the villager saw him driving on Sundays along the road that leads from the fortress to the port town of Villa de Porto because his family lived there.

On the way back to the estate, Nuno hardly spoke to either Estela or Luis. He still couldn't get the expression on the dead face of Cristiano out of his head, a simple man he once knew. Something in the whole situation would not give him peace and would not allow him to be distracted. In the end, he decided that he would definitely find the man's family and try to help them in some way, and informed Estela about it.

"When I get home, I'll go straight to the market and ask the people there. Maybe someone knew this Cristiano," Estela said. "From the gossip in city markets, you can almost always find answers."

Luis had managed to get some wine somewhere. Now he was trudging behind the young people, and from time to time took out a clay flask from his bosom, gurgled something, and then continued the story that he had begun at the edge of the forest: "So, the old people say that this is the work of the Red Ghost. He wanders along the seashore and the surrounding groves. He's been wandering for a long time. Some old people saw him as a child. He is red because he drinks blood."

Estela and Nuno exchanged silent smiles. Meanwhile, the sun was sinking into the sea. It became noticeably darker in the forest. In the bag strapped to Luis's saddle, there were prepared torches in case it became completely dark. Estela, hearing Luis's constant hiccups following the sloshing in his flask, giggled nonchalantly, throwing her head back and closing her eyes.

"And now this Red Ghost is wandering around wherever he wants. And they sanctified these places and sprinkled holy water, but all to no avail. Every year, there will inevitably be a dead man, or he will plague the cows, or the donkeys will go berserk. He introduced himself to one widow as a poor traveler, and afterward, she was found in bed without a single drop of blood in her body. In one word -

Red Ghost!" With these words, Luis crashed to the ground. Duarte barked deafeningly.

Nuno immediately jumped off his horse and ran up to Luis. Grabbing the old man by the collar, he began to lift him up. Luis suddenly shouted, "Come on, nothing will happen to me, Nuno! I was once thrown from the fortress wall; I don't care about anything since then." Estela kept laughing louder with her silver laugh.

A little later, lights appeared in the depths of the forest, followed by the sound of a horse trampling through the underbrush. A minute later, Raul rode up to Nuno and Estela, holding a torch over high. "Are you okay? Donna Manuella asked me to search for you." Raul informed them.

* * *

When Nuno and Estela returned, joining the family at supper, they saw that the former guests, as well as new people, including the housekeeper, the steward, and Nuno's tutors, were all sitting at the table next to Leandro and Senhor Bianco. Everyone had already had supper and, judging by their high spirits, even walked to the winery, which was located just behind the vineyard, no more than a hundred steps from the stable.

Leandro was telling the Venetian something, and the others looked from one to the other. From time to time, they agreed with the head of the family, or, interrupting each other, supplemented his dialogue with their own judgments. Senhor Bianco's smile never left his face. On the surface, it might seem that he was an important gentleman from the capital, who especially came to listen to the complaints and wishes of the provincials. The musician, sitting on a chair, was sleeping with a childish smile on his face, and no one even tried to wake him up.

When the young duo entered, Manuella looked first at Estela, then at Nuno. She seemed a little upset. Leandro, at the sight of his son, put his hand on the hand of Senhor Bianco, who was answering something, and said sympathetically, "Excuse me, Senhor. Well, Nuno? What happened there?"

"We found a dead man," Nuno replied. "It was a man I knew as a kid. The villagers said he may have served at Leiria Castle."

"In any case, Don Daniel must be informed of this as soon as possible," Leandro concluded. "Not only could it be his soldier, but he also keeps order in our villages. Call for Francisco."

"I'm here, Your Grace," the forgotten steward stepped out from behind Leandro's chair.

"Send a messenger… Send Raul to Leiria. Raul already knows everything, doesn't he? Have him tell them at the castle about what happened here."

"Yes, Don Leandro."

Having put an end to the matter, Leandro again turned to the Venetian, "I'm sorry again. And allow me to object; The state system of the Republic of Venice seems to me more perfect than ours. Truly, no man is a prophet in his homeland, is he?"

Senhor Bianco nodded, "Oh, yes. This tragedy is ubiquitous."

"Two years ago, our glorious King Afonso died, and Joao II ascended the throne. I must say that the new king already had a good reputation by that time."

"Absolutely right!" Manuella nodded. "By that time, Joao II had already become famous not only at jousting tournaments and in battles, but also as a patron of the arts, sciences, and navigation."

"And Fernando II de Braganza, three years earlier, had inherited immense wealth and all titles from his late father. His family was the largest ruling family in the kingdom. The duke himself already earned the same privileges as the greatest of the king's generals. He accompanied King Afonso on overseas military campaigns and distinguished himself there more than once. There the duke fought hand in hand with the royal heir, Joao II ..."

Suddenly, a goblet fell from the tray in the maid's hands, followed by other empty dishes. She shrieked, apologized from the bottom of her heart to the gentlemen, and began to pick up the dishes from the floor. Leandro was not surprised; she showed such carelessness at least once a month.

"Well, Senhor, the Duke of Braganza has become the most venerated leader of the nobility. They strive to preserve the influence and wealth received under the late king. I'll be honest, I myself am not only a friend of the duke, but also his supporter in the field of public affairs. In my opinion, the collegial rule of different estates, whether nobles, clergy, or merchants, is much better than the undivided power of the monarch. Such rule contributes much more to the prosperity of the state and the people than sovereign rule. Isn't the power and wealth of your fatherland the most obvious example of this?"

"Thank you, Senhor," Bianco replied with a smile on his face. "The Envoy will definitely hear about your sentiment towards both Duke de Braganza and the Republic of St. Mark."

"However, the new king and his party hold different views," Leandro said. He took a leisurely sip from the goblet and continued, "As soon as he ascended the throne, the king began to reconsider the grounds for the privileges of the great lords, which they had received from the late Afonso V and the previous monarchs. Needless to say, doesn't all of this cause worry for the nobles of the kingdom? Their families? Their distant relatives? Their household people and peasants? Isn't there a threat of unrest when the king encroaches on the estates of his nobles?"

"It's so good that there is the Cortes in Portugal, and you can freely discuss class claims there," Senhor Bianco concluded sympathetically.

"That's not quite true again," Leandro said gloomily. He could have said that the king, perhaps, had completely forgotten that his subjects had the Cortes, but refrained and simply added with annoyance, "Close, but not so."

Everyone fell silent. Only Nuno and Estela, sitting at a distance from the guests, were whispering about something. They laughed from time to time. They were rolling with laughter, the kind that sometimes makes young people who are full of life laugh for no particular reason.

Leandro, already quite tired of the conversation, looked at his son. Why do his father's affairs and worries concern his offspring so little? Time goes by, and one day Nuno will have to do what his father is doing now. Manage at least the estate, not to mention public affairs. As long as

Leandro himself could remember, his life was spent in labor and worries. Leandro's mother died early, and his father, shocked by the death of his beloved wife, never fully recovered. He neglected his business and responsibilities, leaving everything in the care of the steward, and the estate began to decline. When his father died, Leandro was the same age as Nuno today. Having dismissed the steward, he himself zealously took on the duties. He got up at dawn and walked around the arable land, barnyards, orchards, and vineyards of his father's estate.

Over time, Leandro realized that not only fields and pastures could bring profit. Portugal, a maritime power, was gaining strength and needed a fleet, both military and commercial. Soon wagons loaded with brackets for ship planks, hooks, and chains for ship equipment, went from the forges Leandro built on his lands to Lisbon, Porto, and even to Castile. Leandro would return to his house after dark daily, and he still didn't have enough time to finish his business duties. Sometimes he had to spend several days inspecting remote holdings, and during these few days he was away, he always noticed things on the main estate began to go awry. In his opinion, only bad things were done, and the good things were never done.

Leandro was not yet thirty when he was chosen to represent the local nobility in the Cortes. It happened after he met Duke de Braganza. The management of the farm again had to be trusted to someone else's hands, because now, Leandro spent all his free time drafting laws, traveling to the Cortes in Leiria, and countering inquiries from the king's party.

However, there were other things going on in the Cortes in Leiria. Often Leandro helped landowners and merchants to achieve their own personal goals in the Cortes.

Sometimes, with his help, they received new lands from the king or even titles of nobility. Leandro, who knew well the value of the labor and efforts of intermediaries in all kinds of cases, did not refuse remuneration, knowing full well he would benefit as well as the Cortes. Regardless, wasn't the power of the Cortes strengthened by new landowners or when the wealth of current landowners increased?

But what about Nuno? Nuno did not want to grow up and did not want to listen to adult conversations. No matter how hard Leandro tried to imagine his son in his place, he could not. He was not cut out for such trials and did not seek to learn how to manage the economy. What would need to happen for him to change? Nuno had too soft a character to force lazy men and drunkards to honest work, punish poachers and village thieves, force men to marry defamed virgins, and properly support children and the elderly, and no amount of exercise would help in this matter. That's just how Nuno had grown up. He would never raise his hand against another person – just as no one had ever raised a hand against him. Leandro had never thought about the correctness of his upbringing, but now he couldn't help thinking, "Is Manuella right this time too? Can marriage really fix Nuno? And why not? With Estela, of course ... To a strong-willed, smart, and, probably, kind girl such as Estela is. Who else could make a more worthy pair? Yes, but Estela's father is a supporter of the king ... And who else knows how high the sprouts of the current civil strife, which he himself told Senhor Bianco today, can ascend?"

"Estela!" he suddenly had a realization, "You visit the capital more often than we do. Tell me, what do they say about the rivalry between the king and his nobility? And what do they say in Leiria?"

"The common people, Don Leandro, admire the new king," Estela answered loudly, distracted from joking conversations with Nuno. There was still a hint of laughter in her voice. "They always rejoice when their masters are pressured by someone stronger, and everyone at the university is just crazy about the king. After all, Joao, even during Afonso's lifetime, strongly supported the local pundits. As for Leiria, you know my father. He is also pleased with the new king. And my father's subordinates support his opinion, as it should be for serving people. No matter what they think to themselves."

"...Her father is pleased with the king," Leandro summed up in his mind.

Not only were Leandro and Manuella concerned about Nuno's future that evening. Estela was thinking about him, too, about him and only him. In the calculus of the al-Khwarizmi systems, she had far surpassed her fellow students. Her maths was better than anyone who was present in the dining room of Leandro's house that evening. She had long ago, with the help of her mother, assessed the condition of wealth together of both her father and Leandro. It turned out very well. As for her rank in society, high society, of course, because Estela could think of nothing less, she might be among the highest in the kingdom of Joao II. Her opportunity... that first kiss Estela had hoped to get from Nuno today, was so close. And some silly ribbon with stupid drawings prevented him. Well, she'll have to wait for another chance. An event after which an engagement would be inevitable. Of course, Estela's parents thought that she was wasting her time on trips to Don Leandro's estate. Her mother had told her straight out that Nuno would never marry her, but they still couldn't offer her anything suitable or better. Her only hope was to go toward her goal without looking back at her parents.

Estela waited for Manuella to shake her head wearily once again and turn away from her husband. She caught Manuella's eye and smiled at her brightly, still flush with laughter, although perhaps a little melancholy. Manuella gave her a motherly smile back.

A Moment from the Past - A Cut-off Lifeline

Down the street, past the monotonous houses covered with thatched roofs, ran a middle–aged ticitl *healer*. He was in a hurry. From time to time, he stumbled and fell, but got up and ran toward his destination again. Finally, he found himself in front of a palace surrounded by a high hedge. At the gate, he was met by guards armed with spears. Two women peeked out from behind them. Without giving the ticitl a chance to catch his breath, these maids led him to the palace. All three of them walked through several spacious, luxuriously furnished halls and finally entered a bedroom.

An older woman was lying on the blankets that covered the floor in this spacious room. A man in rich clothes was lying and snoring next to her. He was clutching a cup in one hand. Judging by the smell that filled the air, the man was drunk. The room was lit by a fire burning in a ceramic bowl.

Wet rags lay here and there on the blankets. The woman was moaning in pain. At the sight of the ticitl, she let out a scream. The maids tore off her blanket, and the healer knelt in front of her. Her labor had begun. They did not rush but worked swiftly. Presently, a baby cried in the ticitl's arms. "Girl!" The maids said in unison. The woman in labor leaned her head back on the pillow. Tears streamed down her face, distorted with pain. But these were not tears of joy.

The man snoring rhythmically next to the woman in labor did not wake up, but the cup fell out of his hand.

Three people came out of the next room. The first was an old man dressed simply as he is at his home. Tufts of gray hair peeked out from under the tunic at his chest. The old man's arms and body were decorated with faded tattoos, and his head was uncovered. It was Moctezuma, Weyitlatoani of Tenochtitlan, his wrinkled face revealing his fatigue. The maids immediately left the room.

Moctezuma was accompanied by another man, slightly younger. Unlike Moctezuma, he was dressed as if a festive gathering was waiting for him there. It was the cihuacoatl of Aztlan, the weyitlatoani's main chief assistant.

The last one was a young man of about fifteen years old. "Help your mother," Moctezuma said to the young man. "Cut off the lifeline." The young man approached the naked older woman lying on the blankets. He looked at the newborn girl who was still streaked with blood and the boy's face distorted with a grimace of disgust. The young man took out a translucent blue obsidian dagger from its sheath and cut off the umbilical cord.

"Moctezuma, this is a very bad sign," said Cihuacoatl in his exquisite dress. "The priests promised the people a boy would be born, and after the troubles that have come to our land, after locusts, drought, frost, and the flood on Lake Texcoco, the people will not bear this news. The birth of a girl will cause an uproar. Before people find out about the newborn, you have to take as many citizens as possible and leave the city for war. Take the warriors away with you, so that they don't start an uprising. While you are away, Atotoztli will be able to deal with the affairs of the courts and trade."

After finishing his speech, Cihuacoatl looked at the woman on the blankets. Only now she was able to pull the blanket over herself to cover her naked body. The pain on her face was replaced by despair. The drunk lying next to the woman muttered something, rolled over, and began to snore again. Moctezuma looked at him with hatred.

Meanwhile, the ticitl cleaned the newborn's body and wrapped her in a piece of clean cloth. She wasn't crying or screaming anymore. Her eyes did not look in different directions, as happens with ordinary newborns. The girl's gaze was focused on the ticitl's face. She was smiling. Her little nose twitched curiously as if the child was trying to smell new smells. The ticitl had never met such a calm newborn.

"Axayacatl can start helping Atotoztli," Cihuacoatl continued. "Axayacatl is already quite a mature young man. As you know, our priests have already agreed that they will support him as the next Weyitlatoani of Tenochtitlan. He is the youngest son of Atotoztli and will rule longer. He can start learning how to rule our lands now."

The young man stepped up to Moctezuma and, boldly looking into his eyes, said, "I promise that I will do my mother's will in everything!" With that, he sheathed his blue dagger.

Moctezuma looked at the ticitl, then he looked at Cihuacoatl. The last nodded. The newborn girl and the ticitl must be killed.

"No!" Atotoztli shouted. Her voice was authoritative, and her aging face, illuminated by the glare of the flames, was stern but still beautiful. Cihuacoatl, who was about to call the guards, froze. Moctezuma looked at his daughter with a surprised look. "After the priests made their choice of the next weyitlatoani, I became a cihuatlatoani," Atotoztli continued resolutely. "And I forbid you to kill my daughter.

She will live! My word is also law now. The only person, not from our altepetl, who will know about this secret will be the ticitl, and I oblige him to raise the girl until there is a need for her. Then, the ticitl will also witness how everything happened." After finishing her speech, the woman looked at Axayacatl with apprehension.

He felt his mother's gaze but did not respond to it and continued to stare at Moctezuma. Moctezuma sensed and understood Atotoztli's anxiety. Because of Axayacatl, she feared for the child's life. Moctezuma looked questioningly at Cihuacoatl. He shrugged his shoulders. Atotoztli did not wait for their verdict. "Ticitl, what's your name?" she asked.

"Chimalli," the ticitl replied.

"Chimalli, you will hide the newborn at home. You will raise her as your daughter. I will immediately send you a reward for taking care of me and my child, as well as a wet nurse and necessities for the care of the girl." For the sake of the child's safety, Atotoztli decided to settle them in another city, and even in the presence of the cihuacoatl and Axayacatl, she would not talk about it openly.

Atotoztli gave Moctezuma an imperious look. He waved his hand and started to go into another room but paused for a moment. He thought it would be better to take the young man away so that he would not harm his mother. The warriors and citizens of the city should also be sent away, so that they could not ignite unrest among the townspeople, incited by dissatisfied priests. After all, they all have been wanting to get rid of him for a long time. He understood this from their looks during meetings and festivals.

Moctezuma said to Axayacatl softly: "You will help me deal with the Totonac and Zapotec tribes who don't want to celebrate our festivals with us. They are in the land where the large stone head the size of a house is buried. Beyond their land lies Big Water, stretching into the sky. From there, Huitzilopochtli comes to us. There we will build a new city. It will be a city on the water, similar to Tenochtitlan. And one day this city will meet Huitzilopochtli. Get ready. In this campaign, you will be my tlacochcalcatl." Moctezuma's beautiful deep voice matched the look of his expressive, intelligent eyes.

No matter how hard Axayacatl tried to keep a serious face, he could not restrain from breaking into a joyful smile. Bowing to Moctezuma, he quickly left the bedroom.

"Thank you, Father," Atotoztli said to Moctezuma.

"We don't have much time left," Moctezuma replied, looking after his grandson who had just left. "A few years maybe. And they will fly by quickly, like the flow of drops in a waterfall. And when Axayacatl becomes the weyitlatoani, there will be no one to protect you." Moctezuma again looked at the man snoring on the floor with a look full of hatred and then left the room.

Chapter 3. The Captive

Tupac, the otomi of the military group, entered the chambers of the ticitl, Chimalli. At the entrance, Tupac raised his palm with outstretched fingers to the level of his chest, decorated with the Nahui Ollin necklace, and said, "Tonatiu kuautik!" Tupac's shoulder was tied with a strip of maguey cloth, brown with dried blood. On top of Tupac's head was a shock of black hair, tied with a red ribbon.

Chimalli, a man in his late forties, stepped up to Tupac and took his uninjured hand. The hands of the guest and the host intertwined in greeting. Chimalli led Tupac to a bench in the middle of the room, sat him down, and examined the wound. "An arrow?" Chimalli instantly assessed the cause of the injury.

"Yes."

"Anacaona!" Chimalli called, and a girl in a light skirt and short-sleeved dark shirt came out of another room. The young woman's outfit, like her other garments, was emblazoned with a bizarre design. A lock of hair brushed her dark, friendly face like a raven's wing. The girl's face was decorated with peculiar, elaborately made tattoos, the last of which indicated her seventeenth birthday.

"Tupac!" she exclaimed.

"An arrow was taken from the warrior's shoulder," Chimalli said. "We need to heal the wound."

Anacaona rushed to the shelves that completely covered one of the walls. There were a lot of ceramic vessels on the shelves along with large and small bags, and hanging were bunches of dried medicinal herbs. On other shelves were strange-looking tools made of copper, silver, and flint, and the sharpest ones, made of pieces of cooled lava, the obsidian glinting in the light. Broken bones and punctured skulls were next to them, and on the walls hung fabrics and sheets of amatl, covered with drawings that represented wounds in different places of the human body with inscriptions.

The walls, ceiling, and floor here were completely made of stiffened bamboo stalks of different thicknesses. The bamboo floor was covered with a substance that had a red-orange color. It was a solidified mixture of rubber and a special powder. The secret of the powder was revealed only to a select few ore miners. This mixture turned into a glue that became solid and allowed long structures to be firmly connected and did not let water through.

Along the other walls were two small low beds covered with woolen bedspreads.

The young woman brought the necessary vessels, herbs, and a piece of canvas to the table next to where Tupac was sitting. Chimalli untied the knot on the blood-soaked bandage and yanked it off his shoulder. Tupac winced but didn't make a sound, and Anacaona found herself echoing the grimace of pain on his face. Chimalli looked at his daughter questioningly.

Under the ceiling, coming out of one wall and disappearing into another, crossing the whole room, ran a long bamboo stalk with a cork stuck in the middle. Anacaona raised her hand to this cork, twisted it, and took it out. Clean water poured out of the hole. Collecting water into a small jug, Anacaona inserted the cork into place. Then she washed the wound, shifted Tupac's hand to the table, and opened one of the clay vessels. The girl sniffed the contents of the vessel with her eyes closed and seemed to nod affirmatively to herself.

Now the ticitl himself took up the task. He plunged a long and thin wooden spatula into the jar, lifted a clot of black ointment at its end, smeared the ointment on the wound, and began to rub it. Tupac's eyes narrowed in pain, but he courageously remained silent. The wound began to ooze with dark black dirty blood and then with regular dark red blood. "The bad blood has to come out," Chimalli explained.

When the bleeding stopped, Chimalli opened another jar and took out another ointment; it was dark green in color. He quickly rubbed the ointment into the wound and said to his daughter, "A bandage." Anacaona took a length of thick white cloth from a clay pot. She wrapped it around Tupac's shoulder and tied the ends of the bandage. Her work was done.

Tupac smiled and stood up, but Chimalli said, "Sit down a little longer. We must wait until the drug takes full effect. You can lie down if you need to," and Chimalli pointed to the low beds against the wall. Tupac did not answer but leaned back on the bench where he sat.

"Tupac," Anacaona asked, "have you been ashore in Huitzilopochtli's domain?"

Tupac nodded gravely. "Yes, we were on the shore, behind which the sun rises. There is a big wall of black stone, but at the top, beyond it, there are beautiful spacious fields and a forest with unusual trees."

"And Huitzilopochtli?" Anacaona whispered.

"We met two people there who were sitting on large unknown animals. They speak an incomprehensible language and do not dress like us. They had a formidable weapon in their hands, but we tamed them." Tupac spoke concisely and with dignity. "We brought one of them for the Tezcatlipoca festival. This person will be the ixiptlatli in this Toxcatl for Tezcatlipoca. Currently, he is a guest of Coatl in his house."

Tupac never answered the question about Huitzilopochtli. This omission implied a negative answer.

"I'd like to see this ixiptlatli," Anacaona said to herself loudly. She walked up to Tupac and wiped the last traces of blood from his shoulder with a piece of damp cloth. Tupac felt goosebumps run through his body from the touch of Anacaona's gentle hands. When the girl left the room, Tupac watched her go and sighed, confusion and disappointment written on his face. Noticing this, Chimalli involuntarily smiled.

* * *

Anacaona was walking on the bamboo flooring covered with the solid red-orange coating. Every so often she would enter some hall, only to soon come out again the floor continuing under her feet throughout. It brought her to the next hall, and each hall was more spacious than the other. Inside, they looked the same, just like the chambers of the healer Chimalli: bamboo walls, ceilings, and floors. They differed only in size and decor, each with skins, amatl, and large pieces of cloth hanging on the walls.

A particular breed of turkeys was bred in one of the largest halls. In addition to meat, they also provided feathers, which were no less beautiful than a peacock's plumage. These turkeys, idling in their pens, were cared for by many people.

"Tonatiu kuautik!" From time to time, people greeted Anacaona.

As she exited the hall with turkeys, a young man approached her. Shifting from one foot to the other, he said that he would visit her father tomorrow. Anacaona nodded. She knew this man suffered from knee pain. Not so long ago, Anacaona and the boys were chasing a rubber ball while playing ollamalitzli, and this young man was playing with them. This was probably the cause of his knee pain. She would prepare the necessary medicines for him in advance.

Strangers who met this friendly, sociable girl for the first time could hardly believe that she was not afraid of blood and would steadfastly endure the screams of the wounded and the death throes of warriors. Her father began teaching Anacaona the art of healing when she was only six years old, long before Anacaona went to telpochcalli, the only school in their small suburb of Texcoco. At the same time, she began to accompany her father on military campaigns and help him treat the wounded warriors. By the age of ten, she already knew how to do almost everything – prepare healing potions, set dislocations, as well as set broken arms and legs and put clay molds on them. In peacetime, Anacaona carried carcasses of captured animals on her back alongside the hunters. She always found her place in groups of people. The older people loved her for her constant willingness to help and the young for her dexterity in games, her intelligence beyond her years, and her easygoing nature. To everyone, she was, at a glance, beautiful, attractive, and cheerful. As soon as they met Anacaona, everyone began to love her the same way they loved children.

Anacaona entered the next hall. The path she was walking along was fenced off on both sides with bamboo bars. Behind them lay mountains of potatoes, on which a man walked with his feet wrapped in a lot of rags. Anacaona adored potatoes in all their forms, except dried.

As Anacaona entered a room almost adjacent to this hall, she inhaled a sharp but pleasant smell. In the small round mills that stood by the aisle, women tirelessly ground cocoa beans. They made chocolate here, which Anacaona also loved. There were jugs on the shelves against the walls, and Anacaona knew that chocolate was cooling in them. No one drank it hot except Itza. For other chocolate lovers, there were hard blocks of it on the shelves.

In one of the halls through which Anacaona passed, women were weaving cloth, some made from imported cotton and some from cactus or palm fibers. Once upon a time, Anacaona, along with other youths, was also taught this skill at the telpochcalli. Anacaona didn't really like this work. Passing by the weavers, Anacaona coughed; the women were surrounded by clouds of dust, especially noticeable when it was pierced by the sun's rays penetrating the room from somewhere above.

Not only fabrics came out from under the hands of weavers and other craftswomen, but carpets and blankets were also woven here. Clothes were sewn for local residents and warriors, and colorful ribbons with drawings that warriors and townspeople wore on their upper arms were prepared. The owner could present it when he was in another city, and it was clear to everyone who he was. Additionally, the signs on the ribbon told where he lived, when and where he was born, and his main occupation. By putting a number of lines and dots on the ribbon, the owner could also show how many captives he had taken in battles. Right now, as Anacaona watched, Patli, having removed his ribbon from his shoulder, handed it to the craftswoman and poked his finger at the spot of dried blood on his shoulder, requesting a new red point on his ribbon.

The next room was completely reserved for dying fabrics. To obtain fabrics of the desired color, they were soaked for a long time in ceramic vats filled with colored liquids. Scarlet fabric was especially appreciated. For that hue, the dye was obtained from beetles that were bred here. Dyes were also made from shellfish, plants, clay, and rocks which were pounded in mortars and mixed with special additives in specific proportions.

In other halls, where small gardens were located, fruits and vegetables were grown. They grew on the ground, planted in special wooden containers.

Usually, these numerous spacious rooms were, as they were now, in the open air, but if necessary, during excessive heat or prolonged rains, they were covered with light panels, from which it was possible to instantly make a roof. In some places, openings in the walls were also covered with such panels. These were also treated with the rubber mixture and did not let water through. Storerooms were also made with similar panels, where rainwater was collected, so it could flow through the bamboo trunks into rooms and workshops. This was water for drinking only; touching water in storage tanks or using it for other purposes, such as watering gardens, including vegetable gardens, was strictly prohibited.

There was no place for a fire in any room. It may illuminate a room at night better than the light of the moon and stars that penetrated through open roofs or long windows, but a fire here could lead to the end of their world. Fire could only be obtained in one place – in the chambers of Coatl's assistant, Cihuacoatl Tlaluacatli Camaxtli. After receiving the fire, the person had to return to Camaxtli and inform him that there was no need for the fire anymore, and it was extinguished.

Finally, Anacaona left behind the artisan's workrooms, and the bamboo forest spread out green in front of her. It was dissected by paths leading away from where she stood and toward the center. At the edge of this forest, Anacaona saw men who were harvesting the trunks of the stiffened stems. Cutting the stem at the bottom, they did not let it fall but carefully pulled it aside. The tops of the stems were held in place by a huge rope network that didn't allow the forest to sway. The bamboo grew at an incredible rate. A sprig, barely emerging from the ground, could become a stalk as tall as an adult in a couple of days.

Bamboo was the main construction material in Tlaluacatli, their current home. While one grove of bamboo was being used for repairs, the next one was growing and would be suitable for use in a couple of weeks. Therefore, bamboo stocks were always ready at people's fingertips. In Tlaluacatli, it grew even faster, because the forest was irrigated with water with special supplements. Such water was also used in vegetable gardens, along with fertilizer created from bird droppings and animal manure, which was carefully collected every day in the halls.

In the center of this bamboo forest stood the house of Tlatoani Tlaluacatli, the ruler of this town, a man whom everyone obeyed. He was the priest and judge Coatl.

Anacaona was walking towards his house now. The closer she got, the more she saw other people flocking to the house. All of them walked only on paths. No one dared to walk on the soil where the bamboo forest grew. A small one-story house with a thatched roof was already surrounded by a roaring crowd.

After learning about the ixiptlatli, a man captured on an unknown shore and brought here for the festival, people were greatly alarmed. No one had told them anything yet. Now one of them was trembling with fear and said that the captive was a servant of Teotl or was his messenger. And people said he was almost strangled! They say he fell from an unknown animal, hit the ground hard with his shoulder, and is now immobilized. Teotl can be angry!

Others rejoiced – after all, the ixiptlatli, even if they could not yet understand him, could bring good news telling them how to protect themselves and their children from ordinary adversity, how to end outbreaks of hunger and disease forever, how to achieve universal prosperity, and how happy Tezcatlipoca would be with this gift.

Approaching the crowd, Anacaona said loudly, "Ticitl for ixiptlatli!" People turned to her and parted. Many nodded to her affably. Almost everyone knew this young woman and her father. Anacaona climbed the steps and walked into the house. Before the threshold, she got down on one knee, lowered her head, and kissed a small bag lying there. It contained sacred land gathered in the middle of Huey Teocalli in the center of Tenochtitlan.

Getting up from the steps and entering, Anacaona looked around. In a spacious room, Coatl and Ocotlan were sitting on low benches. Coatl held a small bundle of brown leaves in his hand, smoking at one end. He made fire with the help of a fail-safe flint, the device which was known to him alone. From time to time Coatl raised the cluster to his lips and sucked in the smoke. The men were sitting at a low round table covered with a blue tablecloth with yellow patterns. There was a jug, two bowls, and a platter of fruit on the table.

Together with Ocotlan, Coatl examined the armor and weapons brought from the shore — two swords, knives, and a crossbow. All the equipment was lying near the table on one of the carpets that covered the floor. There was another table nearby, rectangular and without a tablecloth. On it lay a large gold plate with the image of a pyramid protruding from the waves of the sea.

There were three similar rooms in this house. The walls of these rooms were extremely richly decorated. On them hung ornaments made of gold and multicolored stones, weapons, stuffed animal heads, and large sheets of amatl covered with drawings and from time to time repeated glyphs.

In the corner of the room, there was a large bed partially hidden by a partition made of mats near the headboard. There was a table by the bed. The captive was lying on the bed, and his fair-skinned face and hands immediately struck Anacaona. Two ladies were fussing around him. One of them, Milintica, was also an assistant to her father. She was tying up the black-and-blue shoulder of the captive, clearly the result of a very strong blow, with a strip of light fabric, under which there was already packed a bunch of medicinal herbs.

Another lady had just poured a drink from a jug into a mug and was now holding it out to the captive with a smile. The captive was smiling; apparently, he had already consumed more than one mug of this drink. He was also obviously enjoying the company of the two ladies, and they even encouraged him. Taking the mug, he looked at the lady with the jug and said something in his language. However, the ladies appeared a little bit worried.

"Coatl, tlatoani Tlaluacatli, can I help heal ixiptlatli?" Anacaona asked.

Coatl blew a cloud of smoke from his mouth and said, "Anacaona, daughter of Chimalli, your help is welcome. Help Milintica heal ixiptlatli and help Teyacapan cook him the best chocolate dinner. Also, bring him another pitcher of octli. See how glad he is for it."

"Tonatiu kuautik!" Anacaona said to the captured soldier with a smile.

He also smiled from ear to ear and said something. Before, ladies rarely spoiled him with this much attention.

Then Anacaona noticed another person. He had been standing against the wall in the shadows, and now he came to the table where Coatl and Ocotlan were sitting. He wore a hat made up of four rings of different fabrics. Long wavy hair fell over his shoulders, framing a beautiful, young, slightly feminine face. His body was covered from shoulders to knees by an unusual sand-colored shirt. Along his collarbone hung a necklace, from which brown fringe swayed, and a similarly designed belt covered his torso. From his back hung a cape made of the skin of some animal. In his hand, the man held a ritual staff with an obsidian knob. Despite his rich clothes, he was without shoes. This was Camaxtli – cihuacoatl of Tlaluacatli.

"Coatl," he said, "as you ordered, I checked our supplies. We have about one winal of water left if we use it as usual. There is also no shortage of food, and no shortage is expected, because everyone who creates it works tirelessly.

However, the people have been worried since you brought the ixiptlatli."

Coatl, looking directly at Camaxtli, raised an eyebrow, but did not break his silence.

"To appease Huitzilopochtli," Cihuacoatl continued, "offerings are needed. We all depend on his benevolence. Perhaps Huitzilopochtli is already angry with us for the trouble we have caused on his land. People are afraid that Huitzilopochtli will spew a terrible fire and bring down the sky on them. We're all scared!"

"Huitzilopochtli is not angry with those who observe festivals!" Coatl said. "And we do! Go, and don't be afraid! Prepare Tlaluacatli for the Tezcatlipoca Festival. And don't forget, Tlaluacatli was built specially to meet Huitzilopochtli. That's why we're all here!"

Camaxtli hesitated for a moment, turned around, and silently left the room.

"Even if Huitzilopochtli does not come to us, our endeavors will not have been in vain," Coatl told Ocotlan. "We will take new captives from those who do not follow our festivals in Uehkatlan and research their land to understand how they mine and craft their metal."

Ocotlan grabbed the jug on their table and filled his cup. After drinking its contents, he pointed his finger at the sword lying on the floor and said, "Yes, these macuahuitl and ichkahuipilli are made of very strong metal. I've never seen the likes of these before. Even if we found out right now how they mine it, it will take a long time before we learn how to make weapons and armor from such metal by ourselves. Their macuahuitl is more dangerous than a snake's tongue, than the paws of a jaguar, and the teeth of a crocodile. They are superior to ours in almost everything!"

Ocotlan glanced briefly at the soldier wiping his lips after another mug of octli, a cloudy white drink made from agave juice. "And if they all turn out to be our enemies," he continued, "we will not be able to resist them. We will not be able to repel their attack in open battle." Ocotlan raised the cup to his lips again and took a sip. This was the same drink that was being served to the captive.

"Besides, they are armed with these strange bows," Coatl said, pointing to the crossbow. "We must learn how to craft and use it."

Ocotlan picked up the crossbow from the floor and began to examine it closely.

"Arrows from this bow fly faster than the arrows of our bows," he said. "They fly faster than the strongest wind. Tupac couldn't even fathom that an arrow could have been fired at him from such a small device, and these arrows are much smaller than ours."

Ocotlan turned the taut bowstring between his fingers. "I already understand how this bow works," he continued. "Such a bow could only be made by very smart people with agile hands. They also use the same metal that their macuahuitl are made of. Without it, it would not work to make such bows. Look how springy this bow is. To bend it and put an arrow in this chute, you need either the strength of a giant or cunning. To release the arrow, you need a hook made of the same hard metal, and here's a plate…" Ocotlan turned the crossbow back over, "that holds the arrow." Ocotlan casually hit the plate with his thumbnail, and it made a ting like an arrow against metal. "Our metal can't sing like that," Ocotlan concluded, "because our metal is soft and malleable."

Anacaona took a piece of chocolate, put it in a stone bowl, and crushed it into small pieces. Then, she handed the captive a handful of chocolate shards. He looked at them in surprise. Anacaona took a piece from the bowl, put it in her mouth, and began to chew. The captive did the same. A smile spread across his face again, and the captive's lips began to turn black from the chocolate.

Meanwhile, Anacaona was furtively examining the captive's face and hands. The outlines of his face and body were not very different from the people of Aztlan, but his skin was strikingly fair. "Maybe they have different diseases, too? Different from people of Aztlan?" She thought silently to herself.

"These people have skin the color of the metstli," *the moon,* Coatl said as if confirming Anacaona's thoughts. "You can't expect rabbits to fight bravely." Ocotlan appreciated the joke and smiled. The rabbit among the people of Aztlan was a symbol of the moon. "Rabbits run away at any sign of danger. All we need to do is run faster and catch them," Coatl finished. Ocotlan continued to smile.

"This morning," Coatl continued, "his friend tried to escape as soon as our warriors were ready for battle. The metstli tlapalli, people the color of the moon, are not brave people. You will lose if you have superior armor but are not brave in battle."

Coatl got up from his chair, went to the bamboo trunk, which, like in Chimalli's chambers, passed under the ceiling, and filled his bowl with water. After quenching his thirst, he lay down on a mat covered with a wool blanket that was spread out on top of the carpet not far from the bed.

Ocotlan put the crossbow back on the floor and looked at Coatl.

The priest stretched and yawned loudly. He didn't even look at the women, because they were macehualtin, commoners. Moreover, Coatl did not pay attention to the captive, yet started speaking about him," We will try to meet Huitzilopochtli again, but before that, Tezcatlipoca will receive a treat..." Coatl squinted at the captive. The soldier was placidly chewing chocolate and gawking at Anacaona as she was listening attentively to the priest. The bandage on the captive's shoulder was beginning to slip, and the grass under it had quickly rubbed to dust. Despite the monstrous bruise that covered his shoulder, he did not seem to pay attention to it.

"... And then the teteo will favor us," Coatl continued. "They'll come out from the other side of the wall and meet us. We will celebrate so loudly that the sky will hear the sounds of our joy. Yes, they will come!"

Ocotlan stood up and respectfully lowered his head. Coatl greatly admired the obedience of the tlacochcalcatl warlord and his shrewdness. "After the festival is over, I'll go meet you near your boats," Coatl directed. "You will be waiting for me there with your warriors."

Ocotlan nodded and picked up the bowl again. Ocotlan was a pilli; his class was equal to that of Coatl but of a lower social rank. He might not bow to Coatl, but he still emphasized his loyalty to Tlatoani, and the latter liked it very much. After taking another sip, Ocotlan asked, "Now, may I go and select the warriors and prepare them for the next visit to Uehkatlan?"

Coatl raised his hand. His fingers were spread out approvingly. "Tonatiu kuautik!"

"Uehkatlan," Anacaona repeated in her mind, "The land beyond the sea. I have to go there with them! I, too, must go with the warriors and see the land of Huitzilopochtli!"

The servant, Teyacapan, looked at the smiling captive's face and poured the remains of the intoxicating octli drink into his mug.

Opening the door, Ocotlan went out onto the porch and began to descend the steps. The crowd, two heads shorter than Ocotlan, respectfully parted before the mountain of muscles. "What is he?" people shouted after him. "Is he a Teotl or a man?"

"Metstli tlapalli pan ueyatl Uehkatlan," *a white man from a far country across the sea,* Ocotlan replied.

A Moment from the Past - Ocotlan Becomes a Cuauhocelotl.

Several warriors with their leader, a sixteen-year-old youth, came out of the jungle and approached the river. All of them wore simple combat clothes, and, in addition, the young man, had a scarlet ribbon tied around his arm. It was decorated with different drawings and a single dot. Ocotlan, this tall young man with highly developed, beautiful musculature, had already captured his first captive in this war and consequently received the military rank of Tlamani.

Everyone in his squad was wondering whether Ocotlan would bring this captive as a gift to Teotl at the next festival or retain him as a slave.

The warriors stopped at a river, rapidly flowing down from the mountain. The water was no more than seven or eight paces wide, but it was very fast. The warriors, armed with spears and macuahuitl, entered the water and began to cross. The current of the cold water was so strong that it literally knocked them off their feet. It occurred to Ocotlan that if the enemies noticed them now, they would be easy prey. Spears thrown from afar by the atlatls, spear throwers, would hit his warriors without a miss. They would not be able to escape or hide under the water either.

After crossing the river, the group went deeper into the jungle. The warriors had walked quite a way when the thickets became less frequent. The smell of smoke reached them, and a clearing with people around a campfire appeared ahead. A spit holding a wild piglet was visible above the fire. Ocotlan raised his arm, bent at the elbow, and his squad froze. Looking closely at those sitting in the clearing, Ocotlan realized that these were warriors of the people they were now fighting – the Zapotecs. There were at least twice as many of them as there were warriors in Ocotlan's squad. While waiting for dinner, the Zapotecs talked nonchalantly, and the noise of the rushing and roiling river did not allow them to hear the enemies.

The warriors of Ocotlan did not take their eyes off their leader. They clearly did not want to get involved in a battle with such a large detachment. Ocotlan also understood that an open battle would most likely end in their defeat. He raised his half-bent arm again and twirled it in the air, gesturing to retreat. The warriors, crouching to the ground, had already returned to the river when suddenly Ocotlan again raised his arm, bent at the elbow. The squad froze again. Ocotlan turned to the warriors. There was a devious smile on his face.

Is he really going to give the signal to attack now?

Ocotlan took out a wooden tube a couple of cubits long from behind his back. The warriors also took out their pipes. Ocotlan opened the bag hanging on his hip alongside his knife. There were several darts in the bag. He chose a red-feathered dart and showed it to the warriors. The tip of the dart was smeared with poisons, including the poison of a golden poison frog. This poison was very strong. It was potent enough that just touching the tip of a dart on the frog's back passed the poison to it, and the dart became a formidable weapon. A mixture of the golden frog's poison with other poisons allowed the captor to keep the victim alive and yet temporarily deprive him of mobility. The warriors also took out darts with red feathers.

Dividing the detachment into two parts, Ocotlan ordered the warriors to take shelter in the thickets along the bank of the cold river. He then covered them with grass and mud, leaving space for the warriors to breathe while they peered from their hiding places, but invisible to those watching from the shore. At the same time, Ocotlan pointed out a sharp turn that the river made far downstream.

Then Ocotlan hid his own weapon and went to the clearing. He walked loudly, deliberately stepping on and breaking dry branches and roots. When Ocotlan approached the clearing, the enemies, alarmed by the noise, were already on their feet. He and the Zapotecs were now only twenty paces apart. At the sight of Ocotlan, the Zapotecs grabbed their weapons and rushed at him. Ocotlan raced back toward the river. Remembering where the river began behind the bushes, he ran straight out of the brambles and threw himself into the water. Ocotlan jumped with such strength that the current did not even pull his body downstream, and he safely surfaced at the other shore.

The Zapotecs ran up to the river and began to slowly wade through the turbulent stream. When half of the pursuers climbed ashore, and the others were still struggling with the current, Ocotlan's warriors raised their blowguns and began silently shooting poisoned darts at the enemies still wading through the water. The Zapotecs on shore didn't even see them, as the warriors were shooting behind them. It was impossible to miss from such a close distance. The Zapotecs that had managed to cross the river were already headed deep into the jungle on the other side in the hope of catching Ocotlan and did not see that their immobilized tribesmen, who could not even call for help, were caught up by the current.

Soon, Ocotlan and his warriors regrouped around the bend of the river. They now had eight bound Zapotec captives in their custody. The captives already had one ear cut off, and Ocotlan's warriors used the blood to make marks on their forearms, where the ribbons were tied. Now, Ocotlan awarded each of his warriors a captive slave, and he himself became a cuauhocelotl.

Chapter 4. The Pyramid

Early in the morning, a column of horsemen, infantrymen, archers, and their commanders, numbering more than a hundred and fifty, left the fortress of Leiria and headed for the seashore. The soldiers shivered from the morning chill, which was intensified by their iron helmets and armor. At the head of the company rode the castellan himself with his deputy. Don Daniel was to command the exercises, which he regularly conducted in the fields, then in the woods, and finally on the seashore. The castellan was gloomy. Although his wife cooked him breakfast and made the sign of the cross to protect him on the road, Estela, despite her mother's urging, did not want to get up at such an early hour and kiss her father, and that saddened him greatly.

The column had to traverse the five leagues separating the fortress from the sea and settle down on the shore. On the second day, the soldiers had to repel an imaginary landing of the Moors from ten ships at once. The distance to the sea was short. Moving at an average pace, according to Daniel's calculations, they should have reached the shore in half a day. However, delays immediately began along the way. One of the soldiers had a cold, and six horses limped and had to be reshod right away. And where there was work, of course, there must be time set aside for lunch, which also required gathering firewood for a fire and cooking.

It was already evening when the company, having finished with half of a small supply of provisions, felt the sea wind. A sprawling but low hillock appeared ahead. It was the hill of the Big Turtle. The hill got its name from the volcanic rock along the shore. The black stones approaching the water were licked by the sea, carving crevices and contours resembling a turtle shell. To the right of the hill was a dark forest. A road crawled out of it, that went along the shore and then followed the entire coast of Portugal. This was one of the main land routes between the cities of the kingdom.

"Ricardo!" Daniel shouted to the orderly.

"I'm here, Senor Castellan."

"Send a messenger to the fortress that we are camping at the Big Turtle, on the lands of Don Leandro of the Sinta estate. Have them send provisions here for three days."

Half an hour later, Daniel was already giving orders to his sergeants, and they were running away to command the soldiers. Infantrymen, cavalrymen, and archers were setting up tents while cook chiefs were making fires. Chains of soldiers with buckets created a line to a barely noticeable small river that came out of the forest and then was lost into the fields.

Pairs of guards were assigned to two shifts. The first guard was to guard the camp, and the second was to patrol the road. Sergeants checked the soldiers' weapons and armor until dark. Someone was ordered to sharpen arrows, swords, and spears again, and check the serviceability of halberds, crossbows, and arquebuses. Someone had to sew up torn clothes and mend boots. The cavalrymen fed the horses and checked their equipment. Some cut grass, which was then left for the hobbled horses. Since an attack had to be expected at any moment, it was impossible to let the horses graze freely.

Don Daniel sat in the tent playing dice with his deputy, whose eyes blinked shut with fatigue. There were mugs and a jug of wine on the camp table. Don Daniel strictly ensured that only sergeants drank wine, and even they did not drink more than one mug.

Finally, the camp quieted down. Soon, two soldiers in armor and semicircular helmets with wide brims came out on the Big Turtle Hill. They stopped at the edge of the cliff to relieve themselves. "Well, Pedro," said one to the other, "they say Cristiano of the cavalry was killed on this hill, and Jose, who was with him, either escaped, or drowned, or something. Have you heard?"

"Who hasn't heard?" Pedro replied," And they also say that the Red Ghost showed up. Cristiano is dead, and Jose, apparently, is so scared that he still hasn't stopped running. He's probably already reached Castile. The cavalry are always cowards compared to the infantry. All their courage is in their horses, and even those limp, heh-heh-heh ..."

"Look!" his partner shouted. "What is that?"

Pedro raised his head. The sky in the west lit up with a red light — as if a huge bonfire was blazing somewhere beyond the horizon. A fire in the sea?! "What is it?" Pedro muttered. "Sunset?"

"It cannot be the sunset! It's been completely dark for already half of the patrol shift. Santa Maria!"

* * *

Coatl stood at the top of a regular quadrangular pyramid. It was a steep pyramid, and each step required a sweeping step up. A separate staircase with smaller steps led to the place where Coatl was standing, and then it passed through the middle of the pyramid. On Coatl's head sat a huge, incredibly opulent headdress of long black, white, and scarlet feathers. The feathers radiated from the headpiece, which was topped with a human skull. The shoulders, back, and chest of the priest were covered with a ritual cape made of leather and precious stones. On each step of the pyramid, there were ceramic pots with fires inside. In addition, each step was decorated with massive drawings, ornaments, and signs.

On the lower steps, at the foot of the pyramid, a throng of people dressed in festive attire was crowded around. Ordinary warriors wore simple clothes, but the bodies of the jaguar warriors were wrapped in the skins of predators, and the heads of the eagle warriors were decorated with their feathered headdresses. Some of the others in simple clothes also wore bright headdresses with two rows of long feathers. Music was resounding; someone was banging drums, rattles were echoing in time, and a bamboo flute was shrilly warbling in the hands of a flutist. Women and young people danced rhythmically to their sounds. Some stretched out their hands toward the top of the pyramid.

There was an estli ahkopechtli, a sacrificial table, in front of the entrance to the room in the small temple on the pyramid. It was in front of this that Coatl stood motionless. After surveying the crowd below, he raised his head and shouted into the sky, "We welcome Tezcatlipoca! This month we have prepared a good treat! We grant you the ixiptlatli. It will be the metstli tlapalli pan ueyatl Uehkatlan!" *a white man from a far country across the sea!*

At this, Coatl pointed to the room behind him. Two warriors, a jaguar and an eagle, led the captured soldier to the landing in front of the temple. His body was covered with blue paint. The soldier was so drunk that he could barely stand on his feet. "Take our ixiptlatli, metstli tlapalli, full of tart drinks and food," the crowd shouted together, "and let's remember this first Toxcatl in our city of Tlaluacatli near Uehkatlan!"

The warriors laid the soldier on his back on the wooden altar and, without letting him out of their hands, stood to the sides. Coatl picked up a ritual knife and raised it over the soldier. The musicians stopped playing; Silence resounded, broken only by the cries of seagulls. Coatl plunged the knife into the soldier's chest, and he let out a shrill scream. Coatl cut open his chest, and the warriors began to break his rib bones. Coatl took the heart out of the soldier's body. It continued to beat. The back of the soldier's head fell onto the table, streams of blood flowing from his body. Coatl raised the heart at arm's length. The crowd roared with delight. The music started again, and the crowd began to dance with renewed vigor.

Coatl took a ritual axe by its patterned handle, a short weapon bristling with obsidian plates, and decapitated the lifeless body with one blow. Then, with skillful movements, the priest removed the scalp from the head and placed the bloody skull on the tzompantli, a stand for skulls at the entrance to the room. Stepping up to the headless body again, he began to scoop up the blood that was dripping from the wooden altar and smear it on his face, arms, and legs. Finally, he stepped back and raised his hands to the sky. The priest's assistants grabbed the headless body and threw it on the side steps of the pyramid. The body rolled down. Falling from the last step, it hit a seagull and, flying off the stern, finally fell toward the sea, tumbling through the air for several more seconds with the last beats of the cut-out heart.

The seagull took off and flew away. From the height of her flight, one could see a pyramid on the deck of a giant ship, motionless on the ocean, made up of two hulls covered by a common deck. There were huge spaces on the sides of the pyramid and on the stern of each of the twin hulls. Through them, daylight or moonlight would fall inside the ship. Next to these giant spaces were wooden panels, which could be used to cover these spaces in case of bad weather.

The pyramid stood near the double stern of the ship and directly on its axis. Apart from the pyramid and the platform in front of it, there was nothing else on the stern. The spaces for the light were connected by a path along which inhabitants of Tlaluacatli could reach the panels to cover openings. The entire ship was covered with several layers of bright red, almost orange sealant made of rubber. In the light of the fires that sometimes illuminated the pyramid at night, the ship, from afar, looked like a bright red rock between the water and the sky.

Still holding out his hands to the sky, Coatl shouted, "Inin mouikpa, Tezcatlipoca!" *This is for you, Tezcatlipoca!*

"Teuan mitsika!" *We are with you!* the crowd shouted back.

Coatl descended from the pyramid. On the deck, people gave way to him without ceasing their dancing. Moving away from the pyramid a few steps, Coatl entered another staircase that led downward. Below the deck, along the hulls, there were wide docks, nearly touching the water that created berths for boats. Heavy ropes that hung from overhead swayed slightly, brushing the edges of the piers. The moored boats, floating just below, were empty. However, there were many warriors standing on the docks. They wore combat attire, and their bodies were covered with not only tattoos but also bizarre painted patterns. The jaguar warriors held maccuahuimeh and shields in their hands, and the eagle warriors were armed with bows and atlatls. The warriors looked at the bloody Coatl with delight.

"Aztlan warriors!" Coatl shouted, raising his hands again. "Sons of the Sun! We are going to meet Huitzilopochtli!"

"Teuan mitsika!" The crowd of warriors roared.

"Xia!" *Go!* Coatl ordered as he took off the skull and feathered headdress and put on his jaguar battle helmet. Then he grabbed the rope hanging over the boat, and swinging from it, he flew onto the bow. His warriors followed his example. Each boat could accommodate ten people, and as the boats filled, those remaining on the dock hauled the ends of the freed ropes up onto the ship.

Ocotlan got into the same boat as Coatl. On his hands, Ocotlan wore combat gloves armored with three short obsidian blades. He wore a yellow ichkahuipilli, the color indicating his rank and position: shorn ones tlacochcalcatl. He also sported a cuauchic hairstyle, a narrow strip of short-cropped hair running through the middle of his shaved skull. The companions of Ocotlan and Coatl were comprised of eagle warriors.

Tupac got into another boat. The face of Tupac was covered with yellow and blue paints, and he was dressed in a gray ichkahuipilli, the outfit of several otomies who sailed on this ship. He commanded the squad that included all the jaguar warriors.

The boats began to float out from under the deck of the giant ship, the size of a town, called Tlaluacatli. The people who continued to dance on the platform in front of the pyramid let out cheers and waved their hands at the sight of the boats. The musicians came to the edge of the deck, where they dramatically accelerated the rhythm of the melody and crescendoed their sounds to near deafening.

Chimalli and his daughter, Anacaona, were sitting in one of the boats. The ticitl wore a long, ankle–length red dress, but Anacaona dressed much more modestly in a dress made of simple linen, decorated with embroidery, and belted with a simple rope. Both, like all Tlaluacatli people, were wearing jewelry made of gold, silver, and precious stones. In the other boat were two of Chimalli's other assistants.

In total, six boats came out from under the deck of Tlaluacatli into the sea. Inside each of them stretched a rope, evenly covered with knots. Grasping and pulling these knots, the warriors drove the boat forward. In this way, they powered the astern propeller, their efforts transmitted through a special round mechanism with small blades at the ends. The warrior sitting at the stern of the boat had his hands on the helm. The engine was so simple that it practically could not fail, and yet, there were oars inside the boats. They could be used if the rope broke or if it was necessary to sail without noise.

The boats were rushing forward. From the body of Coatl, washed by splashes of seawater, the blood of the ixiptlatli flowed to the bottom of the boat. Anacaona waited with bated breath for a meeting with new teteo, a new land, and new people. The girl's excitement was great. From time to time, she dipped her palm into the water and put it to her forehead. Who knew what awaited them ahead? It wasn't long before the boats landed. The warriors began to jump out of the boats and go ashore.

"Get together!" Ocotlan commanded his warriors. "Keep at a distance of five steps from each other. Tupac, you're the first" Ocotlan raised his right hand, tied with a yellow ribbon, and pointed it at the cliff, under which the black wall began. Tupac gave the command to his squad of thirty jaguars. After getting out of the boats, they immediately climbed up the cliff and lay down there in the grass, carefully looking around.

"Ticiti will stay in the boats. They will be called if anyone is injured," Ocotlan commanded. "Jaguar Ikkohtli! And you, the eagle, Cipactli! You will stay here and guard the boats with the ticiti, and you, ticiti, do not dare to leave from here!" At the menacing look of Ocotlan, Chimalli shivered. Ocotlan raised his hand with the scarlet ribbon. The eagle warriors, occupying two boats, rushed to the cliff. Coatl followed Ocotlan. Anacaona really wanted to go ashore and see where the warriors had gone.

"Freeze and don't move," Chimalli whispered to her.

It suddenly occurred to Anacaona that for every opportunity in life, the first time could also possibly be the last. Who could know? Perhaps the warriors would return from the shore, climb in their boats, and sail back, and she would have seen nothing of this new land.

She could be on the precipice of the most important event of her life, and to experience it, she needed to act!

Soon, Anacaona noticed that Chimalli, who had been fidgeting on the bench, squinted and stared fixedly at the top of the cliff the warriors had climbed. The jaguar and eagle did not take their eyes off the black wall either, and also carefully watched the sides of the shore. It was quiet. Anacaona heard only the whisper of the waves rolling on the night shore. After waiting for some more time to be sure, Anacaona silently, without splashing, plunged over the side of the boat into the sea and dived deep. Under the water, she swam away from her boat left in the care of the eagle and jaguar. When the suffocation became unbearable, she quietly surfaced and took a deep breath. The warriors and other ticiti should not have noticed her. The boats were already far away, and Anacaona swam away from them toward the shore. Soon the boats were completely hidden behind the crests of small waves.

As Anacaona came ashore, a wall of black stone, several times the height of a man, rose up in front of her. Here the shore was no longer stone, but sandy. Anacaona touched the wall. It was the obsidian she knew well, solidified lava. Having bypassed this hillock, Anacaona ran in the opposite direction from the boats, looking for a convenient place to climb. After finding a spot and climbing up, she finally felt the soft ground under her feet. Her sandals sank into grass that tickled her ankles. The smell of fields and forests came from the shore. Anacaona closed her eyes for a moment and began to inhale the air of this plain. This girl had a gift, a special sense of smell, which helped her to recognize the healing qualities of plants. In her head, the smells turned into patterns and colors, and now, new smells were entering her head with amazing shapes and colors that she had never experienced before. All these smells were completely new to her. When her nose stopped eagerly exploring the air of the plain, she opened her eyes again.

Lights could be seen in the distance. It seemed that windows were glowing because the lights had a square shape. The bonfires couldn't be square, Anacaona decided. Of course, these are people's homes. Anacaona was scared. Are these the servants of Huitzilopochtli? Who would know how they would meet her? Anacaona looked around, hoping to see the boats, but she couldn't see anything in the dark. "Don't be afraid!" Anacaona ordered herself, "I need to find out who lives here!" And with that, Anacaona went forward, towards the lights that excited her imagination.

Meanwhile, Chimalli, not finding his daughter next to him, was extremely frightened. It was not just that Anacaona violated Ocotlan's order! Anything could have happened to her in this unknown land! Having mastered the art of silently walking, diving, and swimming in his childhood, Chimalli also silently rolled over the stern and began to quietly swim away from the boat. He didn't know that Anacaona had swam in the opposite direction.

* * *

Dawn was breaking. The warriors of Coatl could already clearly distinguish the tents pitched on the field between the forest and the sea and the houses standing in the distance. People began to come out of the tents. They were soldiers, as their attire clearly indicated. "Coatl," said Ocotlan. "These are the same people we met last time. Look! They have the same hats and the same clothes."

Horses appeared in the distance. The soldiers led them to the tall grass clumps that marked the bed of a barely noticeable stream. "And the animals that those two rode are the same!" Ocotlan said.

"Who are they?" Coatl asked himself out loud.

Ocotlan continued to watch the camp, and soon Tupac crawled up beside them. "There are many of them," he whispered. "There are at least five times twenty of them here, and there are more and more of those scary animals."

"And they have the same weapons as those two," Ocotlan continued, "we'll have to go back. We can't fight them."

"We're not going back to Tlaluacatli without more captives," Coatl said menacingly. "People will not forgive us for an unsuccessful campaign. You know that yourself."

Ocotlan understood perfectly well what the priest was driving at. If they returned without more captives, Coatl's influence would be shaken. Then the worst would happen; people would lose faith in their tlatoani! Ocotlan knew it was better not to disturb Coatl with idle conversations anymore. After all, he was a priest, a judge, and the tlatoani of Tlaluacatli. Ocotlan, the tlacochcalcatl, the chief of the military in this campaign, had to follow the orders of his tlatoani.

Coatl needed new captives? Great! Ocotlan's task was becoming clearer than ever: to get more captives like the one who was recently presented to Tezcatlipoca at the top of the pyramid. How should he do it? Attacking them was not an option, so they would have to be lured into a trap and captured so that nothing would be noticed in the camp. Where could this be accomplished? Only in the forest. Fortunately, these soldiers kept running into the forest and back.

"Zolin! Achcohtli! Iuitl!" Ocotlan commanded, turning to the chiefs of squads, "Order your warriors to go down to the shore. Under the cover of the cliff, we will reach the forest and capture as many metstli tlapalli as we can. No one at the camp of these people should notice that we captured their brethren in the forest. We'll take them to Tlaluacatli. Follow me!" Ocotlan crawled back to the shore silently and imperceptibly, never once rising above the grass; the warriors followed him. Once at the shore, below the level of the plain, they straightened up to their full height and ran along the edge of the sea, following their commander.

* * *

The sun had not yet fully risen when Ocotlan and three dozen warriors lay down at the edge of the forest. They stared at the camp and its inhabitants with all their attention. Ocotlan understood that it would not be possible to capture many captives; soldiers from the camp went to the forest alone. Therefore, it would only be possible to capture one or two, not more. If too many people did not return from the forest, the camp would definitely be alarmed. Well, we'll have to limit ourselves to these...

"Ocotlan!" Chief Zolin whispered, "What is that strange sound?"

Ocotlan listened. From the direction of the forest road, which his squad had crossed unnoticed, there was a strange creaking sound. He raised his head and then saw a strange structure roll out of the thicket and into the clearing near the exit from the forest drawn by a huge four–legged monster, the larger brother of those animals on which the other two had been sitting, the ixiptlatli and his partner. It was a wooden platform, under which four wooden discs rotated.

There were sacks of some kind on the platforms that the brothers of the monsters were dragging behind them. A tethered bull trotted behind one of the sleds. The team was accompanied by a soldier metstli tlapalli in armor. He had put his helmet on the platform and was now wiping his sweaty forehead with his sleeve. This team was followed by four more of the same.

At Ocotlan's command, his warriors got close to the road. After waiting for the teams to catch up with them, Ocotlan sounded a signal call. Eagles immediately fell from the trees onto the teams. Making giant leaps, jaguars silently jumped out from behind the bushes. The soldiers in the wagon train did not have time to react, as their hands and feet were wrapped in ropes or vines, and their mouths were stuffed with lumps of rags. Ignoring the platforms and bags, Ocotlan's warriors dragged the captives into the forest. The capture lasted less than a minute, and all was done. The horses left without their owners, continuing to pull the carts onward, and the bull continued to wave off the gadflies with his tail. Finally, the wagon train crawled out of the forest.

* * *

Don Daniel was resting on a soft bed in his tent when he heard the orderly whisper, "Your Grace! We have trouble!"

"What is it?" Daniel woke up instantly.

"A supply train has arrived from Leiria, but none of our soldiers are with it. A soldier's helmet was found on one of the carts and nothing else."

"What the hell! Where are they?"

"I don't know, Your Grace, but the wagon train is completely untouched." The supply carts were indeed intact. Even the location of the bags of flour and cereals tied with ropes indicated that none of them were missing, but the wagon train soldiers seemed to have sunk through the ground.

Panic seized the camp on the seashore. Who would threaten the soldiers, except those damned Moors, who had not been seen here for a long time? "Yes, it can only be the Red Ghost," the experienced fighters said, "it is his handiwork, or maybe his teeth."

Spewing curses, Daniel ordered a detachment of three dozen soldiers to comb the forest, and the cavalry split into two groups to inspect the road in both directions.

* * *

After getting out of the water, Chimalli climbed a hillock. He didn't see any of the warriors at the top. In the distance could be seen tents and figures of people in shiny armor, who scurried between them. To the left, the forest approached the camp, and Chimalli realized that his tribesmen could only be there. They couldn't hide anywhere else. Crouching down to the grass, Chimalli crept towards the forest. Chimalli was already very close to the thicket when suddenly several four-legged monsters rode out to the edge. On their backs sat men dressed in shiny armor. Their complexions were similar to the pale hue of the metstli.

"The Red Ghost!" One of them exclaimed in horror, pointing at Chimalli.

"Hold him!" another shouted.

The horsemen rushed to Chimalli. Dismounting near the terrified ticitl, they knocked him to the ground and began to beat him. The blows were so strong that the ticitl began to lose consciousness. "And you say a ghost! Look how the blood is gushing out of him!" one of the soldiers said. The soldiers tied up Chimalli, put him across the saddle, and drove him to the camp with joyful hooting.

* * *

Meanwhile, Anacaona was approaching a village that stood far from both the sea and the military camp. The people she saw from afar, even at such a distance, were like the ixiptlatli presented to Tezcatlipoca some hours ago. The same white faces and long beards. The women, clothed in unusual dresses, were distinguishable by the same light color faces. Anacaona immediately understood what these people were doing. They were macehualtin, farmers and herders.

Someone, despite the early hour, was already cutting the grass. Some women carried water in strange metal jugs. They drew the water from pits with evenly outlined rims and carried it to their farmsteads. Some fed the birds that scurried under their feet, and a little boy with a twig in his hand was driving birds of a different kind to the meadow. These large birds waddled, pulled up their necks, and babbled in unison. The older boys were driving larger animals, which Anacaona had also never seen before, into the meadow. These animals were docile, moved slowly, chewed grass constantly, and would sometimes moo loudly. On the other side, across the road, girls in odd dresses were spreading long pieces of canvas on the grass.

Soon the sounds of hammering and clanging began to sound from the village. An experienced ear would have recognized them as the blows of a blacksmith with his hammer. The noise of looms could be heard through house windows facing the sea, and despite the early hour, this noise was accompanied by a mournful female song. All these unfamiliar sounds to Anacaona both frightened and interested her at the same time.

Anacaona decided to get closer to these people and their homes, but suddenly a detachment of military men in shining armor atop four-legged monsters rode out of the forest. They raced along the road that passed through the village. One of these monsters knocked down a little boy but did not stop, even when the boy's roars could be heard by the whole neighborhood. Anacaona was petrified by the horror that these creatures and their behavior instilled in her.

Bending down below the grass, she hurried back to the side of the cliff, the top of which was clearly visible against the sky.

Descending from the cliff, Anacaona came out on a stone shore, similar to the back of a giant turtle. Searching her memory, she remembered that their warriors disembarked from boats not far from here. However, there were no boats near the shore anymore. Anacaona looked out to sea. Far away, between the crests of the waves, boats disappeared and reappeared, looking like seed husks from her place on the shore. The warriors and her father, there could be no doubt about it, were returning to Tlaluacatli.

What could Anacaona do? Of course, in no case did she want to catch the eye of those cruel savages whom she had managed to see, so she decided she would have to hide in the forest.

A Moment from the Past - Anacaona's Dream

When Anacaona was nine years old, she and her father, the ticitl Chimalli, lived on the outskirts of Texcoco. One night she had a dream that she remembered so vividly it was as if it had happened in reality. In this dream, Anacaona left her house and launched into the sky. She didn't have wings, and she didn't have to move her arms. Anacaona controlled her body with her mind and could fly in any direction. She flew over Lake Texcoco, and the majestic Tenochtitlan appeared ahead. Anacaona flew over the long bridge that connected the shore to the city. The city was in the middle of a lake, like a big island, a big, beautiful city on the water. In flight, Anacaona felt as if she were gliding over the waves of a sea. Rushing downward, she picked up speed, then abruptly soared up toward the stars. The sky was brightening behind the silhouette of the mountains; sunrise was beginning.

Anacaona was flying over the city now. She sailed over the chinampas – huge floating gardens on the water that surrounded the outskirts of the city. Chinampas always amazed Anacaona. They were artificial structures. Piles were driven into the bottom of the lake, connected with wattles, and then earth was filled in. Everything that farmers and gardeners needed was planted on this land. In the case of high water, the plantings were not washed away by the currents. The crops simply floated on the surface along with the land on which they grew. Harvests were always plentiful. One benefit of the chinampas was that the land was fertilized by what was collected right there from the bottom of the lake.

Below Anacaona, gardeners were sailing their boats to the thickets of mango, banana palms, orange, and fruit trees. Some of them were rubbed with the juice of plants to protect them from mosquitoes and midges. Where the long and wide chinampas ended, the market began. Anacaona noticed some merchants pointing at her. However, many did not even pay attention to her, as if the girl's flight over the city was an ordinary event. The merchants had more important things to do. They laid out vegetables and fruits on their counters, both locally grown in the chinampas and brought from the shore.

Turning right, Anacaona found herself above a long straight street. Someone was just leaving home below her, many were on their way to work, and someone, conversely, was returning home from night service. A woman standing on the side of the road was shaking out a rug. It was unwise to do this in her yard because infants who lived in the house spent most of the day in the garden, which occupied part of the backyard, and it should always be clean there!

Reaching the end of the street, Anacaona turned left. Now there were artisan settlements below. Anacaona liked to walk among their homes and workshops with her father or her friends when they were allowed to go to Tenochtitlan for the day. However, this rarely occurred. This beautiful city was very far away, and it took a long boat ride to get to it. Things made by craftsmen were often displayed in front of the houses. They would be exchanged for other goods, and among these items was everything that the townspeople needed. Beyond the artisans' settlement, the market could be seen. Craftsmen from other cities of the large expanse of

Aztlan brought their crafts there, and the more the state grew, the more diverse the goods in this market became.

Right behind the market, there was a large, magnificent building that housed the calmecac – the school for children of the city's nobility. This school was attended primarily by boys who would replace their fathers in the civil service, the sons of priests, councilmen, judges, and personal ticiti of tlatoque. There was also a court not far from the school. Flying over the courthouse yard, Anacaona saw how the judges were taught to put on their intricate clothes. To Anacaona, who saw mostly the clothing of ordinary people, the judges' caps and their boots with bows seemed funny, although they were interesting in their own way.

Just a moment after, Anacaona was already flying over the center of Tenochtitlan. There were government buildings and a whole block of temples. In the very center of this block stood Huey Teocalli, a giant pyramid, decorated with reliefs, stretching into the sky with two smaller temples. These were temples of Huitzilopochtli, the teotl of sun and war, and Tlaloc, the teotl of rain and fertility. Leading up to the pyramid, on a platform there was a terrifying exhibition of human skulls. This was the largest tzompantli in the city.

Suddenly, at the top of this pyramid between the temples, Anacaona saw the silhouette of a female figure. Anacaona immediately recognized her mother although she had never seen her. Yes, Chimalli had said she died in childbirth, but Anacaona stubbornly continued to believe that there was some kind of mistake, that her mother was alive, and that one day they would meet. So, this is what their meeting would be like! Anacaona rose so high that she was level with the top of the pyramid and accelerated her flight. Her mother's face was glowing; it glowed so brightly that it seemed as if she would go blind when she looked at it, but

Anacaona flew toward this light. She landed at the top of the pyramid and rushed to her mother, but suddenly Anacaona's hands and feet seemed to have turned to stone. She tried to run as hard as she could, but she could barely move. The pyramid literally anchored Anacaona to its blocks of stone.

"Anacaona," said the silhouette of a woman, "You must wake up!" The voice was beautiful, just like her mother's voice in her other dreams. She often cried in her sleep when she thought that she would never be able to hear this voice in reality.

"You must wake up!" the woman's voice repeated, and then the pyramid began to shake. One block after another began to fall from it. The silhouette of her mother crumbled into thousands of small fragments, and these fragments cascaded down like corn kernels. From the top of the pyramid, Anacaona saw the destruction of the city over which she had just flown. Roofs and walls of houses fell, burying people under them, and statues of teteo fell, collapsing into pieces as they tumbled down.

Above the surface of the lake, always serene, a wave suddenly surged, rushing toward the city. Anacaona realized that not a single person on the island could escape from this giant wave. Everyone was doomed!

"Anacaona, you must wake up!" She heard her mother's voice again in her head.

Anacaona shuddered and woke up. At the same moment, fragments of the wall of her home rained down on her. Anacaona jumped up and rushed to the exit of the house, but the roof caved in and blocked the way to her escape. The straw fell on the coals of yesterday's fire and immediately ignited. Anacaona rushed to the window and

managed to jump out of the house before the flames
engulfed it and left it in ruins.

The street was in the same chaos that Anacaona had
just seen from a bird's-eye view in her dream. Voices
screamed all around her, women ran around with children in
their arms, and some men tried to pull a man screaming in
pain out from under the ruins of a house. The earth was
moving like the waves of the sea. Even the mountains that
were visible on the horizon seemed to be shuddering. Those
who kept their wits about them had already begun to flee into
the jungle; others followed them. Anacaona fled to the jungle
with everyone else. She ran, but she smiled because, for the
first time in her life, she had finally seen her mother.

Thus began the most terrible earthquake in the
history of her people.

Chapter 5. The guest from Overseas

Anacaona, who had been dozing off, opened her eyes. The forest surrounding the girl now was not at all like in her homeland. Instead of arches of mangrove trees, under which an entire village could freely pass, this forest consisted of low pines and other trees that grew between. There was no wet springy jungle ground under the girl's feet. These trees and squat bushes grew on sandy scant soil. There was also no fog in this forest, even now, at dawn, as was usual in the jungles of her homeland. Anacaona closed her eyes and sniffed the scent of the forest. New smells, unfamiliar to her, spread out in colored patterns in her imagination. The color and shape of the patterns gave her clues about what particular plants, grasses, or foliage could help heal. Out of the huge variety of new smells, she felt something very strong. This particular smell told her that there was a plant in this forest that could cure the most difficult ailments. Where could she find it?

However, the events of the previous morning began to disturb Anacaona with renewed vigor, and her study of smells had to be postponed. The boats had returned to Tlaluacatli, and now she was completely alone in an unexplored land! What to do? The military men, prowling through the forest with their bright long macuahuitl, did not notice her in the predawn twilight, but it could happen during the day! As if to confirm Anacaona's terrible conclusion, the wind carried the sounds of human speech to her.

Before dawn, Anacaona, exhausted, had sat down on a sandy hummock and immediately dozed off. She didn't notice that she had stopped near the road, and now the metstli tlapalli were passing by her. They walked either in pairs or individually and held spears, coils of rope, and various sticks with three or four unknown metal ends, and some carried huge, but hardly heavy boxes on their backs. A man galloped along the road, overtaking these people, riding a huge four-legged animal that Anacaona had already noticed early in the morning from afar. The people on foot gave way to the man, and some took off their hats and bowed to the rider.

Cautiously glancing at the road, Anacaona began to retreat into the forest thicket. After making sure that she could no longer be noticed from the road, she began to inspect and study the unfamiliar trees and grasses. Anacaona was very thirsty, but she didn't see any traces of water nearby. Sorting through the vegetation, the young woman began to pull out their stems. If they didn't taste bitter, Anacaona would eat their juicy flesh.

* * *

"Luis, do you really think that our old clothes will be useful to his family?" Nuno asked. The horse under him had strained his legs the day before and was now limping on the front right, which was why Nuno fidgeted in the saddle every now and then.

Luis, who was riding next to him, shrugged his shoulders, "Who knows? Everything comes in handy on the farm, especially for poor people. Well, the rich definitely don't become soldiers, that's a well-known thing. It would be better, of course, to give a purse with gold or, at least, silver."

"There's silver, too," Nuno answered. He reached into his bosom, took out a small but heavy bundle, examined it carefully once more, and put it back.

"And to tell the truth, you don't have to give too much," Luis continued, "after all, the son was killed in the service of the king, so let the king help them. Otherwise, they might become proud and quit working. They will think that they themselves have become the masters... Oh, trouble, trouble…"

Suddenly, a scream came from the depths of the forest. Nuno and Luis exchanged glances. The scream was undoubtedly from a woman. Nuno spurred his horse and, bending down to his withers, rushed into the thicket. Luis rode after him. Among the juniper bushes, they saw an unfamiliar, apparently alien, dark-skinned woman. She was dressed in a simple linen dress, with gold bracelets adorning her arms and a necklace of precious stones around her neck. The young woman's right leg was clamped in the jaws of a trap.

"Damn poachers!" Luis swore. "They were banned from the lands of Don Leandro! Under his father, such people used to be flogged for trapping one rabbit, just for show, to prevent others from hunting in the lord's forest."

Nuno jumped off his horse and ran up to the woman. The wound on her trapped leg was bleeding. With the help of Luis and a strong oak branch, Nuno parted the jaws of the trap and freed her leg. From a bag strapped to his saddle, he took out a flask of clean water and a piece of clean cloth. Nuno always carried this bag with him after an incident where he was unable to help a wounded peasant. After washing the wound and wrapping a cloth around her leg, he finally asked the girl, who was recovering, "Are you from around here? How did you end up here?"

The young woman wiped tears from her eyelashes and said something in a language unknown to Nuno. She could tell from the stranger's face that he didn't want to hurt her.

"Luis, do you understand anything she is saying?"

"No. Maybe she is a Marrano girl, or maybe from the Moriscos. Although to tell the truth, she doesn't really look like them either. Dark, but not the same."

Anacaona tried to get up from the ground, but her wounded foot was pierced by such a sharp pain that she screamed and fell unconscious on the soft forest ground.

* * *

When consciousness returned to Anacaona, she saw a canopy of exotic, almost transparent fabric above her. She was lying on a soft bed that smelled of flowers. She raised her head and saw an elderly woman sitting next to her on a chair. Anacaona immediately remembered that she was on Uehkatlan. The woman worked quickly and silently with knitting needles, from which a wide fluffy piece of handwork hung. There were balls of yarn on her lap. Next to the woman sat a young man, whom Anacaona recognized as her rescuer. He was holding a board in front of him and moving a stick with a piece of gray clamped to the end of it.

Noticing that Anacaona was awake, the woman raised her head and looked at the young man. "Your guest is awake, Nuno," she said indifferently. "Maybe she needs something? Otherwise, I'll go to my room."

The young man got up and went over to the bed. "You may go, Graca," he said. "Tell them downstairs to bring fruit, meat, bread, and a jug of lemon juice with honey."

Approaching the bed, Nuno timidly pulled back the curtain. "How's the leg?" he asked.

The girl smiled and said nothing. She tried to get up, but as soon as her foot touched the floor, she winced in pain.

"Graca! And a new bandage with healing ointment!" Nuno called after the maid. Cautiously glancing at the dog dozing at the threshold, the maid left the room.

Soon Anacaona's wound had been treated again. Nuno personally served her food and poured a drink into the girl's cup, which she clearly liked. By the way the girl ate, it was obvious that she was hungry. Nuno showed Anacaona the board with a piece of paper on it. In the outlines of the figure depicted on this sheet, drawn with the stick, Anacaona immediately recognized herself.

"I... "Nuno tapped his chest with his fist "Nuno."

Anacaona nodded and put her palm to her chest, "Neuatl tokaitl Anacaona" *My name is Anacaona.*

"A-na-ca-o-na," Nuno repeated diligently.

The girl laughed but nodded affably. She took the board from Nuno's hands, drew a leg on paper, and said, "Ikxitl" *Leg.*

"Ikxitl" repeated Nuno. Guessing the meaning of this word, he said, "A leg!" Anacaona nodded happily. Nuno wrote next to Anacaona's drawing, "leg."

Then she put her index and middle fingers on her palm and began to step over them, "Xinenemi" *Walk.*

Nuno wrote down this word as well. Making more drawings, the young people soon began to understand the meaning of unfamiliar words, which they identified by these drawings. There was something menacing and beautiful at the same time in the melody of the language the girl spoke.

"How did you get here?" Nuno asked and looked at Anacaona's big, beautiful eyes.

Anacaona realized what the most natural question would be. She showed the waves of the sea, and the boat with her hands and said, "Uey Atl" *Big Water.*

Nuno took the portrait of Anacaona, surrounded it with figures of a man, a woman, and children in a few strokes of a quill, and looked questioningly at the girl. "Kampa no senyelistli?" *Where is my family?* Anacaona guessed at his question. She again depicted the sea and the boat, and then strongly, as if she were driving someone away, waved her arms to the side.

Nuno understood that the girl came from an unknown country across the sea; Nuno thought she was probably from Africa. He also learned that she was seventeen years old and that she had no mother, only a father.

With the help of drawings, Nuno told her that he was also seventeen years old, that he was the son of a man who owned a large estate, and that he had a dog named Duarte. At the mention of his name, the dog poked his wet nose into Anacaona's sore leg and happily wagged his tail. Nuno simply forgot all about Estela and the fact that Anacaona was settled in Estela's room.

The servants' conversations about the foreign girl that Nuno and Luis found in the forest quickly reached Leandro and his wife, and they both came to see her. "Maybe she got into the forest with poachers?" Leandro asked his son suspiciously.

Manuella went up to the girl, looked into her eyes, took her hands in her own, and examined them. "This girl is not in the habit of rough work," Manuella said, "and she has not been abused either. Most importantly, she's wearing jewelry. Did she run away from her rich parents' house?"

"So, who is she?" Leandro wondered. He brought and showed Anacaona a rough map of Europe, but it turned out that the shapes on the paper did not mean anything to her. However, in the corners of the map were painted all sorts of monsters that, judging by the fins, came from the sea.

"Maybe these people also hold their own festivals?" Anacaona thought as she looked at the monsters. Anacaona pointed her finger at the image of the hippocampus, a sea creature with the head of a horse and the tail of a fish, and looked questioningly at Leandro. He exchanged glances with his wife. Manuella only understood that this animal was a mystery to Anacaona, the same as anyone. One riddle continued to generate another, and they multiplied, multiplied, and multiplied.

Something, however, was clarified when Anacaona was examined by a doctor summoned specially for her. When he re-treated the wound on her leg, he wrapped it with a bandage and began to tie the ends. Anacaona resolutely stopped him. She unwrapped the leg, then bandaged it again, and when the bandage began to run out, she tore the rest along the middle with a sharp movement. Lastly, she tied the pieces at the base, brought one of them towards the other around the leg, and then tied the ends. At the sight of her skillful binding, the doctor was speechless. "This girl knows things beyond our skills," he muttered. Indeed, such a method of securing bandages, a very sensible one, was not yet known to him.

In the evening of the same day, Estela also had a chance to experience a shock. Estela met Manuella at the entrance to Leandro's house, and the girl immediately noticed the unusual expression on Manuella's face. The lady of the house was clearly bewildered. "Estela," she said, "you won't be able to stay in your room today, maybe in the room of one of the maids?"

"What happened?" Estela asked with surprise.

"Nuno found a strange young woman in the forest. She speaks an unknown language. She's hurt, and Nuno put her in your room to heal."

Even if there was still some uncertainty about Nuno and Estela's engagement, Estela considered her room in this house to be her own. Needless to say, she was understandably shocked! But Estela was very good at controlling herself. Entering "her" room, she greeted Anacaona with a smile and, tapping on the cross on her chest, told the girl her name. After looking closely at the patterns embroidered on Anacaona's dress, Estela took the scarlet ribbon she had found on the shore from under her sleeve and showed it to Anacaona. Estela still carried this ribbon with its incomprehensible writing with her, so as not to forget to show it to the instructors at the university.

Anacaona gave a startled cry, "Kampa Tupac?" *Where is Tupac?*

Estela didn't say anything. She briefly grasped Nuno's elbow and, without looking at his face, left.

"Well, what can you say about her?" Manuella asked. She had waited for Estela outside the door.

"First of all, she identified that strange ribbon that Nuno and I found on the shore not far from the dead soldier," Estela said. She took the ribbon out from under her sleeve again and showed it to Manuella. "That is most important, and this connection will have to be investigated by Don Diego, my father's deputy, who oversees the deanery in this region. As for the girl herself, dark skin suits some girls." Estela sighed and continued after a short pause, "Her wound will heal soon. However, I don't understand. When a girl wanders into the forest, it usually happens to a simpleton, but this girl is wearing so much gold jewelry that she can only come from a very rich family… And maybe…"

"Maybe what?" Manuella could not wait for Estela to continue.

"You say, according to Nuno, that she came by sea. Maybe she's a merchant's daughter? Or maybe she strayed from some family of Marranos or Moriscos who are now fleeing the country from Castile?"

"But what are the Marranos or Moriscos doing here? Leandro says they're running away from us too. They are running only to the north. Why would they come to our land?"

"Anyway, this girl is in trouble," Estela said calmly, "and the Lord will bless your family for the fact that you have aided her. I hope she got her gold jewelry in an honest way. Sometimes such girls are used by the most notorious villains. I'm sure you know that, Donna Manuella!"

In Leandro's house, Estela passed the endurance test through to the end despite the fact that no matter what conversations she started with Nuno, the young man's gaze soon began to fog up, and he strove to return to his other guest. Estela refused to spend the night with the maids or in the room that was prepared for her. That evening she went home accompanied by the servants, who had not even rested after their hard day.

"Leave me alone, Mom!" she shouted to her mother, who was surprised by her sudden and very late return. "Nuno has a new bride! A mix between a monkey and a wharf girl from the poorest port! And in order not to be found out, she pretends to be a foreigner!" With these words, Estela rushed to her room, slammed the door loudly, and sobbed.

Nuno had a hard time that night, too. Having seated their son on a chair in front of them, his parents told him how much Estela must have been offended by the appearance of Anacaona in her room. "Even if Estela didn't show it to you, my son, she's deeply offended." Leandro was saying. "She's a very tenacious, strong-willed, but restrained girl, and you have to respect that. Anacaona should leave."

Looking at her husband's face, Manuella nodded in agreement.

"This Anacaona does not speak our language, and our customs are alien to her," Leandro continued. "We don't know who she is, where she came from, or how she came to our land. She must leave our house as soon as possible. She could be dangerous to you."

"I don't see any danger in her," Nuno kept saying, "while we don't know who else can help her or where she needs to return to, we will put her in more danger by forcing her to leave now."

"And what about Estela?" said the mother. "Believe me, son, nowadays such acquaintances and such girls are not easily found. Oh, if you only knew how many stupid, uncouth, and boring fools there are for each one such as Estela! If you only knew! You can't imagine what happiness Estela can bring you! Yes, you are just spoiled by your comfortable friendship with this most worthy girl! You've seen too few unhappy families! Don't you understand that it is the wife who makes her husband a man and a member of society?"

Don Leandro blushed deeply, "And then, what if your Anacaona is a girl from a Marrano or Morisco family?" he hastily interrupted Manuella. "Can you guarantee she's not from their community? After all, you know that Isabella of Castile is currently expelling them from her country. The cup of patience for her people has overflowed! I am sure that our king will do the same soon. Those infidels drink the blood of Christian babies! Didn't Padre Pablo tell you this?"

"By the way, in Castile, anyone who decides to marry a baptized girl from the Marranos will have to bring la limpieza de sangre," Manuella echoed her husband, "a certificate of purity of blood. So far, this is only in Castile, but soon such laws will reach us too. And how, for example, will the same Anacaona provide that if she came from nowhere, does not believe in the only God who exists, and does not speak our language?"

"Manuella, we are not talking about marriage!" Leandro shouted. "We're just talking about…"

Nuno jumped up from his chair and ran out of the room.

"Leandro!" Manuella cried. "Maybe this girl will only stay with us until her family is found. Maybe then Nuno will calm down and she will go away?"

* * *

Anacaona stayed at Don Leandro's house, and it surprised her at every step. The clothes of the household and even Nuno himself seemed too warm to her; Anacaona would have suffocated in them. Her tribesmen always left at least half of their bodies exposed, despite the fact that they wore more jewelry than garments.

These people's faces, hairstyles, and jewelry did not tell Anacaona to which social class they belonged, but their clothes and demeanor seemed to indicate it was not the lowest one. Chains and thin bracelets made of gold were worn only by Nuno's parents and their guests, and they were worn with incomprehensible pride as if they were awards received from Weyitlatoani himself. However, ordinary people often had metal tools in their hands for which Anacaona's people would have given a fortune in their homeland. So sturdy and durable were all these scissors, fireplace tongs, jugs, cups, and tools of the peasants! Even the door handles were made of it.

Benches, cabinets, carpets, tapestries, and ornate caskets – Anacaona guessed the purpose of all of these things. These were found in her house as well. However, it bore the imprint of a completely different world here. The only thing that really struck Anacaona was the mirror. When Anacaona first saw her reflection, she cried out in fright, "Tleuatl?" *What is it?* and she pointed her finger at the mirror.

Nuno laughed, "It's a mirror, Anacaona. Mir-ror." He picked up a board with a piece of paper, and wrote down "Tleuatl" and his translation, "What is it?" Nuno went to the mirror and stood next to the young woman. She cried out again. Nuno waved his hand, and Anacaona did the same, bursting into loud laughter. Seeing their shared reflections,

Nuno suddenly realized that he would now be very lonely without Anacaona.

"Chipauak atl" *Clear as water*, she said. "Tleka amo atlanteittani" *But why doesn't it leak?* Anacaona touched the mirror with her hand and looked questioningly at Nuno, who, meanwhile, was quickly drawing on the paper with a quill. He was writing down the new words and making drawings. Anacaona's mind was already swarming with hypotheses about how these people possibly melted the stone, making it smooth and hard again, and how it then was polished. That was how mirrors were made in her homeland.

Nuno abandoned all his usual activities, hunting, pigeons, trips to artisans' workshops, and visits to the stables. Even books became tiresome to him, and now he only took up paper and quill to make drawings for Anacaona and memorize new words. The language of Anacaona was easier for Nuno to learn than the Portuguese was for Anacaona.

Anacaona began to walk slowly, although with a slight limp, and they walked together through the surrounding groves and fields. Nuno showed Anacaona fruit trees and vegetables growing in their fields. Anacaona tasted an apple for the first time in her life, which was surprising for Nuno. Apples, in his opinion, should grow everywhere. He also took her to the village, where they laughed together at women who snatched up children and ran away at the sight of a dark, incomprehensible girl with tattoos. All this, too, was understandable to the keen, laughing Anacaona.

Mysterious animals harnessed to platforms on wooden circles no longer frightened her. In her homeland, the wheel was not used, and the pochteca, merchants, carried loads on their backs. But as a child, Anacaona had a toy, a wooden animal, that could be rolled on the floor because it was put on wheels. It was just such structures on wheels that the local pochteca used.

Nuno gave Anacaona the opportunity to get to know the horses. The girl almost cried when she felt the tender lips of the horse, and it ate the piece of bread she held out for it. Soon, Anacaona was riding, and she immediately began to hold herself in the saddle more confidently than many cavalrymen held themselves.

In the evenings, they looked at drawings in books by candlelight. The main book in the Nuno family, of course, was the Bible. Nuno told Anacaona about Christ, and she agreed that it was impossible to save humanity without sacrificing a person. In confirmation of her words, she told Nuno about the rituals in her homeland. However, her stories did not explain much to the young man. The concepts that Anacaona tried to convey with gestures, several dozen words, and drawings, turned out to be too complicated to understand.

Nuno completely lost his head for this beautiful, kind, and amazingly understanding young girl, and Anacaona liked him more and more every day. Her life had never been so carefree before! In this house, there was everything that the body and soul could wish for, and no one demanded anything from her in exchange. However, the more Nuno and Anacaona became attached to one another, the darker Don Leandro's face became when he looked at the couple from afar, and his father's attitude toward Anacaona did not escape Nuno's attention. He firmly decided he would leave his father's house with Anacaona once the girl finally recovered and would not return until Anacaona found her family and secured reliable protection.

A Moment from the Past - A Storm Off the Coast of Africa

Afonso V and his son, Joao, the heir to the throne, were standing on the deck of the royal caravel. With gloved hands, the royal duo grabbed the tarred ropes as an unprecedented, strong storm raged, bringing with it a furious downpour.

The armada numbered about four hundred ships, and each one was threatened with destruction. Here and there the ships buried their bowsprits in the sea, tilted sideways, touching the waves with the tops of their masts. Waves rolled over the decks, washing away people, horses, barrels, and debris, and there was not a man on these ships now whose heart did not shrink with horror. On some vessels, soldiers arbitrarily launched boats or tried to swim to shore, but it was all in vain. The sea seized them on the spot, pushed at the small boats, and rolled them over. People, both on boats and ships, threw off their heavy armor in panic. Those who managed to do this could still possibly stay afloat. Less fortunate soldiers went under the water without ever having time to shout the name of the Saint Virgin Mary, or their mother or wife…

"Look!" The drenched king shouted to his son, "Look, Joao! I have been preparing this endeavor for years, and now everything I collected for this purpose is going underwater. Do you know how much this cost me and my country? And what this means for all of us! Do you know?!"

Sixteen-year-old Joao did not answer. He knew perfectly well that his father was not waiting for an answer, and the king couldn't even shout or curse in despair like the simple sailors. "Fernao!" The king exclaimed, trying to shout over the noise of the storm. Fernao, the assistant commander of the armada, came out of the cabin on the upper deck of the caravel. He was pale as death. "Fernao, once we are on the shore, you will first count the number of ships remaining in service," the king ordered, "then, you'll fix them up, and also tell me how many days of supplies we have left. If there is not enough for a month, you will have to return to Lagos and replace what we have lost."

"Yes, Your Majesty," Fernao croaked. Holding his stomach with both hands, he wandered back.

Suddenly, a cargo ship hit the broadside of the royal caravel. The cargo ship's mast snapped and began to fall on the caravel. The king and his heir barely managed to dodge out of the way as the mast fell to the deck and cracked it. Judging by the rumble below, the hull was deeply damaged. Fernao's deafening shouts reverberated over this roar as the falling mast grazed him, the end of the second sailyard from above landing right in his mouth and tearing him almost to the ear. Blood gushed onto the deck. Fernao rushed into the cabin where he was quartered with the captain and the doctor, and the squall immediately slammed the door behind him.

The deck became a little quieter. Joao turned his gaze to his father. The king continued like nothing had happened, "Even if we don't have enough supplies, we'll still attack Asilah tomorrow!" The king shouted stubbornly in his son's face. "We will attack the city with what we have left. Having besieged the fortress, we will not last long. We need the provisions they keep in the city. It's all or nothing!"

Joao nodded. He saw his father's despair and was very scared, but Afonso's last words inspired Joao with hope, if not for a successful military campaign, then at least for a successful landing and solid ground under his feet.

Next to the royal caravel, vainly struggling with the waves, a horse floated among the debris and broken parts of ships. She tried to neigh but choked as an indescribable horror froze on her face.

Chapter 6. The King and His Navigators

In the castle of St. George, at the bottom of a regal staircase, there were two guards in armor and with halberds in their hands. These stairs ascended to the upper landing that opened on the left to a great square hall. The hall was illuminated by the sun's rays, freely penetrating through the huge windows that were as spacious as the entrance. Swallows sometimes flew through one window, only to immediately disappear through the opening of the other.

This was the king's study. In the middle of this spacious hall, there was a long table covered with dishes of food and jugs of drinks. The stone walls were decorated with carpets, tapestries, antique armor, and weapons. Along the walls, there were chests, caskets, and open cabinets, in which were stored large and small scrolls of papers and stacks of documents.

Between the two grand windows, there was an exit to a spacious balcony. Walking along it, one could walk around the tower and explore Lisbon; from this height, the entire city could be appreciated at a mere glance.

There were three people sitting at the table dressed in the usual attire for the time. At the end of the table, on a large, comfortable chair, sat the king, a young man in a simple white shirt, ordinary pants, and boots. If the king's bearing had not been truly royal, a foreigner, seeing Joao II in this costume, could have mistaken him for one of the guests. The king was meeting with the most famous navigators of

Portugal. "Today I will have to make an important choice," the king said. "I will need your help, Senhors. You will tell me again what the goals of your voyages are."

The king raised a silver goblet to his lips and took a sip. His guests stood up and also drank from their cups. "Bartolomeu, where do you want to sail your ships?"

Bartolomeu Dias, a 33-year-old sailor, stood up and spoke respectfully, "My goal, Your Majesty, has not changed in recent years. I, like you, believe that we should build forts on the African coast. They will guard our merchants and missionaries and protect them from both savages and our European rivals. We have recently built the fort of Castelo da Mina. It is the first of many. To raise that fort, it took ten caravels and two cargo ships to be sent to the predetermined place on the coast of Africa. The land in the vicinity of the fort has no name yet. During the journey to this land, we did not meet any other ships, and therefore Your Majesty has every reason to consider this land as belonging to the Portuguese crown. I propose to call it the Gold Coast because it is very rich in gold. As for the rest, I want to continue moving toward the south of Africa."

The king nodded and took another sip from his goblet. It was clear he liked what the navigator said.

"We will move south along the African coast," Dias continued, "and make maps of rivers as we traverse along them into the utmost depths of Africa. We will find out who lives there, what riches they have, and what benefits we can bring to each other. Most of all, we need free hands now. They will allow us to extract the gold scattered along the gold-bearing rivers and deliver it to our forts and trading posts to be shipped to Portugal."

"But this single fort is too weak for such defense," the king said. "Even if you start bringing gold into it, it will be very easy to lose control of it. Soon, after us, the Castilians, Moors, and only God knows who else, will sail there. We are not the only ones who have suitable ships. You must know this. By "free hands" you probably mean black slaves?"

Bartolomeu Dias nodded respectfully.

"Well, these slaves will have to be fed," the king grinned. "We'll have to pay their guards. Won't your "free hands" cost the treasury too much?" The king got up from his chair and went to the window under the stone arch, covered with amazingly fine carvings. The navigators were silent. Standing at the window, Joao II admired the view of his beautiful capital. Vessels of all sizes, merchants' longboats, and fishermen's skiffs scurried along the Tagus River below.

"The only thing we have over our rivals now is time," the king continued. "We were ahead of them and therefore we were the first to build a fort there. Now we must strengthen it in every possible way. Then we must build new forts, fortresses, and strong trading points. What is needed for this? First of all, ships, and we will need more and more of them. The more fortresses we have, the more ships we will need. We must have carracks and cargo ships because I can't use warships to transport cargo and goods. Not only would it offend the navy, but it wouldn't be wise. Warships are not donkeys or draft oxen. Their business is to fight, not to transport goods. Besides, warships are needed here in Portugal first of all. They have to protect our shores."

"Yes, but gold is also capable of bringing protection," Dias dared to object.

The king stared at him. Dias cleared his throat and calmly smoothed the lace collar on his chest, worn only for the occasion of his visit to the palace. This collar spoiled the simple, comfortable, and rough style of the sea wolf, who had more than once looked into the eyes of death itself. Dias wasn't scared this time either.

"As soon as the gold from Africa flows into your treasury, Your Majesty," he continued in a firm voice, "ships can be built with tenfold strength, both the carracks and cargo vessels. Young Portuguese already want to be shipbuilders rather than soldiers. There are hereditary masters among them, and there are more and more of them because they are in demand. If you leave them idle now, they will go to build ships for the Castilians, Sicilians, or Genoese, or even for the Moors. What happens then? We invest our strength and soul in them; they spend time learning, devoting their strength and their parents' money to studying ship trades, and then they leave Portugal."

The king's other two guests looked down. Each of them knew that Bartolomeu Dias was telling the absolute truth. He said what they didn't dare to say.

"Gold loses its value if you look for it too long," one of the sailors finally objected, "and if it is found quickly and in great quantity, it also becomes worth less."

"Vasco, what are you suggesting?" said the king.

Vasco da Gama rose from the table, a bearded young man of twenty-three who already had a reputation as one of the most daring and skillful sailors. As always, he was dressed in a sand-colored doublet girded with a wide belt. At the sight of large white diamonds on the black sleeves of his shirt, fashionably visible, one might have thought that they were signal flags de Gama used to command all the ships of his fleet at the same time.

"The transportation of goods can bring even more income than gold mining," Vasco da Gama answered. "Of course, we need fortresses in Africa, but they will be needed not only to protect merchants and their goods but also to pave new sea routes from one coast to another so that it will be possible to replenish ships with supplies during long crossings. The farther away we have trading posts, the better. Who knows, maybe one day we will even be able to pave a sea route to India."

The king and the navigators looked questioningly at Vasco da Gama.

"India is known to be surrounded by the sea," da Gama continued, "so ships must be able to get there, and I am sure that it is possible to get there by sea even now. However, this is only on the condition that the discoverers of this path are accompanied by ships with sufficient supplies. This requires a whole armada! If there are fortresses with warehouses for the captains headed to India, they will have much less need for their own cargo ships."

"We don't know yet if it's possible to get to India by sea if we keep going south along the African coast," Dias objected. "Many people think that that coast has no end."

"But after your exploration, we will also confirm or deny just that. Isn't that right, Bartolomeu?" Da Gama answered, looking into Dias's eyes.

Dias nodded with a smile. The king shuddered, having noticed Dias's teeth, beaten by scurvy, the scourge of the pioneer navigators.

"Therefore, I propose first of all to find a sea route to India," da Gama said, addressing the king, "while this path is not yet open, while no one knows where the unknown path will lead. There may be nowhere to put new fortresses, and such fortresses may be useless. However, there is no way to do without them on known paths. Whether they will carry gold, goods, or slaves through them, all this will require maps, which are not yet available."

"Maps can be drawn simultaneously with the construction of new fortresses," Dias interjected. "One project will only help the other."

"We will lose the lands in Africa that we have already opened if the Castilians get ahead of us," the king interrupted the navigators. "We will lose both gold and goods that can be brought from there. Yes, we know that there may be a sea route to India, but no one in the world knows for sure yet. Time is on our side now, but it won't always be like this. I know Isabella of Castile. If she hears rumors about a route to gold, she will send ships for it immediately!"

The king scratched his nose. He wanted to continue but suddenly stopped. "Christopher!" he exclaimed, "How would you prove, for example, to my gatekeeper that the land is round? After all, you seem convinced of this yourself?"

The man sitting next to Bartolomeu Dias was his age. Answering the king's question, he also stood up and spoke with a smile on his long expressive face, "Very simple, Your Majesty. I would show him a ship at sea, going in any direction. As soon as this ship moves away to a distance of five thousand vara, that is, about six thousand steps of an adult, the ship is lost from sight. First, its hull disappears, then the sails, and finally the tops of the masts." Christopher Columbus spoke Portuguese well, but still, it was clear from his accent that he was not Portuguese. It seemed Columbus was afraid that his answer to the king was not clear enough. In addition to his words, he spread his hands, in one of which he continued to hold his black hat which matched the color of his doublet.

"And where are you going with this?" The king frowned. Columbus was a rather tall man, and the king had to look up from below.

"This means that the land is not flat, but has the shape of a ball, Your Majesty. That's what I would tell the gatekeeper."

The navigators gave Columbus a puzzled look.

"I do believe," he continued, "that sailing south along the coast of Africa means finding a free exit to the western coast of India sooner or later. However, because India is washed by the sea from both the west and the east, a trip to the west will also lead to India. Because the land is round, this voyage will lead to the east coast of India."

Dias and da Gama looked at Columbus with increasing surprise. He did not share his idea of going west with them before the meeting.

"I have traveled a lot throughout Europe during my life," Columbus continued. "I've been to the North, too. The Northerners, who once sailed the seas in drakkars, their long galleys, told me that many centuries ago their ancestors visited a land they called Vinland. They reached this land in this way, all the time going by sea to the west. One of these northern sailors even brought a bride from Vinland, and I was shown their distant descendants. These are descendants of Indians; their faces are different from the Northerners'. I am sure that if we sail west from Portugal, we will definitely reach the east coast of India."

The king folded his arms on his chest and began to pace the hall in silence. The navigators did not take their eyes off him. At last, the king went back to the window and, without addressing any one of his guests said, "Vasco and Christopher want to go to a place from where they may never return. At the same time, Portugal will spend a lot of money and effort on these voyages. If your travels are successful, the new sea routes will be able to cover these costs in one year, of course. But what Bartolomeu suggests involves less risk but with a lower and slower reward though. Besides, our rivals are also thinking about this path. I declare; I am sure of it. What if they build their fortresses on the African shores and reach its riches before us?"

The king went to one of the cabinets and took out a paper scroll from it. Then he spread it out on a spacious table. On the paper was a drawing of a ship. The navigators had never seen ships like this before. "Look here," the king pointed to the level of the middle deck. There were a lot of squares drawn there with ropes hanging over them. "Do you know what these are?"

"Cargo hatches?" Vasco da Gama suggested.

"Gun ports," Columbus said affirmatively, "but why are there ropes on these hatches?"

"This battery occupies the entire middle deck!" Bartolomeu Dias exclaimed.

"You are all correct," the king chuckled. "This is my new ship, the Santa Catarina. She has no equal in the fleets of France or Castile. She is bigger and faster than any Carrack or similar ships of other navies, and its main advantage is its rate of fire. There will only be cannons on the middle deck. This battery will be able to fire volleys, shooting continuously, because, at the moment when some cannons are firing, others are reloading. The ropes at the hatches, Christopher, are designed for closing them during a storm. With the ropes, it will be possible to close and open them fast at any time without crawling on the hull."

The king let go of the edges of the paper, and the drawing folded by itself. "I showed you this drawing so that you know what kind of fleet will be built for Portugal soon. This fleet will make our country invincible at sea." The king put the drawing back on the shelf in the closet. "And Portugal will not know its equal at sea for another hundred years. There will also be such ships to protect the caravans of merchant ships that will go along your sea routes, both old and new ones. And do you know what I need to build them?"

The king looked around at the navigators. "Money, first of all, money..." The king fell silent. Seagulls screeched, and shouts of sailors could be heard from the port. "... And time," the king continued. "There is no time to lose because we have very strong opponents. If I pay for all the trips you have planned, nothing will be left to build the new fleet," The king jerked his finger in the direction of the cabinet with the drawings, "and the children and apprentices of our shipbuilders will run away to the rivals, as Bartolomeu correctly noted."

The king went back to the window. "We will start preparing your sea trips," he said from there. "One of them will be prepared in one and a half or two years. At the same time, we will start to build new ships. Bartolomeu said that it is possible to open new paths and build fortresses at the same time. This also applies to ships."

"Exactly so, Your Majesty," Dias bowed his head.

"Yes, I would like to sail the sea on the Santa Catarina!" Vasco da Gama exclaimed. "That is exactly how I imagine the best ships in the world to be, the ship of my dreams."

"You may sail on such a ship," the king told him without looking at Vasco, "but there is no time to waste," and his gaze shifted toward Christopher.

Columbus guessed; the journey he proposed was to be postponed indefinitely.

"Afonso!" The king shouted loudly. A man's footsteps could be heard coming up the stairs. "Senhores navigators, you may go," the king announced to his guests. "I will tell you soon which of your proposals I can support. But some..." and the king looked into Columbus's eyes, "should not expect my answer anytime soon."

The navigators bowed and left the hall. The king went back to the window. He was overcome by heavy thoughts. In front of him was a beautiful city, the capital of Portugal. It was not a poor city, but in order for the king's subjects not to starve, citizens had to work hard, and still, there were dark days within their families. Meanwhile, there were idle rich people in Portugal, very rich. People who never wanted to think about how to bring prosperity to Portugal. Some of them believe that the Cortes would help, but did the Cortes have the money for such help? Did they have an army and navy to fight the Moors or open new trade routes for those same rich people? So, he, the king, was expected to spend the treasury's money to make them even richer?

The king chuckled. No, on the contrary! It was he who would take away their surplus property and money. He would spend their wealth to make the whole country strong and rich, and if these people resisted the will of the king, they would disappear. No matter what they said, mired in empty talk and bribery, in their Cortes. Portugal would become strong and beautiful, like the new ship, Santa Catarina. Ships like this would guard the trade routes that glorious sailors would pave to the new shores of Africa and India.

General Afonso, the namesake of the former king, entered the hall. The forty-year-old general wore steel armor. Afonso left his sword with the guards. Entering the royal chambers with a weapon would be considered committing a crime. Looking at the general's face, the king shuddered; it looked very much like the death mask of his father, and indeed of any man the king had ever seen in agony.

"Afonso, my friend," said the king, overcoming his fear. He went up to the general and embraced him. "Today, I entrust you with an important mission! We are starting a very important business. Someday you'll be proud to have taken part in it."

"Your Majesty!" Exclaimed the general who was very touched by such words of the king. "I am always happy to serve you." The general's bird-like face radiated joy and devotion.

"But tell me first, what's new in the South?" the king asked.

"The Castilians, Your Majesty, are still not complete masters of their country in the south. Although they considered the Reconquista already completed, Granada remains under partial control of the emirate and a hotbed of rebellion. To suppress the rebels, the Castilians have to keep a large army there."

"Is it true that many local residents are also opposed to the final Reconquista in Granada?"

"Yes, Your Majesty. To overcome them, the Castilians are not only taking military measures but also spiritual ones. The Castilians are calling these measures the Inquisition. Isabella suppresses Jews and Mohammedans with an iron hand. The Jewish have no place on her land anymore, but now the Jews are trying to infiltrate into our land from there. We catch them and drive them away or convert them either to the true faith or to slavery. We are forced to execute those who do not obey. Now we have so many slaves that there is nowhere to keep them and nothing to feed them. All the garrisons of our fortresses are constantly in full readiness…" General Afonso stealthily but meaningfully examined his armor and finished, "We will not allow heretics and Moors to gather in groups and gangs."

"Great!" The king exclaimed. "No mercy for heretics! You're talking about the Inquisition. I know too little about it, but I will learn more in time. Isabella will surely only strengthen it. Tell me, Afonso, how many soldiers are left in the garrison of Lisbon after we transferred another thousand soldiers to Algarve a month ago?"

"Six hundred and forty, Your Majesty, one hundred and twenty archers, seventy horsemen, and the rest are infantry. Perhaps we should move our troops from the Algarve back to Lisbon?"

"Then who will catch heretics in the Algarve?" the king asked. "The army in Algarve will stay there, but I repeat, I trust you to perform a secret task, you and only you. Only you can successfully complete it in the name of the king and Portugal."

"Yes, Your Majesty!" The general snapped to attention.

"You will gather the garrison of Lisbon, all the soldiers except the guards at the gates, towers, and bridges. With this garrison, you will march today to the district of Evora, to the castle of Vila Viçosa!"

"Your Majesty...?" Afonso could only mutter, dumbfounded.

"Yes! And no one, not a single living soul, including your soldiers, should know about the ultimate goal of your campaign. Nothing threatens Lisbon at the moment, but still, leaving the capital without a garrison is a great risk. Therefore, your assignment will remain a secret. I can entrust the command of the garrison in the campaign only to the most loyal of my generals. To you, Afonso!"

Gnashing his armor, Afonso made another bow, "Your Majesty!"

"In the castle, you will have to capture Duke de Braganza and execute him, the duke, and all his family."

General Afonso was so shocked that he leaned on the back of a chair that had just been vacated by one of the navigators. "To capture and execute Duke de Braganza?" he gasped.

"You will have to execute Duke de Braganza and his family right in the castle, right in front of the soldiers. They must see that there will be no mercy for enemies of the state or those who do not support the King of Portugal!" Joao II remained silent about liberating the wealthy landowners of their property solely based on his own fictional accusations.

The general continued to listen to the king with his mouth open. De Braganza was considered the most influential duke in Portugal, and now he, General Afonso, was tasked to capture and execute this man. Afonso continued to listen to the king, not believing the king was actually saying this! A couple of years ago, during his father's lifetime, King Afonso and the Duke of Braganza were good friends, and this would not have happened.

"If you are not allowed to enter Braganza castle," Joao interrupted him from his thoughts, "you will have to besiege it, but do not storm it. There is no need to destroy what will soon belong to us. I will keep the fortress for the sake of Portugal, but there will not be the means to restore it if it is destroyed during a siege. In addition, we will need new places for soldiers who will help strengthen the border. Surround the castle, but don't attack it. It is not enough to waste the lives of our people on this rat. If he doesn't want to give up, let him starve to death in his own castle. I am also satisfied with this outcome."

General Afonso was struck by the evil grimace that now distorted the handsome appearance of the young king. "And if he wishes to surrender," Joao II continued, "tell him that you have brought a personal message for him from me. He will meet you, Afonso; that is absolutely unavoidable, and when he comes to you, you will execute him with this sword." The king went to one of the cabinets and took out an old Roman Gladius sword. The hilt of the sword was covered with rubies. They covered the hilt so thickly, the sword could not be turned in any direction where the rubies did not reflect the sun's rays. General Afonso recognized this sword. Joao had received it as a gift when he was knighted.

"And don't be afraid for Lisbon, Afonso," the king continued, handing the sword to the general. "I have declared an increased readiness on all ships of my fleet. I have ordered men to check any ship, any vessel, or even a small boat, approaching our shores from either the north or the south. The warships of our enemies will not escape the attention of our fleet."

"Yes, but the nobility… Many of the nobles are grateful to Duke de Braganza and support him," General Afonso said, knowing this firsthand. "How will they react?"

"They will be even more grateful to the king," Joao II snapped. "They only need to be made aware of the troubles that the duke was preparing for the people, and those who loved the duke will then love me. The same people who praised him will be shoveling coals into the fire, which the duke will assuredly ascend. I am also sure that he makes dubious acquaintances with heretics."

Judging by Afonso's face, the general wanted to object, but the king raised his voice, "It would be better if the capital's garrison marched at night. From two to four in the morning, during the dog watch hours, this city of sailors sleeps especially soundly."

General Afonso had already completely regained control of himself. "May I go to carry out your order?" he asked, holding the newly obtained sword like a knife — blade down and back.

The king nodded, "Yes, but don't kill Braganza's soldiers. We will need them in the south to suppress the heretics. Now you may go, Afonso."

"Yes, Your Majesty!" The general exclaimed. Clanking his spurs, he left.

Joao II watched his general with a derisive look and went back to the window opening. Wrinkling his forehead, the king continued to summarize today's conversations with the best men of his kingdom. The funds that he would gain from the elimination of Duke de Braganza would allow him to equip the new campaign of Bartolomeu Dias and establish the next fortress on the African coast, maybe even two forts. He, the king, would go to the castle of Vila Viçosa himself to estimate the funds that would be received as a result of General Afonso's campaign. If, God forbid, his soldiers, those drunken louts ready to defect to the enemy for a penny increase in salary, doubted the generosity of the king, he would, perhaps, ignore the heretics flooding in from Castile until the people became outraged. Only then would he rise up against this invasion of infidels, the soldiers would rally behind their king, and the people's love for their victorious monarch would become even stronger. First, he needed to accomplish this in Lisbon, then in other cities, the hearts of which held fortresses. With the powerful support of the king by the people, the nobles would have to do the same. They would have no other choice.

Yes, but what was this inquisition that Isabella had invented? Joao had already learned that it was an alliance between those highest officials of the kingdom who knew how to bring the rabble to obedience and the bishops who own people's minds and souls. Undoubtedly, this insidious woman would succeed in both. Otherwise, she would not have dared to unite both for a common cause.

Joao II looked again at the streets of Lisbon, spread out below, and sighed. Thank God none of his enemies knew that the royal treasury was empty. They did not know that the chief treasurer of the kingdom secretly appealed to Marranos who were fleeing from Castile to donate at least a pound or two of gold to maintain the normal course of life in the royal palace. What a shame! But it wouldn't last for long. Soon the king of Portugal would be able to use the main wealth, which was always at his disposal. This was the power of the people's faith in the king and the strength he had gathered in his army and navy. He would end the influence of rich rats on the souls of ordinary people, and those of them who remained alive would crawl to the king on their knees and beg him to take their gold to build a new fleet. How beautiful this new Santa Catarina ship would be! Oh my God! There would come a time when people, looking at a current map of the world, which the king discussed today with the best navigators of the time, would laugh at it, just as Joao himself once laughed at Ptolemy's map.

Meanwhile, the navigators who had just visited the king were already riding out of the castle on their horses. Vasco da Gama and Bartolomeu Dias were talking animatedly and laughing. Dias tore the collar from his neck, blew his nose into the precious lace, and threw it behind the roadside bushes.

Christopher Columbus was walking. His friends, descending from the mountain, were already lost in the twists of the winding road leading to the impregnable castle, and he was only just crossing over the swing bridge of the north tower. Nearby, barely standing on his feet and leaning on his pike, a sentry was pouring a draught with a drunken smile. Crossing the moat, Christopher looked back. In one of the window openings of the tower that housed the king's chambers, stretching high over the walls of St. George Castle, he saw the figure of the king, still looking at the city.

"Yes, there really is no time to waste," Columbus recalled the king's order. "It seems that a visit to Queen Isabella is inevitable." By the time Christopher Columbus descended to the city streets and walked past the houses with their countless workshops, taverns, barbers, and fun houses, he already knew for sure that he would immediately go to the Queen of Castile. It would be to her that he would present his plan of a campaign to the West, the very plan rejected by King Joao II of Portugal.

A Moment from the Past - The Young Duke's First Chess Game

Four carriages entered the southern gate of Paris one after another, each decorated with a coat of arms: a shield crisscrossed with two red stripes. The procession was accompanied by a mounted guard. It was only part of a larger cavalry detachment that remained in the suburbs of Paris. Inside the city, fewer guards were needed.

In one of the carriages sat fourteen-year-old Fernando de Braganza. His father, Fernando the First, second Duke of Braganza, was sitting next to him. The duke was a big man with a face mostly hidden by a thick black beard. He still wore his traveling armor, and a shirt of unexpectedly delicate pink peeked out from under the bright metal. A wide yellow sash was draped over his shoulder – the sign of ducal dignity. He was expected to arrive at this meeting in full regalia. The family carriage went first, followed by carriages with other family members and retinue.

As the wheels slowly tapped on the cobblestones, Paris rose up above the travelers in all its splendor. The streets of three and four-story houses were striking and elegant, the impression spoiled only by the clouds of smoke escaping from chimneys. Here and there the spires of cathedrals could be seen. Even the mills were stunning with exquisite architecture.

Crossing the bridge over the Seine, the travelers began to pass women with heavy baskets in their hands. By the smell, it was clear that they were returning from the shore where fishermen were selling their morning catch. True to the Parisian elegant style, even the commoners' garments were alluring.

Young Fernando's eyes darted everywhere. He saw a young man, a little older than him, sitting on the bank of the river and drawing something with a silver quill on a sheet placed on a small tablet. He realized that the young man was sketching a tall temple with two identical bell towers on each side. At the sight of the temple, Fernando cried out with delight, "Amazingly beautiful! We don't have anything like that. What kind of temple is that, Father?"

Fernando's father squinted out the window and answered, "Notre Dame de Paris, the Notre Dame Cathedral."

Young Fernando had never seen such architecture or artists who simply worked right on the street. As the travelers ventured further into the city, the passers-by, the horsemen, and the nobility looking out of their carriages became even more elegant. Soon the boy saw a crowd staring at some street performers. They tossed up one of their comrades who turned over in mid-air and landed sitting on the neck of his partner. Another artist juggled a dozen colored stones at once, not letting any of them fall to the ground. A man with a bare torso, his head wrapped with a white turban, made a frightful expression and suddenly spewed fire from his mouth. Women and children, squealing with delight, tossed small coins to the artists. Some members of the audience awarded them with loaves of bread, apples, and even a large fish with scales that sparkled in the sun. The gaiety of the people, even those who were dressed as artisans or mourners, was amazing.

Finally, the Fernando family's carriage drove up to a huge estate surrounded by a high stone fence. The carriages rolled into a spacious courtyard in front of a magnificent palace, the corners decorated with two small round towers. Compared to the splendor of Paris that young Fernando had already seen, this was an even more luxurious building. A fountain was flowing in the middle of the courtyard with water falling from scattered spouts. Young Fernando squeezed his eyes shut, blinded by the brilliance of the sun on the water.

Fernando the First, often jealous in matters of honor, whispered at the sight of the other carriages emblazoned with the coats of arms of other aristocratic families, "The Spencers... the Churchills... The Egmonts... Montfort-l'Amorys... Wittelsbachs... Hohenzollerns... Radziwills..."

Young Fernando knew that the highest aristocracy of all Europe would gather at this festive dinner. He wondered why they had made the long journey from Portugal. Judging by the fact that his father, head of one of the noblest families in Portugal, undertook such a long trip, and especially with the whole family, very important issues would most likely be deliberated here. Such meetings usually preceded the meetings of monarchs themselves.

As soon as the travelers entered the palace, the owner of the house and his family immediately greeted them. Young Fernando was questioned by two luxuriously dressed teenagers, "Venez-vous du Portugal? Peut-être êtes-vous le Duc de Bragance? Comment avez-vous aimé Paris?" *Are you from Portugal? Are you Duke of Braganza? How do you like Paris?*

Fernando smiled shyly. He knew little French, so he tried to switch to Latin, "Mihi nomen est Fernando da

Braganza. Ego sum de Portugal." *My name is Fernando de Braganza. I'm from Portugal.*

The teenagers – Fernando guessed from their faces they were brothers close in age – chattered in French again, talking not only to him but also to each other.

He furtively examined their clothes. The younger brother was dressed in a daringly cut doublet made of shiny red, very beautiful fabric. The edges of a snow-white shirt peeked deliberately out from under the exquisite garment. Narrow, tight-fitting yellow stockings covered his legs, and his outfit ended with pointed shoes with barely noticeable heels. The elder brother was dressed similarly, only his stockings were white, and his doublet was blue. The necklines of the doublets would have been much more suitable for a lady and were made from a fine fabric Fernando did not recognize but would later learn was silk.

They were lively, liberated young men, whose facial expressions and gestures were as foreign as their language. The older brother's gaze was somewhat strange; he seemed to be looking through the person he was talking to, or at an imaginary wall behind that person. At the same time, the younger brother made direct eye contact and smiled. After rattling off a mountain of more incomprehensible words to Fernando, he took him by the hand and led him into the courtyard. There the young man began to tell him something, waving his hands at the fountain, well-groomed trees, neatly smoothed paths, and gazebos with benches inside. The Frenchman suddenly exchanged glances with his brother, and both laughed at the same time, and Fernando decided that they were probably laughing at him as if he were just a bourgeoise from God-forsaken Portugal. Fernando remembered his grandfather's admonition, "If a donkey kicks you, and you kick back, you are both donkeys," and he decided not to pay attention to the boys' stupid antics.

Meanwhile, more and more carriages arrived at the estate, accompanied by guards dressed to the nines while the restless Frenchman continued to usher Fernando around the yard. Inside one of the gazebos, the young man showed Fernando a tiny tree. To his amazement, the tree had the shape of a sprawling century-old oak despite being only a span or so tall! Looking at Fernando's face, the Frenchman laughed. It seemed he was bragging about his wealth, and at the same time, taking advantage of the fact that Fernando did not understand French, secretly mocking him. However, Fernando continued to endure the scoffing.

A beautiful girl and another young man came out into the courtyard – both were also the same age as Fernando. While the girl was wearing a vibrant green pleated robe dress, the boy, for some reason, wore gilded armor. The boy in the armor made a strange image; a pale head peeked out of the dark breastplate, and he looked like a chicken coming out of an iron shell. In bright contrast, the beautiful girl had wide eyes accented by long black eyelashes. Her head was decorated with a bizarre pleated white veil, from under which blonde hair escaped in places.

The younger of the brothers grabbed Fernando by the arm and dragged him to the couple. "C'est Fernando" *This is Fernando*, he introduced his companion, "et moi, je m'appelle Yves" *And my name is Yves.*

"Mam na imię Anna" *My name is Anna*, said the girl, "a to jest Henryk" *And this is Henryk.*

"Rycerz Henryk" *Knight Henryk*, corrected the young blonde man, his golden armor shining.

The Frenchman, who Fernando now figured out was named Yves, continued to chatter, and the more he talked, the more it was clear the others obviously understood him. The girl's speech was richly saturated with hissing sounds, and Fernando could not place what country she came from, but it was clear with Henryk: he was a German and from some warmongering territory. Fernando was eagerly taking in all of the amazing sights and sounds around him. However, he could not take his eyes off the girl; her appearance, her grace, and her speech enchanted him. Yves was also obviously fascinated by her, perhaps even brazenly enamored. The girl was likewise captivated by Yves; he was Parisian of course, and they had a reputation. At the same time, she also smiled at Fernando.

Finally, Yves took the girl by the arm and led her into the gazebo, where a pitcher and a dish of fruit were laid out on the table. The girl turned around and looked at Henryk in confusion. Then she looked at Fernando. It seemed the Frenchman was beginning to tire her with his attention. Fernando melted with that look. What to do? How he wanted a moment alone with this girl and a chance to talk to her! But how can he compete with these Parisians and their ability to take girls by storm?

Henryk and Fernando found themselves near a table with a chessboard. Fernando didn't know how to play, but he knew the names of the pieces. He took the white king from the board, showed it to Henryk, and made an inquiring gesture. Henryk nodded gravely, making it clear that he, Henryk, was in fact, nobility. Then Fernando took the figure of the white queen and pointed it at Anna. Henryk smiled and nodded again. He took the hint. Then Fernando took a black rook, pointed at Yves, and placed it between the pieces of the king and queen. Henryk narrowed his eyes suspiciously. Fernando hit the rook with the king's piece, knocking the rook over on the board. He then joined the figures of the queen and the king as if in a kiss. Henryk finally realized what Fernando meant and rushed after the Frenchman. He caught up with him, shouted in a barking voice, and then punched the Frenchman in the face. The Frenchman fell and rolled on the ground, splashed by the spray of the fountain. His doublet and white shirt were immediately covered with dirt. The courtyard resounded with the screams of women. The guests sitting at the tables scattered among the courtyard and gazebos jumped up. From somewhere there was the sound of a sword being pulled from a scabbard. For a moment, everyone froze. Then something completely unexpected happened; Yves jumped up and, shaking off the dirt, ran away to the palace. Immediately, his brother came out into the yard. At the sight of the expression on his face, Henryk backed away but slipped and fell in the very puddle which had just soaked Yves. The yard was filled with laughter from the most astute observers. Henryk got up and hurried away. The brother, without looking at Anna and Fernando, went back to the palace in search of Yves.

Anna looked at Fernando questioningly. Catching her eye, Fernando took a white pawn and placed it next to the queen's piece. Anna laughed. He led her to the miniature tree and pointed at it. At the sight of the curiosity, Anna laughed again and clapped her hands. Fernando realized that not only was she beautiful, but she also knew how to appreciate beauty. That evening, Fernando's hands touched a woman's body for the first time.

Chapter 7. Siege and Escape

In the camp set up around the castle of Vila Viçosa, you could only walk up or down, because the castle stood on a high hill with steep slopes, and this exhausted the soldiers even before the assault began. Cursing each other, the horses, and the authorities, the gunners began to set up bombards in firing positions. Younger warriors, grimacing from the strain, pulled stone stands from carts, struggling to drag them up the steep incline, and arranged them from corner to corner. Meanwhile, the old men skillfully rolled the bombards onto special stretchers and carried them to the stone stands.

The horses, exhausted by the long march under the sun, greedily slurped water and chewed their oats while the cavalrymen removed the saddles and examined the horseshoes. The infantrymen were chopping down trees in a grove nearby and preparing fascines – bundles of branches to throw into the moat under the fortress wall. Soon the archers also came to their aid. The soldiers looked up at the square battlements of the walls and towers holding their helmets so they would not fall off their heads.

The leader of the army, General Afonso, approached the wall accompanied by an entourage. "Hey there!" one of his officers shouted. This officer had already tried to talk to the castle guards but was turned away from the gate.

A sentry's head, covered with a shiny round helmet, hung out of an opening between the battlements of the wall. "What do you want?" The sentry said calmly.

The officer shouted, "Tell the Duke that General Afonso himself will speak to him now!"

A few minutes passed. Another man appeared next to the sentry. He also leaned over the wall and shouted, "Heed our terms! First, all troops are to move away from the castle a thousand paces. Second, General Afonso approaches the gate alone and unarmed, and we will lower the bridge to him. After crossing the bridge, the general will enter the castle and speak with Duke de Braganza. That is all."

Soon the general was granted entry to the castle. Duke Fernando II de Braganza was waiting for him outside the gate – not yet old, still handsome and strong in his armor. A doublet of black brocade embroidered with gold peeked out from under his iron breastplate. Orange trousers shaped like Chinese lanterns encircled the duke's hips. The duke was known for his indulgence in the most lavish fashions and remained true to his reputation even now.

"Speak up, General," the duke began immediately.

Under de Braganza's gaze, the general took off his helmet. The wind chilled his scalp under his sparse sweaty strands of hair. "The king's terms are as follows:" Afonso declares, "The king promises to discuss everything peacefully with you if you leave the castle and come to him for negotiations. No harm will come to your family. That's the King's word. Additionally, Duke, not a hair on your head will be harmed if you allow my army to enter the castle. I swear on the honor of the general."

"Oh, is that it?" de Braganza said thoughtfully. "Well, I also promise that not a single hair on your head will be harmed, but only if you depart promptly with your army. In addition, I promise you that you will keep your position when the Cortes elects a new king. But, again, only on the condition that you immediately take your army back to where you came from."

"The king is supported by the whole of Portugal," the general said, involuntarily pulling himself to attention under the gaze of the duke's intelligent eyes. "The people won't support you. The king will not uphold the promises I have proposed if you do not allow my army to enter the castle. Think about it; I have received exceptional powers from His Majesty. Don't force me to storm the castle. Our bombards have pierced walls stronger than yours."

"The Portuguese will never give up," the duke said. "That's what makes them as brave as you, General. They will never surrender. When they come to the battle, there is no backing down, no room for cowardice."

Thanks to his well-established military intelligence, the duke already knew that Afonso's army was not large enough to take the castle by storm. Time was beginning to work against the general and his king because carrier pigeons were already carrying the duke's notes to the castles and palaces of his powerful associates. However, the Rubicon had been crossed, and the duke understood that the matter could no longer be solved with negotiations. War was unavoidable; either the king or the duke, and their supporters in the Cortes and elsewhere, would win while the other would almost certainly face death.

As soon as the general crossed over the bridge, his horse's hooves echoing on the planks, it immediately began to rise. The haste with which this was done was insulting, since the general was alone, and his army had retreated to a distance that made the horse seem no bigger than an ant.

The duke was also in a hurry. As soon as the gate was closed behind Afonso, an officer wearing shiny, almost mirrored armor entered the archway under the wall. It was Stefan, the commander of the Vila Viçosa garrison. As expected of an officer in the presence of a superior, he kept his helmet on his bent left arm. "Did you hear everything, Stefan?" Fernando asked him. The duke's short brown hair seemed to the officer like a halo in the light of the sun's rays that broke over the walls.

"Yes, Your Grace," Stefan replied. His loud commanding voice echoed in the archway.

"I'll have to leave the castle," the duke said. "During my absence, you will receive ten... no, a hundred gold cruzados daily. This is not counting the payment to your subordinates. While I'm gone, you will continue to hold my flag over the keep. Let them think I'm staying here."

Duke de Braganza had a remarkable ability to do several things at once. And now, giving orders to the commander of his garrison, he was already thinking about where he would go to raise an army to expel General Afonso's troops from the vicinity of the castle and further resist the king.

In the dead of night, the duke and his family walked through an underground passage. Ahead, lighting the way with a torch, walked a page. Fernando's wife, Isabella, trotted behind the duke. She held two-year-old Dinis in her arms. The duke's eldest son, four-year-old Jaime, strode bravely beside her. From time to time Jaime ran his finger along the bricks of hewn stone – exactly the same as the walls of the castle here – leaving soot on his finger. The procession was brought up by servants, a nurse, and a wet nurse. The duke's court physician carried a leather bag with medicines and tools, not trusting it to anyone.

The footsteps of the company reverberated with a strange, seemingly endless echo. Ten minutes later, the underground passage ended in a wide spiral staircase. Upstairs, near the open hatch, the duke and his family were greeted by his secretary, Beniciu. Above, the fugitives found themselves in the middle of a spacious but almost empty stable. Next to Beniciu was the duke's servant, Evandro, dressed as a simple soldier. Evandro had a twin brother, Jorge. In the village, the two brothers were never seen together – this was the rule of their secret life. Currently, Evandro was preparing horses for the fugitives' journey at the stable on the outskirts of the village, and Jorge, who was posing as a visiting owner of a stable of dray horses, was snoring in a neighboring house after a day shift of hard work. At the duke's request, everyone except his wife left the stable for the courtyard which connected the stable with the village buildings.

"Isabella," the duke said when the couple was alone, "you and the children will have to go to your friends, to Castile." Isabella nodded. She had already anticipated this. The duke continued and shadows ran across his face, as the draft stirred the flames of the torches every now and then, "Because I'm staying in Portugal. I'm staying to fight the tyranny of this madcap, our king."

"Do you really believe that you will be supported?" Isabella asked.

"Yes! Many times over, yes! The nobles and their representatives in the Cortes will support me. The nobles have money and a sufficient number of patrons who can make up an army. Yes, there are more peasants who support the king, but they have nothing. And for that same reason, the injustices of the king do not frighten them in any way. So far, the nobles are not a threat until the king starts extorting them. With their money, he will want to expand his army, build a new fleet to incite fear in all the coastal countries, and spy on every free-thinking subject. If we manage to unite the nobles, we can overthrow this king and choose a new one. The Cortes has the authority to do this."

"Do you think the new king will take the Cortes into account?" Isabella whispered, adjusting the collar around her husband's neck.

"A new law will be created explicitly for this. According to this law, the opinion of the Cortes will weigh exactly as much as the opinion of the king, no less, and this will be just the beginning. In the future, we will curb the king, following the example of England. He will not be able to lift a finger without the consent of Parliament. This is the only way to protect Portugal and its people from fits of insanity, which from time to time afflict the monarch in one country or another, including ours as well. Judge for yourself: isn't it madness what Joao II started, having just ascended the throne? Would his father have dared to encroach on the rights of the nobility, on the privileges of his nobles, on their estates?"

The conversation between the duke and his wife was brief; soon the duchess, accompanied by servants and guards, set off. The duke's secretary rode ahead, and Evandro brought up the rear. There was a single carriage in the middle carrying Isabella and her children.

* * *

After a sleepless night spent on the road, and then a whole day of agonizing delays in Lisbon, the duke lay in a bed, unable to fall asleep. His faithful servant and bodyguard, Proshperu, on the other hand, slept peacefully on the floor across the room. The remainder of the duke's retinue slept in other rooms of the inn.

Throughout the day, the duke did not receive a single message from his friends in the capital. The messengers the duke secretly sent to them invariably returned with the same result. General Dacosta, Admiral Pascoal, the third, fourth, twentieth general, admiral, courtier – they had all left Lisbon.

Five hundred people! To save Portugal, the nobility, and the people, the duke only needed five hundred people! Such a detachment would have been more than enough for the duke because, by noon on the last day, he was convinced that the garrison of Lisbon had left the capital. In Lisbon, the duke did not see a single soldier; there were usually no fewer soldiers among the passers-by than the ubiquitous monks. It was possible to smuggle so many soldiers out of Lisbon, but it was impossible to hide an army of several hundred people. So, it was the Lisbon garrison that was besieging the duke's castle.

For the duke, the absence of a garrison once again confirmed the danger of Joao II – both for the whole of the people and for the king himself, because even after being mentored by his father, he remained a stupid man and a narrow-minded monarch, a king who thought that the people really loved him enough to fight for him at the first call – as if the people's love for the king is worth anything without the support of the royal army, and even more so in the absence of troops.

Now, if the duke had the same number of soldiers under his command – even if not seasoned, battle–hardened slashers, but just grown, strong men armed accordingly – overthrowing the king would be the easiest thing. He didn't even have to be overthrown. The king had to be forced to reckon with the Cortes and issue a special law on this account, that's all.

The duke understood that now fate had given him an unprecedented and unique opportunity: the king, hoping to deal with the most dangerous of his enemies, that is, with Duke de Braganza, left himself unguarded. Finally, it dawned on the duke that they must go to Porto as fast as possible before the fooled General Afonso guessed that the duke was not in his castle. The duke had many friends in Porto; it was a huge city. He surmised there would always be a thousand people there who were ready to enlist in any army for good money. "Proshperu!" The duke shouted, "Get up! We're riding north to Porto."

Proshperu immediately jumped up, energetic and ready to go as usual. "Shall I wake the others?"

"Yes, Take Janeiro and Branko with you."

* * *

On the way, remembering friends he could rely on, the duke did not immediately think of Leandro, a prominent member of the Cortes of Leiria. It was not often that the duke and the simple landowner Leandro met, even though he was one of his ardent supporters, but at the end of the next day, when the duke was traveling to Porto and passed the vicinity of the fortress of Leiria half-way there, he already knew that he would spend the night nearby at Leandro's estate in Sinta.

They arrived at the estate after sunset. Leandro, dazed with joy – there had never been such distinguished guests in his house before – ordered dinner to be prepared. Meanwhile, the duke and his retinue were able to rest for a while. After dinner, Leandro and the duke continued their conversation.

"Of course, the representatives of the nobility in the Cortes now have every reason to refuse to oppose the king," said the duke, "but it won't help them. Sooner or later, the king will take everything from them, and then begin to exterminate the nobles and their families."

"But why?" Leandro asked.

"To create new nobles which will depend entirely on him. Such bloodletting occurs from time to time in many countries. When the old ways of common existence for some reason stop working, the king tries to get rid of the best people in the kingdom and the best people have to attempt to dethrone the king. That's why my friends and I have decided to fight him to the bitter end. I have already told you the goal of this fight, and I will not repeat myself. I have only one question for you, dear Leandro: are you with us?"

"Of course, Your Grace!" Leandro exclaimed.

"In that case, you should start assembling your own mercenary army yourself. Let it be small, but it must be combat-ready. You will have to find people yourself, collect them, and keep them on your estate right now. Do you have enough accommodations?"

"Yes, of course. But unfortunately, I myself am not as healthy as I was just a few years ago, Senhor. I won't be able to sit on a horse anymore, but I can gather a small army to support Duke de Braganza and his companions. Tomorrow I will send my assistant Raul to Leiria. He will walk through its streets and all the taverns there. Let's see how many mercenaries he can gather that way. Meanwhile, his father, Francisco, will go around all my villages and also select strong guys that are more loyal to money than the king."

"Fine, I never doubted you!" de Braganza said. "You have always been my good friend!"

Leandro broke into a smile. The noblest nobleman of Portugal called him the holy word "friend."

"When we assemble the main army in Porto and move from there to Lisbon, your detachment will join our army, as other factions will also join us everywhere along our route," de Braganza continued, "Are you saying that you are no longer fit for military work? But how are your sons?"

"I have only one son," Leandro sighed. "I am ashamed to say this, but he has not yet been trained in the art of war."

The duke's look said that he either did not believe Leandro or was grieving over the disgrace that had befallen the gentleman's family. But the duke decided not to ask unnecessary questions.

"If our army is late, and you are waiting for it here in the meantime, you will be in danger. I am sure that the castellan of Leiria will remain loyal to the king, and that your preparations will not escape the attention of his spies. He will be able to find out that you are gathering a mercenary army at your place before my army approaches you."

"I'll warn Raul and Francisco," Leandro replied. "They won't talk too much. Besides, they are local, and already know roughly who in our region would agree to become a mercenary."

"We don't have much time," the duke continued. Judging by his face, he was already preoccupied with something else. Thinking a little, he asked, "You've been to Porto da Vila?"

"Of course; the village is very close. Fish are brought to us from there every three days."

"My caravel is docked at Porto da Vila. She's there alone now, you'll find her right away. In case of danger, you can pick up the family and transport them to this caravel, and then get to us at Porto by sea. I'm sure you agree, this will be a much less dangerous path than traveling by land."

"I agree," Leandro nodded. "Thank you, Your Grace, for taking care of my family. I hope your family is in a safe place too."

"Tell me, do you have enough funds to raise an army?" the duke finally realized his discourtesy.

"Yes, of course. I won't need any help in that matter," Leandro said, smiling less virtuously than was required at the moment. After all, now Duke de Braganza himself was becoming his debtor. "And in general, I am ready to help you in all your endeavors."

"Thank you. That's all I need. I think I'll stay with you for one more day. I will send my assistants on the same errand to other estates and wait for them here. Once I receive news from them, I will continue my journey to Porto."

It was already quite dark when the soft clop of horses' hooves was heard outside the windows of Leandro's house. The duke sent two messengers from the estate: one to Porto, and the other to the most influential of his friends in central Portugal. Both messengers conveyed the same task: first, to immediately begin to assemble a mercenary army, and secondly, to convey the same message from the duke to his other friends. In the bosom of the messengers, there was a letter written by the duke himself and certified with the imprint of his family ring. The idea of sending messengers came to the duke when he thought that the letters sent by pigeon mail may need confirmation.

A Moment from the Past - Anacaona's School Years

When Anacaona turned fourteen, she, like all her peers in Aztlan, began to attend the telpochcalli, the school for the macehualtin, the commoners. The school consisted of a few simple houses with thatched roofs, similar to other houses in the outlying areas of Texcoco where Anacaona lived with her father. There were three times five students in each telpochcalli house. They usually sat on carpets or blankets as they listened to their teachers. There was nothing else in the house except jugs of water and sometimes dishes of fruit.

Teachers of the telpochcallin, who moved from town to town on the shore of a large lake, came to one school and then to another, and there they shared their knowledge with the children and teenagers. During the day, children moved from one schoolhouse where a subject was taught to another. Boys and girls studied separately, but sometimes their home classes were in the same place. When the teacher ended a story in one of the schoolhouses, the children moved to another house, to a new teacher. If a new teacher did not come on one of the days, the children went to any of the other teachers who were telling stories on that day.

However, parents always provided primary education to their own children. Before the children came to the telpochcalli, their parents, according to the law, were obliged to transfer basic knowledge and skills to them. Parents had to pay special attention to their children's behavior when preparing children for school. The students were expected to respectfully listen to the teacher, not make noise, and not interfere with other students. Telpochcalli teachers closely followed the development of their students and their character. Truly gifted children could be transferred from telpochcallin to the calmecacs, the school for children of the highest social stratum. Studying at the calmecac provided connections and acquaintances with children from noble and wealthy families, which meant that it was possible to achieve a higher social position in the future.

The rapidly growing state needed a large number of educated people – workers, merchants, and artisans. Therefore, studying in the telpochcallin was strongly encouraged. The school reforms initiated by Weyitlatoani Moctezuma were further established and increased by his grandson, Axayacatl, the new supreme ruler of the state.

Anacaona liked to visit the telpochcalli. However, after the military campaigns that she went on with her father, school seemed too childish for her, and studying was like a game although she still studied with great interest. Other teenagers from her community studied with her. There were children of pochteca, the merchants and artisans, macehualtin, the farmers, and tlacotin, the slaves. However, studying was not always easy for Anacaona. She didn't really like working with lines, dots, and drawings that looked like trees, or when she had to draw all sorts of circles, squares, and triangles, to do calculations. Fortunately for Anacaona, though, the telpochcalli for girls taught housework first of all, and only then these shapes. Anacaona grew up without a mother, so there was no one to teach her cooking and knitting, and the school helped her with this as well. Special attention was paid to these subjects in the women's telpochcalli. The boys were taught military affairs and construction skills.

There was one subject in which Anacaona had no equal among the other students. This was the structure of the human body and the treatment of ailments. By the age of fourteen, Anacaona still could not bake delicious bread or weave the simplest cloth, but she was already able to apply a variety of bandages, knew all the internal organs, and could restore broken bones, not to mention her knowledge of medicinal herbs. Even as a little girl, she surprised her father, the experienced ticitl, Chimalli, with the correct balance for mixing many medicinal herbs. He had never taught her that. She found exactly the plants that were needed to heal the disease, dried and ground them, or alternatively, took their juice, and mixed them in perfect proportion. Her medicines had always been strong and effective remedies. Besides that, Anacaona was a good student of her father and readily learned his skills. What else could she learn during military campaigns since she was with him more often than at home? Anacaona also mastered military discipline from childhood, and in her telpochcalli, it was highly appreciated.

Another science that Anacaona liked was taught at school by an old man. He had poor eyesight, and when he appeared in the telpochcalli, the children always helped him find the right house. Long ago, the old man came to Texcoco from distant lands inhabited by the Itza tribes. He talked about the stars and the calendar, the seasons, and the ways in which the sun and moon travel. The old man was always holding a pipe at the ready, in which a pinch of some greenish leaves was smoking. He would suck in the smoke, let it out from the corner of his mouth away from the children, and continue his story, slightly narrowing his cloudy white eyes.

He taught Anacaona how to find the right path and understand directions depicted on sheets of amatl. Anacaona herself then learned to represent the roads and streets of her own city in this way.

The old man showed them a round calendar; around the inside, there was a ring with twenty pictures that represented days. The days were illustrated in the form of animal heads or other objects. He said that these drawings not only named the days but also showed the directions of different paths. The Path of Huitzilopochtli was depicted at the top of the calendar, leading to where the sun rose in the mornings. The calendar should always be laid down or put on the ground and turned in that direction. The word "xotl," or foot, meant a path on land, and the word "atl," or water, meant a path on the water.

Each path should be chosen according to the name of the day and in accordance with the direction of the Path of Huitzilopochtli, that is the sunrise. For example, the Iztli Koyotl tribes, with whom Chimalli and Anacaona once went to war, are on the Path of Xotl Mikaztli from Texcoco. And the cities of the Itza tribes, where the old man came from, are on the Path of Xotl Ollin from Texcoco. He told them if they put a stick in the middle of the calendar, then by the shadow of the stick, which moved with the sun during the daytime, they could divide the duration of the day into parts and always accurately determine them.

The old man also said that the way by the stars was more accurate than by the Sun, and talked about Big Water that never ends. He said Lake Texcoco was just a small puddle compared to Big Water. Anacaona found it hard to believe, but she then dreamed of seeing Big Water.

She learned the stories about Moctezuma's prophetic dream and the history of the Mexihkah tribes. From those tales, Anacaona grew very proud of the history of her people. The old man also always reminded them of the strong friendship between the tribes of Mexihkah and Itza, and of the enmity between the tribes of Iztli Koyotl, Zapotec, and Totonac.

After the sun reached its highest point and began to descend, the girls' classes ended, and they headed home. Only boys stayed and continued to listen to the teachers' stories. Anacaona didn't have to run home to help her mother. She liked to stay with the boys and listen to what the teachers told them. She also liked the games of patolli and ollamalitzli that the boys enjoyed after school. Sometimes, they played patolli together with the teachers, a game played on the lined wooden floor in one of the houses at the school. Anacaona liked to throw the bean grains marked with a white dot on one side and see how many dots would fall upright out of the five thrown beans. Then she moved the round stones around the playing field and tried to collect them in her corner. Plain stones replaced the expensive, elaborately made figures that were used to play in the calmecacs. Anacaona played patolli with her teachers several times as well. It was very fun!

However, patolli did not fascinate her as much as ollamalitzli, a game played with a rubber ball. Anacaona would run around the small field with the boys until evening trying to get the ball through a ring on a tree. Anacaona didn't play as well as the boys, but she tried her best. Anacaona knew that in the calmecacs in Texcoco and Tenochtitlan there were special playing fields with stone walls and special beautiful rings for playing ollamalitzli. However, she had never played on one of these real playing fields.

Late in the evening, when the tired Anacaona returned home, Chimalli could not be proud enough of how much time Anacaona spent at the telpochcalli. However, this peaceful life was to quickly come to an end as Chimalli was expected to go on another military campaign soon. He had no one to leave Anacaona with, and the girl would have to go with him again. Therefore, Anacaona still could not finish her studies at the telpochcalli. This went on for several years. Chimalli was very worried about this. He really wanted Anacaona to complete her studies at the telpochcalli like all the other children. Soon she would marry some glorious warrior, and she wouldn't have finished her education.

When Chimalli found out that the brother of the tlatoani of Texcoco needed an experienced ticitl in the new small town of Tlaluacatli, far from Texcoco, where there had been no war for a long time, he decided to enter his service, away from the big city and eternal military campaigns. This was how Anacaona finally saw Big Water, the very one she was told about by the teacher from the land of the Itza tribes.

Chapter 8. The Visit of the Castellan

Both Anacaona and Nuno turned out to be exceptionally capable students. Soon they had used up almost the entire stock of Don Leandro's watermarked paper for drawings and inscriptions, and they could understand each other's language, once foreign, without much effort. While listening to Anacaona, Nuno made notes and drawings, collected them, and clarified things he had not understood before. He decided that later he would rewrite this information on separate sheets in the form of a complete tome of stories and make a separate dictionary with drawings of all the words studied.

From Anacaona's stories he learned that almost thirty years ago, the inhabitants of her country held a Fire Festival ceremony. This is how Anacaona's people celebrated the coming of Xuihpohualli, the new century, according to their calendar.

On the night before the ceremony, the weyitlatoani, the leader of the Mexihkah people, named Moctezuma, had a prophetic dream. In this dream, Moctezuma, surrounded by residents of the capital city of Tenochtitlan, stood in front of the largest pyramid of Huey Teocalli. At the top of the pyramid stood a skinned man. In his hand, he held his own beating heart. Moctezuma and his countrymen were naked. Each was smeared with fresh blood from head to toe. Crocodiles, jaguars, and other animals moved around the people; poisonous snakes crawled under their feet, but these creatures did not harm the people. In the dream, Moctezuma realized the people were protected by the blood applied to their bodies.

"Huitzilopochtli does not take my blood or my heart!" The skinned man from the pyramid shouted. "Quetzalcoatl, the teotl of humanity, wants me to come back! Our blood is Tlaltecuitli, from the teotl of the earth. Our blood is the blood of the teteo, and the teteo don't want to drink it. Tlaltecuitli protects us from the moment of our first breath! Teteo don't drink each other's blood!"

The next day, Moctezuma told his chief adviser, the astrologer and priest, Quetzalcoatl, about his dream. From this dream and its details, Quetzalcoatl concluded that the Mexihkah should no longer sacrifice people who participated in their festivals because they were no longer ordinary people, they were half-teteo. From that moment, human sacrifices ceased among peoples who believe in the same teteo and followed the same rites, and with that, the internecine wars that had plagued Aztlan for more than a century stopped. A huge state began to develop rapidly, and its inhabitants began to live better and better. Labor and trade brought them more and more prosperity, and then wealth. People lived much longer, and enlightenment spread on a scale never seen before.

Other cities began to join the state of Aztlan, whose altepetls, city-states, followed the same beliefs, and whose festivals were held on the same days as in Tenochtitlan. After all, the capital offered protection for them and allowed for duty-free and open trade throughout the vast lands of Aztlan. Among the newly united territories and cities were altepetls of the Itza people, a great nation of astronomers and mathematicians. Among these peoples, the calculation of time on circular calendars had the same number of days, and numbers were counted in the same manner, but the great culture of these Aztlan neighbors had begun to decline long ago.

Drought was tormenting the country more and more often along with mass diseases. In addition, people were fleeing from the cities, troubles, and civil strife. Joining Aztlan was a salvation for the people of Itza; it put an end to internecine hostility and brought peace and prosperity to the people. After the people of Itza joined Aztlan, the common state reached unprecedented proportions. Now it was washed by Big Water both by the paths of sunrise and sunset. All new lands and islands joined the state, including Amotlaxtlauas. From Anacaona's story, Nuno realized that this was not one island, but many.

"But not all the neighbors celebrated our festivals, and that's why they couldn't join Aztlan," Anacaona continued. "There are many tribes in the Path of Xotl Mikaztli from Tenochtitlan called Iztli Koyotl. These are very angry and scary people. They often manage to unite and attack us. Our warriors take them as captives, and they are made slaves, or those who refuse to become slaves are brought as gifts to the teteo at festivals."

"Many years ago, the council of our chief priests decided that we should meet with Huitzilopochtli. This was agreed upon by the main people of our country, our weyitlatoani Moctezuma, and the high priest Quetzalcoatl. To meet the teotl of the sun, the best men of our country decided to go to the place where he lives, where the sun rises. For this journey, our people, together with the Itza, built Tlaluacatli over many years, a city on the water, and Coatl became the tlatoani."

"We started our journey to sunrise five by five days ago after the Tozoztontli festival," Anacaona drew five long lines. "It happened after we passed the last island of Amotlaxtlauas, and we continued to go further on the Path of Huitzilopochtli in Big Water…"

Listening to Anacaona's stories, Nuno was surprised to find he could translate for himself not only the words but also the images that formed from her descriptions. South, North, West, East, maps, compass, time – all this was there in the language of Anacaona and her people, but it was all said quite differently. It seemed, according to Nuno, all too long and not very accurate.

At this most interesting hour in Nuno's life, Anacaona continued her story about miracles, which had been interrupted the night before. "That night, when there was a full moon, we came very close to your land. At first, mosquitoes made themselves known, beginning to annoy us for the first time in many days. Then the birds appeared. Some branches began to appear in the waves and then whole trees that had been carried into the sea by the flow of rivers. Coatl realized that the coast was close. Finally, your land appeared in the distance. We decided that our city should not approach it yet. Coatl called on a squad of warriors to reach your land by boat and went with them himself. My father, a ticitl, was also called to join the group. I went along with my father, because I, also, know how to give help to wounded and sick people …"

Here Anacaona paused and looked questioningly at Nuno. Numerous hoofbeats came from the courtyard and a group of horsemen rode up to the house. Judging by the noise, it was a considerable party. Nuno went to the window. The morning sun was already breaking through the trees. At least a dozen armed, armored horsemen were pacifying their horses in the courtyard. They were led by Daniel, Estela's father. Daniel jumped off his horse, threw the reins to the soldier accompanying him, said something briefly to him, and walked resolutely to the entrance to the house.

Nuno turned around, "Anacaona, I'll be right back." he said, but his face showed he was worried about something.

From the gallery that circled the rooms of the second floor, Nuno saw Daniel. Francisco, the steward, was bowing to him. After hearing the answer to his question, Francisco left for the main hall. He soon returned, "Don Leandro will come out to you now," he bowed again.

Almost immediately, Leandro came out of the doors of the main hall. When he saw Daniel, he smiled and gave him his hand, "Good morning, Senhor Castellan. What brings you to my home, dear Daniel?"

"It's a long story," Daniel answered in a soldierly manner. He smelled the aroma of fried chicken coming from Leandro, and his stomach rumbled. Daniel spoke louder to cover the indecent sound, "But I don't have time for long words. The main thing is that my camp on the seashore was attacked."

"Who attacked your camp?" Leandro asked with astonishment.

"The devil only knows!" Daniel exclaimed with annoyance. "That remains to be seen because they have disappeared."

At that moment, Leandro and Daniel noticed Nuno standing on the gallery. "Hello, Don Daniel, very glad to see you!" Nuno said, and with that, he strode away.

Daniel was surprised by such a brief greeting from the always sociable young man. He nodded after him and turned back to Leandro, "There was a wagon train with provisions going to our camp. It was driving on your land, dear Don Leandro. The wagon train was just leaving your forest and headed to our camp near the Big Turtle."

"What turtle?"

"Oh, my Goodness! The hill that is on the shore, beyond which is a cliff directly above the sea. This is your domain, isn't it, Don Leandro? Did you..."

"Oh, yes, yes... there, the day before..."

"Yes, they found one of my soldiers slain." Daniel nodded.

Leandro looked at where Nuno had just disappeared.

"...And the other one disappeared in the same place," Daniel continued. "So, the wagon train was traveling through the forest, but only horses and carts were left, and the guard had disappeared. Can you imagine?"

"With great difficulty, dear Daniel."

At this moment in the room from which Leandro had just come out, there was a crash of falling dishes and, at the same time, a woman's exclamation. Daniel looked at the door behind Leandro with surprise, then at his impassive face, and continued, "In a word, I have raised my squad, and now my people are combing your properties. Sorry, but it is necessary. Although we are in the service of His Majesty, and I am not obliged to inform you about this, I still thought it necessary to notify you about this."

Leandro nodded silently.

"That's why I came to you. Tell me, Don Leandro, do you know anything about any suspicious persons who may have appeared on your property in recent days? Maybe your people told you something..."

Leandro shrugged his shoulders, "Fortunately, we have not seen any robbers."

"In that case, allow me to take my leave!" Daniel actually gave Leandro a slight bow and headed for the exit. On the way, he turned around and shouted, "If God forbid, anyone sees anybody, I implore you to inform me immediately, dear Senhor."

"By all means!" Leandro answered.

Daniel turned to the exit door. Then, suddenly, one of the doors opened in the hallway. Daniel knew it was the guest bedroom door. A tall, not yet old, fair-haired gentleman in a white shirt tucked into his trousers came out of the room. Judging by his manner, he did not seem like a guest here. Passing by Daniel, he pretended not to notice his greeting, and together with Leandro, retired to the main hall.

* * *

Leandro and Duke Fernando de Braganza sat down to breakfast, and the fading sound of hooves came from the yard. The horsemen were leaving the estate. "It was the castellan of the local fortress of Leiria," Leandro informed the duke. "He said that his camp was attacked by unknown robbers. They kidnapped the soldiers accompanying the convoy."

The duke did not answer. Looking at his plate, he was thinking about something intently. Finally, the Duke raised his head, "And who do you think could have done it?"

"I don't know, Your Grace. Until now, our region has been famous for peace and integrity. Apart from stealing chickens and fighting rogues, nothing unusual has happened around here. However, recently one of the castellan's soldiers was killed on the seashore. There was another soldier with him, but he disappeared. Maybe they didn't get along with each other. It is unlikely that the killer, if he is roaming through our forests, could attack a whole wagon train. I don't understand what may have happened, unfortunately."

"Leandro, you have a reputation as a law–abiding gentleman and a kind owner of large estates," the duke said, "but still, I want to tell you, in view of the campaign that we are starting…"

"We're starting…," Leandro echoed in his head.

"… We won't have to be as picky as before. Perhaps the people who attacked this castellan's wagon train will be willing to serve us as well. By the way, what can you say about this guest of yours? Isn't he the officer King Afonso himself promoted for his military exploits, and also, as I now understand, made castellan of Leiria?"

"Yes, that's him. The castellan of Leiria, Don Daniel, served in the war in Africa with Afonso's army," Leandro replied. "I must tell you our children are friends, my son and his daughter, they are the same age."

"Is that so? Yes, your situation turns out to be quite delicate. I met Daniel a long time ago, and as I remember, he is a determined man and rules in the simplest manner. And, of course, is fervently devoted to the king."

"That's right," Leandro said with annoyance, "but I don't think he's a threat to us right now. First of all, he doesn't know anything yet. Raul and Francisco have just left to gather mercenaries. Secondly, he greatly values the good relations with my family. He loves his daughter madly and will do absolutely anything for her. I know he would prefer to keep the peace between his daughter and my family, or I don't know these people at all, Your Grace."

The duke stared at his plate in silence. He had already imagined what might happen if the castellan recognized him. He could only hope that the castellan did not yet know about the siege of the castle of Vila Viçosa, or that they were still hoping to get to the duke, unaware he had fled. Otherwise, Daniel would have to capture him right here at the Sinta estate. After all, it was under the jurisdiction of the castellan as the local guardian of order.

Perhaps the king had not yet sent an order to capture the duke to Daniel or the other castellans. However, he would definitely do it soon. Therefore, the Duke had less and less time, and it was necessary to hurry with the recruitment of mercenary troops. As long as the duke's fortress held, the Lisbon garrison would be tied to it, but sooner or later the mystery of the duke's disappearance would be revealed, and the garrison would return to Lisbon.

What if the king had already ordered the duke to be captured, and this castellan were to find out? After all, the military are people of the same social circles, and they have the same interests, and the gossip of their wives, too. Therefore, the only question was, did the castellan recognize the duke or not? If he did find out, the duke would have to run away as soon as possible, but how to escape? After all, the messengers sent to Porto and other friends of the duke must eventually return back here, to Sinta with their news, and it should happen very soon. Maybe even today.

"What should I do?" The duke continued to ask himself this difficult question. And he couldn't find an answer to it.

Daniel rode along the forest road ahead of his soldiers. For some reason, the most interesting thoughts came to the castellan precisely when he was riding, and this was one of those moments. The four recent events in Daniel's mind were now finding more and more in common and becoming more and more connected with one another.

First, an attack on a convoy by unknown intruders. They didn't leave any traces behind. Even the place where they attacked could not be established. It was only clear that it happened near the edge of the forest, because the horses got out of the forest by themselves, obviously under the influence of very recent prodding.

Second was the murder of the soldier Cristiano and the disappearance of his partner Jose. Such things happened from time to time in the garrison, and yet the reasons for such events usually became known immediately.

As these strange occurrences continued to perplex him, he also considered the elderly gentleman with a well-groomed face who came out of the guest bedroom in Leandro's house. Who was this man who dared not respond to the greeting of the royal captain? Maybe he didn't understand military ranks and positions? Or was he a foreigner? Yes, foreigners visited Leandro often, but this man reminded Daniel of someone. Who? Where could Daniel have seen him before?

Finally, Daniel found Nuno's behavior strange. This young man, usually so friendly, did not even come down to greet his close friend's father properly. So close that possibly... he would think more on that later... And Leandro himself did not invite Daniel to go inside the house. It seemed very easy for him to take on faith the castellan's statement that he did not have time. Strange. Very strange.

Don Daniel praised himself for not telling Leandro about other strange events of the last days and hours, but of course, they too seemed important here. There is nothing, no reason, for ordinary people to devote time or concern to the affairs of the military. For example, Daniel didn't need to tell Leandro about the creature his soldiers caught in the forest. He looked like a man but was intensely black-brown, and his attire was profoundly different, a dress and shiny chains. Also, he spoke in such a way that no one understood him. The soldiers called him the Red Ghost, but Daniel himself still had not had time to deal with him. It was okay, he would deal with the stranger upon arrival back at the castle. He would figure it out!

With that thought, Daniel whipped the horse with a flourish. And suddenly, unexpectedly he shouted, "Braganza! It was Duke Fernando de Braganza!"

A Moment from the Past - Storming Asilah

The rain subsided, and the wind dispersed the last of the clouds over the ocean. From the height of the tower towering over the wall of Asilah, a fortress along the ocean shore, Vizier Shadulla clearly saw the ships of the Portuguese fleet in the distance. Some vessels were lodged on coastal reefs as they continued to fall apart. The surviving ships lined up opposite the fortress, preparing to fire and fill it with holes. The infantrymen who managed to get to shore also gathered in detachments and began to surround the fortress. Their immense columns came from afar and were already walking toward the walls. Despite the recent rain, they raised clouds of dust. Looking closely at the soldiers, Shadulla saw that many of them did not wear any armor, and some even walked barefoot.

There were so many of them that for one defender of the fortress and city, there were at least five enemies. The vizier looked at his soldiers, grimly waiting inside the fortress for the assault at the walls. Just yesterday, their faces were cheerful, and the city was living a quiet peaceful life, but suddenly these Portuguese appeared, and the arrival took everyone by surprise. The city did not have time to prepare for this siege. Many of Asilah's soldiers abandoned their homes or posts at the news of the Portuguese landing and, neglecting their duty, ran away with the ordinary citizens before all the gates of the fortress were closed.

Shadulla thought it was unlikely that the Portuguese would launch an assault immediately. He knew a lot about military affairs and that an assault is always preceded by a long siege. This would give the defenders of Asilah time to gather and strengthen their morale. Suddenly, however, the side of one of the ships was dotted with a number of small clouds, which were immediately blown away by the wind. Then the rumble of cannons reached the city. At the same time, cannonballs began to blow up the ground near the fortress, hit the walls, and fly over the heads of the defenders of Asilah. The Portuguese had still brought their terrible cannons! Peering into the distance, to where the ranks of cavalrymen were lined up behind the infantry lines, Shadulla saw soldiers assembling long ladders made from planks delivered from the ships, but why did they need these ladders now? Weren't they going to besiege the fortress first?

Shadulla, whom Sheikh Muley had left in command of the Asilah garrison, began to clasp his cheeks in despair. Were they really going to storm immediately after they got off the ships? This should not happen this way! The position of the fortress defenders was rapidly becoming hopeless. Yes, he was not mistaken. The soldiers were there with ladders at the ready and on command, rushed forward to join the infantry already standing near the walls.

Young Daniel, with his saber raised, was running towards the wall, his squad following behind. This was the vanguard of Afonso V, who, at that moment, was looking at them through a spyglass from the captain's bridge. Behind the assault squad, the king saw a large red horse, on which his son and heir to the throne, sixteen-year-old Joao, was sitting. The soldiers, inspired by Joao's presence, shouted with delight. However, the strong spiritual uplift did not prevent them from observing line position and order. They did not lag behind Daniel, who had received instructions from Joao before the attack detailing from which side and how the squad would storm Asilah. Despite Joao's youth, the courtiers had predicted he would have a career as a great general. His teachers were the best experts and masters of military affairs in Portugal. Under their guidance, he had already learned the basics of military science, and now the heir passed the final exam as he commanded this assault.

Here the king's son caught Daniel's eye as he turned around and immediately pointed to the gate tower with his hand. Daniel gave the command to his sergeants and continued running toward the wall. Soldiers rushed in with ladders. With a running start, they leaned them against the walls and immediately divided into groups. Some climbed up while others held the ladders stable. Arrows, spears, stones, and construction debris collected for such an intrusion flew at them from above, but no matter what the defenders of the fortress threw at the Portuguese, no matter how they tried to push the ladders away with poles and pitchforks to prevent the soldiers from climbing the walls to the tower, their attempts were in vain.

Daniel had almost reached the top edge of the wall when a stream of boiling water fell on the ladder. Fortunately for Daniel, the boiling water barely touched him. Only on his back, under his armored shell, it felt as if a scorpion's tail dug into his back. One of the soldiers climbing after the commander roared in pain.

"Don't take off your armor!" Daniel bellowed, already putting his foot on the wall.

A saber swung! And another! The Moors, who had rushed toward Daniel, backed away and leaned towards the crowd of comrades bristling with pikes and sabers, but the scalded, brutalized soldiers of Daniel's squad no longer registered anyone in front of them. Daniel barely managed to escape the swing of a halberd that crashed down on the nearest Moor. Uttering wild cries, his soldiers rushed along the fortress wall to the gate tower. New volleys of naval cannons thundered around them, and the towers began to crumble, their stones scattering together with the remains of the defenders of the fortress.

Soon Daniel's squad was running from the wall and down the steps leading to the gate. Scattering stones and logs that supported the gate from the inside, they opened the doors. The cavalrymen waiting outside, who had completely covered themselves and their horses with armor, rushed into the fortress with pikes at the ready. It was simply impossible to restrain the onslaught of these muscles and steel!

"Long live the King!" The cavalrymen shouted all together. "Long live Joao! Rush ahead!!!"

The devastation brought upon the conquered city by Afonso's soldiers was terrible. The soldiers exterminated almost all living things that came their way. Breaking into the mosque and finding where the wives, children, and mothers of the Moor warriors sought refuge, they killed everyone. Thousands of captured soldiers and citizens were surrounded by the Portuguese in the main square and awaited their fate there. They were destined to rebuild the city from the ruins half-starved, and then go to the slave markets of Portugal.

The looting of the city continued for three days. On the morning of the fourth day, a messenger came to the tent of Captain Daniel, who had just barely managed to fall asleep after the terrible and unpredictably fast victory that frightened even himself. "The King is waiting for you, Senhor Daniel," he said briefly. Daniel rushed to the basin of water, but the messenger stopped him, "His Majesty has ordered you to arrive as I find you."

Therefore, Daniel arrived in the middle of the square in the fortress with other officers in the same torn, sweat-soaked, and smoke-saturated clothes. To the right and left of them, on the dais, sat the king's entourage. Directly in front of Daniel, King Afonso V was sitting on the dais. Shadulla was kneeling in front of him with his hands tied behind his back. The vizier squinted his camel-looking eyes in pain but remained silent.

"Captain Daniel!" the herald proclaimed. "Approach the king!" Daniel stepped forward and froze at the dais.

"What happened to your hand?" The king asked loudly, pointing at the bandage on the captain's arm.

"A Moor on the wall managed to hit me before he fell down."

The King shook his head respectfully and continued, "Daniel, tomorrow my son will be awarded his accolade. You fought bravely under him. The courage with which you led your men-at-arms to storm the fortress and open the gates for our cavalry ensured a quick victory. If it weren't for you, my son probably wouldn't have earned his knighthood in this campaign. Therefore, I have issued two decrees…" A young courtier ran down the steps of the dais.

He handed Daniel two scrolls with red wax seals hanging on them. Daniel took the scrolls and saluted the king. He continued, "Daniel, first of all, I'm appointing you castellan of Leiria Fortress. Together with your family, you will receive an improved allowance there. You will also get ownership of a house with the right of inheritance. In addition to your share of the loot, you will also receive a special bonus from me…"

The king swore under his breath, slapped his neck with a flourish, and killed a fat meat fly. The gaping page began to fan the king with redoubled zeal with a large fan. "Secondly, your children will study for free at the University of Lisbon. Our army needs the descendants of soldiers like you. They should be not only brave soldiers but also educated people. This is the content of my decrees."

Chapter 9. In the Name of the King

Captain Stefan, the commander of the Vila Viçosa garrison, lifted his head from the pillow and listened. It was still early, but a discordant chorus of drunken soldiers could be heard from the barracks. They chanted in derision at the pot-bellied nobles and threatened to let the red rooster into the estates of the gentlemen and defame their wives and daughters. Only the name of the king remained sacred to them. Only the king was spared by the soldiers and only on him did they continue to rely. The worst thing was that the soldiers delivered their blasphemous speeches in rhyme. They didn't even invent anything special; they just twisted the words of the drill song, and, of course, a once-uttered obscenity is impossible to get out of your head. Stefan knew this from his own experience.

Last night, when Stefan didn't find a single sentry on the castle wall, he looked into the barracks, and even the duty sergeant didn't come up to him with a report. Only one, the drunkest, but somewhat obedient, soldier tried to get up, and even that was out of some force of habit. What else, damn it? What next?! Stefan knew well that the army was rotten from the inside and falling apart.

After one or two days of idleness, the first cracks would start on even the strongest shelf. One soldier, then another, would stop shaving or mending his clothes and armor. Then, the sullen grumbling of the most irrepressible troublemakers would begin. These would be silently supported by the majority, some agreeing and others following because they were afraid of these loudmouths. There may be only three or four of them, but they would have strong fists and a habit of keeping everyone down. They liked to fight, which most, on the contrary, did not like at all, despite their trade. A week later, a soldiers' revolt would become inevitable, turning the regiment into a huge gang of looters and rapists, terrifying civilians. Once it began, it could only be brought to obedience with the help of regiments that had not yet been touched by corruption, and there was already one such regiment – camped just outside these castle walls.

My God, while he, the commandant, was fussing with his secret, the soldiers had already guessed everything! That there would be no assault and the duke had fled. He was left alone with his lies and looked at the ground. After all, the whole garrison had eyes. Everything the soldiers saw; they would freely discuss. The red line had already been crossed. He, the captain and commandant, would not be able to hang even one soldier-perjurer to impose fear, because he simply would not find any amenable performers.

Stefan imagined being pushed out into the street, into a crowd of drunken soldiers. Everyone was angry at him for some reason or another; such was military service. Everyone kept a stone in his bosom. The soldiers angrily shouted righteous words. They made up a terrible, criminal untruth, but the crowd was unable to see through it, and finally, a noose was thrown around his neck…

For the first time in days, Stefan felt goosebumps running down his spine.

He couldn't help the duke anymore. He was no longer able to carry out his orders. Neither the duke nor his family was in any danger. Yes, the treasurer continued to regularly give both soldiers and him huge sums in gold cruzados, but sooner or later the supplies would run out, and then they wouldn't be able to buy half a dead rat for those damn cruzados.

Stefan remembered how the superintendent shouted at another captain right in front of his eyes. When the officer tried to justify himself by referring to an order he received, the superintendent retorted, "That's why they made you an officer, so that you could decide for yourself which order to carry out and which not!" He meant you had to get yourself out of predicaments! And Stefan started packing.

He had prepared simple peasant clothes in advance, reasoning that they would protect him better than any armor at this point. Stefan just put the armor under the bed, and from there he took out a heavy bag of gold. Stefan took only a dagger for his weapon. Now he had to wait until dark. To reach the entrance to the underground passage, which only he knew about in the castle, it would be necessary to cross the square, where drunken soldiers were walking around now. Stefan didn't want to meet them at all, not in his captain's attire but even more so not in his current dress.

Finally, darkness enveloped the castle. Now it was dispelled only by the flames of the fire on which the soldiers were roasting the last mutton from the remaining stock in the kitchen and washing it down with precious wines from the duke's already looted cellar. Stefan chose the moment when another barrel was being rolled out onto the square. The soldiers, shouting drunkenly, gathered around it, gave unwanted advice to the sergeant kicking the bottom out of the barrel, and pushed each other away. A fight started. One after another, soldiers fell on the cobblestones but then got up and stubbornly crawled back toward the barrel.

Stefan, holding a bundle in one hand and a stick in the other, sauntered past them to the temple. Creaking open the iron door, he went inside, and once there, pulled on a large icon in the lower tier of the altar that opened a secret door. Entering the altar, he confidently took a few steps to the northeast, bent down to the floor, groped for a large wooden hatch, pulled it up, and descended the steps. Once at the bottom, Stefan took out a tar-soaked rag from his bundle and impaled it on the stick. He then took out a flint and began to strike sparks. Soon the underground passage was illuminated by the flame of the torch.

* * *

Jorge first sensed the smell of burnt tar, and then he heard footsteps coming from the same place, from the underground passage. He got ready. The trapdoor cover lifted, and a head appeared in the light of the oil lamps. Jorge threw a silk cord around the stranger's neck and pulled at its ends. A minute later it was all over.

Jorge pulled his victim out of the hatch and immediately, without delay, transferred the body to a cart standing at the stable gate. Two bodies were already lying on the cart. Jorge did not even take time to look at the face of this new victim. He went back to the hatch, bolted it, and extinguished the lamps. Then he threw hay over the bodies, opened the gate, slapped his palm on the rump of Perito's stallion, who snorted with fear and shame for the actions of these people, jumped into the cart, and drove out of the stable. His journey under the starry sky was a short jaunt to the river. That was the duke's order. Duke de Braganza did not give any directives concerning the gold cruzados, so Jorge kept those for himself.

* * *

The day eventually came when there was nothing left to eat or drink. The soldiers broke down the door to Stefan's apartment but found only the abandoned armor there. The captain had escaped.

The patrol riders who regularly made rounds of the castle could not believe their eyes when the de Braganza family flag fell at the feet of their horses. They raised their heads and made sure that it was the same flag that used to hang on the keep. There was no flag there. The fallen flag was brought to General Afonso, and he immediately left for the castle. When he got to the wall, there were ranks of soldiers on it.

"Where is the duke?" The adjutant of the general shouted.

"The duke has disappeared," they answered from the wall.

"Where is the castellan then?"

"Also disappeared," one of the soldiers of the garrison shouted. With that, he threw down Stefan's armor.

"Who can General Afonso talk to?"

"Let him talk to all of us. We're all in this together."

"Open the gate! But no trickery, otherwise our bombards will talk!"

"And what will happen to us?"

After some debate, the soldiers of General Afonso were allowed to enter the castle. The general spoke with two officers of the garrison who had come out of their shelters after seeing the king's soldiers in the castle. The general, on behalf of Joao, promised forgiveness to everyone. Afonso's soldiers began to search the castle in the hope of finding the duke, but their efforts were in vain. Neither the duke nor his family, not even his servants, were found in the castle. In the end, Afonso realized that the duke had managed to escape the castle in secret, unbeknownst even to his officers and soldiers. How did he do it? Afonso contemplated this, although it no longer mattered. He could not complete his task, and the duke had disappeared. Afonso was unable to capture and execute him. Having assessed the situation, the general decided to immediately send a messenger to the king with this news. Afonso himself had to restore order in the castle, assemble a new garrison for its defense, and only after that, go back to Lisbon.

* * *

For King Joao II, the most trying days of his entire reign had just begun. He assembled a council of the remaining generals in Lisbon and worked out a plan of action with them. Messengers were sent all over the country with a common decree for all. In the name of the king, every castellan and every commander of a garrison, regiment, ship, or border guard detachment, as well as every customs official were tasked with capturing Duke de Braganza and delivering him alive to the royal court. Now Joao II wanted to personally execute the duke and make sure that this time the duke would not be able to run away.

In addition, copies of the edict were sent to the Cortes, in which the king declared de Braganza a traitor to the kingdom and a troublemaker. Every subject of the king who dared to grant the duke asylum was henceforth threatened with execution and deprivation of property, regardless of his rank, wealth, or nobility of family. The members of the Cortes had to sign off that they had familiarized themselves with the edict and notified their communities about the pursuit of Braganza.

For the most slow-witted, the king established a reward for the apprehension, or any information leading to the apprehension, of Duke de Braganza.

The King also sent a messenger to Queen Isabella of Castile with a request not to give refuge to de Braganza if he came to her. However, Isabella, with all due respect to Joao II, was in no hurry to answer. Heeding the messenger's pleas, Isabella received him in the throne room, sitting next to her husband Ferdinand of Aragon. This distraction did not tear the queen away from her favorite occupation, embroidery in frames.

Isabella listened to the broken speech of the messenger who read the letter of Joao II to the end, looked at her husband, and bowed her head to bite the thread. "Your Majesty, "she mumbled, "have you heard anything about this Braganza?"

Ferdinand did not answer, but shrugged his shoulders and began to look at the ceiling, covered with Arabic script and ornaments.

"Neither have I."

They were a worthy couple. The Castilian monarchs were second cousins to each other, but despite the remoteness of the relationship, they were similar in appearance. Each had the same rounded, even puffy face, and a similar outline of the eyes. However, unlike the potato nose on Ferdinando's face, the queen's nose looked more like a bird's beak. Her hair, hidden under a helmet-like white cape and a veil of transparent fabric, was the color of straw, whereas Ferdinand was black-haired. The queen was wearing her usual dress of blue silk embroidered with gold patterns. This color didn't go well with the queen's greenish-blue eyes. However, the same could be said about the almost satanic combination of Ferdinando's black eyes and his red clothes.

The Queen admired the azure cornflower she had just finished embroidering and sighed. De Braganza's wife and children were already living in one of the country palaces of the Castilian monarchs, but in his letter, Joao II did not ask about the duke's family. The duke himself was not in Castile. He was still in Portugal, which Isabella also knew. However, the queen had no desire to quarrel with Joao II. He could get angry and, for example, order his fleet to block the exit from the Mediterranean Sea through the Estrecho de Gibraltar. Castile, weakened by the centuries-old Reconquista and recent wars with Portugal, would hardly be able to achieve success at sea now. The alliance of Portugal with England added convincing arguments against a quarrel with Joao II. In any case, such a quarrel would be costly.

"So, what do you say, Your Majesty?" Isabella turned to her husband again.

He shrugged again and said, "First of all, the beneficent King Joao II is our relative." It was a stretch, but Joao II could be considered a relative of the Castilian monarchs. In his second marriage, Afonso V was married to Joanna la Beltraneja, Isabella's half-sister. Therefore, Joanna was Joao II's stepmother.

"And we must," Ferdinand continued, "respect his request."

"Tell the king that as soon as Braganza appears in our domain, we will immediately consider this request," the queen told the messenger. "Paco!"

"I'm here, Your Majesty!" The queen's secretary approached the throne.

"Prepare a letter from the Castilian monarchs with an answer to His Majesty Joao II."

"Yes, Your Majesty!"

Isabella and her husband exchanged glances. They understood each other perfectly. The last wars against Castile in 1476 and 1479 were carried out by Afonso V precisely because he defended the illegitimate Joanna's right to the Castilian throne. Both wars brought him bad luck, but now the monarchs felt they should not stir up the past. However, in the event of a new war, de Braganza, if he finds himself in Castile, may even be very useful to influence the stubborn Joao II. The Castilian monarchs loved the purported "persecuted Christians," but they loved their money even more, and they knew de Braganza had a lot of money.

* * *

After Daniel's visit to the Sinta estate, the exercises at the Big Turtle continued for another day. When Daniel returned with his squad to Leiria, he first yelled at Lieutenant Furtado, the commander of the garrison, who was sitting in the fortress with the rest of the soldiers. There seemed to always be a reason for this, but today it was a prisoner who was caught on the shore. Daniel met Furtado in the desk sergeant's room where this strange dark-skinned man, draped with shiny bracelets and chains interspersed with multicolored stones, was sitting on a bench right behind the sergeant. The prisoner dared to look directly at Daniel with his intelligent, shining eyes.

"Why is he here?!" Daniel shouted to the sergeant, pointing at the prisoner. "How do you know what he is contemplating? What if he attacks you from behind? Do you want a guard to be murdered like in Albufeira?"

The duty sergeant stood at attention and eyed Daniel apprehensively.

"Your Grace, he can't be treated like everyone else," Furtado defended the sergeant. "I don't know who he is or where he's from, but he's wearing gold jewelry."

"What?" Daniel approached the prisoner and yanked the chain from around his neck. The prisoner continued to look him straight in the eyes. "Damn it! It's really gold, and with stones, precious, I suspect."

"Think for yourself what will happen if he falls into the hands of the soldiers down in the cells," Furtado continued. "They have all been wounded and bloodied at the hands of Moors and dream of revenge."

"So, put him in a separate dungeon!" Daniel shouted. "a jug of water for him! A loaf of bread! An armful of hay! And the Gospel. That's it! Let him wait until I come."

"Yes, Senhor! But he doesn't need the Gospel, because he doesn't speak our language."

"And what does he speak?"

"I don't know, and no one can understand him. He's a foreigner, that's for sure."

"Send a messenger to our temple. Some new monk was recently sent to them there. They say he is skilled in languages."

"Yes, Senhor!"

"So. What other urgent matters do we have?"

"Your Grace, you have a letter from the king," and the attendant handed Daniel an envelope.

"What? Why didn't you tell me this first ...?!" Daniel roared.

He opened the envelope and began to read the letter, "To capture Duke Fernando de Braganza..."

Daniel blinked and read again, "To capture Duke..."

He sat down on the desk chair.

Then he read again, "To capture Duke..."

"Come on, let's go!" The voice of the lieutenant brought Daniel back to his world. Furtado kicked the prisoner up, twisted his arm behind his back, and led him out of the room.

Daniel finally came to his senses. Without saying goodbye to Furtado, he ran out of the duty room and rushed to his office. There, Daniel read the letter to the end and reread it again...

What the hell was to be done? Go back to Leandro's estate and grab de Braganza? Yes, because from the moment Daniel read the letter and failed to rush headlong to carry out the order, he himself became a criminal. Leandro is a witness that Daniel saw de Braganza. However, he was not introduced to the duke, and in case anything goes awry, it could be possible for him to say he did not recognize the duke. Therefore, he could safely wait for the duke here, in the fortress of Leiria, if he should happen to come here.

Daniel could possibly meet him on the high road, or the devil knows where else. That's when, if he failed to detain him, Daniel would have disobeyed the order, and Daniel really didn't want to carry out this order because to fulfill it meant involving Leandro in this matter. Then, of course, Daniel would have to capture him too because the decree says, "Every subject of the king who dares to grant Duke de Braganza asylum will be deprived of property and life, regardless of his rank, wealth or nobility of family." Daniel reread the letter. Oh, these nobles! Why must they rebel against the only legitimate king? Of course, they should be executed for this! And he, Daniel, needed to capture not only de Braganza but also Don Leandro! Yes, but if he does so, Estela and Nuno's friendship will be over!

A third possibility remained: to immediately return to Leandro's house and tell him about the king's order. Let him run with this duke wherever he desires. Daniel would turn away and not notice. He would delay for a day or two and only then realize the duke was missing! Go in pursuit of the duke! But Nuno and Estela…

Suddenly Daniel's office seemed to be illuminated by the sun, as the smiling Estela entered through the open door, "Hello, Father!"

"My daughter!" Daniel exclaimed. He jumped up from the table and rushed to Estela. The daughter offered her forehead for a kiss and gently evaded the embrace of her father, who smelled of fire, sweat, and horse.

"I'm glad to see you again. Why don't you go home? I suppose you are probably tired after everything?"

"Oh, daughter, daughter!" Daniel could not find words for the feelings that were bursting from him now. For once, his daughter, who did not particularly give him her attention, came to him directly at the fortress. "How are you doing? What's new at the university? How's Mother? How's Nuno?"

"Nuno is the most interesting of all," Estela said. "At his house, in my... my former room, there is a wounded girl. I'm afraid she may be an accomplice of those criminals who attacked your soldiers. I already heard about the attack." Estela took the scarlet ribbon from her sleeve and put it on the table. "We found this piece of cloth where one soldier was killed and the other disappeared, and the wounded girl staying with Nuno recognized it. Perhaps she is involved in the murder of the soldier on Big Turtle? And also, she looks remarkably like the prisoner who was just led past me."

Daniel, even during Estela's childhood, was never surprised by her constant awareness. Estela's curiosity and inquisitiveness were boundless as were her knowledge and memory. If she were a man, he thought, she would have no equal in the intelligent aristocratic society and would already be working as an envoy to other countries.

"Who hurt her?" Daniel asked.

"I don't know. It doesn't matter. The important thing is that she is not from our area and speaks a language that no one can understand. Also, no one can agree whether she is possibly from the Marranos or Moriscos because of her dark hair and very, very strange clothes, just like your prisoner. When you see her, Father, you will immediately want to take her into custody," Estela said. "I'm sure about it!" she added meaningfully.

His daughter's wishes had always been Daniel's law.

"That's it! When this girl disappears, Nuno will realize that he made a huge mistake," Estela thought. "He won't associate with criminals, and when this dark-colored girl goes to prison, she will be counted among criminals, and the ribbon will be proof of that. I'll help Nuno forget about her! Her room will be mine again. Only the feather bed will have to be changed, and we will have a happy time together again like before."

"Come home," Estela said to her father. "I will ask my mother to prepare warm water, lunch, and a fresh bed for you." With that, she left.

Daniel continued to reason, and his thoughts were headed in exactly the direction that Estela had planned. She really knew a lot about diplomacy.

"Leandro," Daniel thought, "is acting in concert with the duke, there is no doubt about that. The question is, did they not possibly organize all these incidents, the attack on the two soldiers at Big Turtle and the attack on the wagon train? Of course, they didn't need these soldiers themselves, but what if they were just unwelcome witnesses to bigger dealings? What if these attacks were only part of a coup d'etat that, judging by the tone of the royal letter, de Braganza was guilty of organizing? And was this coup already in full swing and occurring right here, right under my nose?" Ideas started to transform from a puzzle to a clear vision in Daniel's head.

"If you don't know what to do, act according to the oath," Daniel recalled the rule that he himself had hammered into the heads of soldiers for years. Indeed, this was really the most reasonable solution. Daniel jumped up and, despite the pain in his leg, bruised the day before by a horse's hoof, ran out into the yard. His orderly was just passing by, "Ricardo! Tell Sergeant Ligeir to get the horses saddled again! Feed them and the soldiers. In half an hour we leave again. Go!"

Then, Daniel was back on horseback, racing ahead of his soldiers. From time to time, midges flew into his mouth, and Daniel spat. Estela would never be in that scoundrel's house again! She wouldn't entertain any friendship with Nuno anymore. His new girl recognized that ribbon. She didn't even pretend! Oh, you robber breed! Was it necessary to come up with such a thing, to encroach on the power of the king? And on the very land under Daniel's supervision! On the power of the king, on whose mercy the fate of Daniel and his family depended! The king! Daniel had always been loyal and would remain loyal until his last breath because the kings, both Afonso V and Joao II, always paid him an honest salary and rewarded him generously for special military labors! No! He was not a noble's son who had gone berserk with fat. He's an officer! An old hack and an honest man! And he would not give his daughter to these troublemakers for abuse!

* * *

Furtado watched the last horseman leave the fortress. It became quiet, and he went to his office apartment. "What has happened to the castellan?" he asked himself. "Once again, he is not acting according to reason. People just returned from a hike, and he has dragged them somewhere else again. However, I could care less about the captain." Furtado still had tasks ahead of him. But he, at forty years old, the oldest lieutenant in Portugal, had almost nothing to look forward to. Soon he would have to retire and live on a paltry penny pension without a home of his own, without a wife, without a family. All of which Furtado once lost forever because he was quarrelsome, weak to wine, and a drunkard. Well, he would venture to change this…

At home, Furtado opened the casket in which he kept his valuables and took out a tiny ceramic vessel, only about the size of a finger. He opened the stopper, brought the vessel to the window, and looked into it. There was something barely splashing at the bottom. That was enough. Even one drop was enough. He would add one drop... no, two drops, just to be sure, to the water of that dirty one who was dragged from the shore and just now taken to the dungeon. Once the prisoner took at least a sip, Furtado planned to take some of his jewelry, not all of it, of course. Some would have to be left. Even one chain from the prisoner's neck would be enough for him for the rest of his life. Enough for Furtado to buy a small house with a garden, a vineyard, and a cellar with huge barrels inside. As for the prisoner... Well, who would miss him, a runaway Marrano or Morisco or whatever? If he were to die, everyone in the fortress would only cross themselves and care less, and after he has expired, there would no longer be a need to guard him. The fewer of them there were, the better. How many of these were found on the roads monthly?

"Senior Commandant!" someone shouted and suddenly knocked at the outside door.

Furtado shuddered, abruptly put the cork back in place, and shoved the vessel into the casket. "Well, come in!" he shouted.

The door opened a crack. The attendant was standing in the doorway and next to him was a blond–haired, blue-eyed youth dressed in a brown wool shirt. Furtado recognized him; it was the new monk expelled to the church of Leiria from Lisbon. They said he was a troublemaker; he didn't get along with his superiors. There was a blissful smile on the monk's face. His teeth protruded slightly.

"This is Brother Pascoal," the attendant introduced the monk, "whom Senior Castellan ordered to be sent to interrogate that prisoner. They say he knows different languages. Would you like me to take monk to the prisoner?"

A Moment from the Past - Saving Joao

For this military campaign, Duke Fernando de Braganza had put on his most beautiful German armor: blued steel with gold engraving. Because of this armor, soldiers had mistaken him for the king or the heir to the throne several times. The duke was pleased. During this campaign, he had remained close to Joao II, in order to readily make acquaintance with the future king.

The cavalry under the command of Duke de Braganza had just burst through the swinging gates of Asilah castle. Knights in armor on armored horses trampled the soldiers of Vizier Shadulla and drove them away with their long spears. Following the cavalry, detachments of infantry rushed toward the gates of the castle. A monstrous battle raged inside the castle. The heir to the throne, who kept at a distance of only a fathom from the duke, could barely cope with his horse. It neighed and shied away from the iron weapons that glinted and rang all around. Behind them, the infantry was already pressing in on Joao II, striving for victory within the castle. Suddenly, the soldiers, including Joao II and de Braganza, were attacked from somewhere by a large detachment of Moors on camels. Hiding behind multicolored round shields, the Moors brandished sabers and uttered wild screams.

King Afonso V, who had been watching the battle through a spyglass, got up from his chair on the bridge. From there he could see that the Moors on camels were rushing toward Joao, because the standard–bearer rode next to the heir, holding the flag of Portugal high in his hand, his horse dancing with fear. The Moors fought their way toward the flag as they realized the heart of the attacking army was there.

The duke immediately assessed the situation and guessed the Vizier's plan. While the duke's cavalry was fighting inside the castle, Shadulla sent his camel riders through another gate to cut off the advancing infantry from the Portuguese cavalry so the Moors would be able to close the gates and kill the Portuguese cavalrymen inside the castle. Indeed, at the sight of the Moors on camels, the Portuguese infantry stopped and bristled with pikes. The first camels, snorting and drooling, immediately crashed into the infantrymen and began to trample them. The riders, clothed in white, began to chop at the soldiers with their curved sabers. Joao II prepared to repel the attack and swung his sword in front of him. At that moment, one of the camels pushed his horse with all of its weight. The horse fell, crushing Joao. De Braganza, who had not taken his eyes off the heir, plunged a spear into the camel. The camel roared, jumped, and threw off the Moor rider. However, the Moor did not let go of his saber. Getting to his feet, he rushed toward Joao II and swung at him, but de Braganza's sword stopped him. The duke cut open the Moor's stomach. The enemy's white clothes bloomed with the stain of blood. He fell to the ground and stilled. The duke pulled Joao II out from under the fallen horse, helped him onto his own horse, and led the horse away under the cover of the infantry, which was taking the brunt of the blow of the troops on camels.

Seeing that Joao II was on the duke's horse and moving away towards the shore, Afonso V, who had been petrified with horror and drenched in sweat, finally sighed and sat down again on his chair.

* * *

In the evening, when the battle had ended in the center of Asilah and there were only small skirmishes occurring and homes being burned on the outskirts of the city, King Afonso V sat down to have dinner with his entourage. It came to his attention that the duke's feat had still gone unnoticed. The king held a goblet in his hand, walked around the long table where the guests were sitting, and clinked glasses with everyone, not allowing them to get up. The king stopped and lingered near Duke de Braganza. "De Braganza, you saved the life of my son, heir to the throne," he said, looking into the duke's eyes.

De Braganza stood up and held out his cup to the monarch. "Who else would have done otherwise?" The duke said with a soft smile.

"So, tell me what reward you want," Afonso said cheerfully, banging his cup against the duke's cup, "To your health, Senhor." Both took a sip.

The duke wiped his lips with a cambric handkerchief he purposely carried for this occasion and said, "Thank you, Your Majesty, but personally, I don't need a reward. The saved life of the heir is already the greatest reward for me."

"De Braganza!" The king raised his voice, "I never borrow from anyone. Tell me how I should repay you."

"Your Majesty! I am not a poor man!"

"Of course!" The king exclaimed. De Braganza's wealth could nearly compete with His Majesty's treasury.

"Once, Your Majesty, you knighted me. Your favor toward me is also a huge reward."

"Ah, Duke!"

"Therefore, I will ask not for myself, but for a friend."

"Have it your way. What kind of friend is this?"

"He lives near the castle of Leiria. This is a humble nobleman named Don Leandro. He inherited a ruined estate that he managed to re-establish and make prosperous. He is a hardworking, diligent, and honest man. He is respected by everyone in the neighborhood, and I ask for your assistance by naming Don Leandro as a member of the Cortes and endowing him with the villages surrounding his estate. Don Leandro, I can assure you, belongs to those people who make up the backbone of our kingdom. There are few such people, but it is they who struggle the most to get to the top because they are honest and modest people. He will ensure the peasants in these villages do not drink but work diligently. Believe me, Don Leandro will not allow them to sleep for long periods of time, idly stagger around, or beg on the roads."

"I will give my consent for your friend Don Leandro to become a member of the Cortes and grant him new lands, but I will thank your family, Duke, too. If you don't tell me how I can, I will decide for myself," said the king. He clinked glasses with the duke once more and took a step towards the next guest.

Chapter 10. Meeting

"Leandro, explain to me what's going on?" Manuella shouted, bursting into her husband's office. "Some frightening people with weapons are coming toward our estate. They don't look like farmhands or peasants; they behave like soldiers coming into camp."

"Calm down, dear…"

"Two sheep have already been roasted for them and a large pot with some type of brew is being prepared," Manuella did not calm down, "and they got wine from our cellars for themselves. They defecated right in the flower garden among the roses, and they have started pinning the girls in corners. Bella, the housekeeper, has already complained to me about them, and Paula, the milkmaid, came running with the same complaints. You were silent this morning, silent this afternoon, and you're not explaining anything right now. What is happening here?"

"I'll explain everything to you," Leandro replied, "this evening at dinner. In the meantime, calm down Manuella. All this is being done for the benefit of our family."

Yes, keeping all this from his wife was a big mistake on Leandro's part, but he was not able to think of anything to say to Manuella in advance. It seemed impossible to let her into the secret! Was it possible to tell her straight out? "The king decided to ruin Duke de Braganza, but I am on the duke's side. You don't know yet, but our family savings, the gold, is already melting away because it has to be spent on those very rude men who gather on our estate. Those are mercenaries. They do not know crafts; they abhor peasant labor so much they would rather kill than follow the plow. They are outcasts of their families… But just such people are needed now. A terrible time is coming, Manuella, and no one can escape from it!"

Leandro gathered his strength and managed to find a way to explain all this to his wife before dinner, and now, the whole family, the Duke of Braganza, and Anacaona were sitting at the table. No matter how shocked Manuella was by her husband's story, she still found warm words for the guests of the house. She watched with a smile as Anacaona mastered European dishes and mealtime etiquette, Nuno helping her with advice and by his own example. De Braganza was watching the girl closely too.

"At this hour, Your Grace, I have managed to gather about forty mercenaries," Leandro was telling the duke. "They have already received half of their pay, and at the same time, a good berating from their commander. They won't get another drop of wine until the end of the campaign. Two of the loudest had to be flogged but were then made foremen. They are already shouting at their soldiers."

"Smart guys," the duke grinned.

"Yes. While it was still daylight, they managed to hold competitions in crossbow shooting. There are some really skilled shooters among them."

"But," thought the duke, "forty mercenaries will not be enough to overthrow the king." The duke hoped that the messengers sent to Porto and his friends were about to arrive here, but what would their responses be? After all, the messengers may not bring him good news. How long would it take before the duke's friends could gather the right size army? By such grains, in twos, threes, fives, or tens?"

Somewhere in the kitchen, dropped dishes rattled. No one in the living room paid any attention to this, only Anacaona smiled.

"Tell me, my dear friend," the duke turned to Leandro, "have you managed to find out what your guest knows about the attack on the soldiers at the Big Turtle? Were they really robbers?"

"Anacaona recognized the ribbon that one of her people had dropped," Leandro replied. "It was found where a soldier from the castle was killed. Anacaona even gave the name of the person to whom this ribbon belonged; it is their badge of distinction."

There was no need to point out that robbers did not wear insignia, but still, the duke asked, "So it belonged to a military man?"

"Yes, Your Grace," Nuno answered for his father. "As far as I understand, it was a group of warriors. Anacaona said that the ribbon belonged to a commander named Tupac, not a very common name." Hearing the familiar name, Anacaona smiled and began nodding her head.

"Nuno, tell their lordships about that ship… the ship that Anacaona came on," Leandro urged his son on, "although I admit, it all seems like a fairy tale to me."

Nuno told the duke what he had learned about the Aztlan country, its structure, and the reasons that made Anacaona and her companions head toward the sunrise. Information about the land across the ocean did not interest de Braganza, but the ship on which the wanderers came to the shores of Portugal could be useful. Having learned that the ship was now just over the horizon, and the warriors were sailing to the shore in boats, the duke began to ask Anacaona about the ship itself, which Anacaona called Tlaluacatli.

"What size is your ship?"

"Ken uey mo accalaza?" Nuno translated the duke's question for Anacaona.

"Makuili mahtlaktli iko chikuase" *fifty times six,* Anacaona replied, using her fingers to mimic taking steps along the table.

The duke looked questioningly at Nuno, "How much?"

"Three hundred steps," Nuno replied. "I also asked Anacaona this question, and I was also very surprised, but she confirmed her answer, three hundred steps."

"And how many people came on it?"

"Kexki tlakatl accalaza?" *How many people are there?* Nuno translated for Anacaona.

"Makuili mahtlaktli iko sempoualli" *fifty times twenty,* Anacaona replied.

"A thousand," Nuno translated.

The duke jumped up from his chair and began to pace the hall nervously. A bold plan of action was maturing in his mind. "And how many of them are real warriors?" he asked.

"Kexki tlakatl teyaochiuani?" Nuno translated, referring to his pictures and notes.

"Yeuan teyaochiuani," Anacaona smiled.

"They are all warriors," Nuno confirmed.

With Nuno's help, she also told them about the jaguars and eagles, the terrifying weapons made of cooled lava, and the rubber shoes that allowed one to jump high and far. She also offered an explanation for the ease with which the foreigners handled gold. It was not a precious metal to them, and this was incomprehensible to the Europeans. The duke already understood everything. He continued to pace the hall. From time to time, he glanced at the owners' faces and smiled at the same time. He also paid attention to the fact that Nuno was very interested in this foreigner, and she also responded to him with fondness. The duke understood where this was going.

A plan had finally matured in the head of the disgraced Duke Fernando de Braganza. Even with the most successful combination of circumstances, the army from Porto would not arrive earlier than next week. Therefore, the duke would promise to help the strangers find what they came for on their miracle ship, and the aliens, in exchange, would join the duke's army. Under his command, they would move to Lisbon to capture the king's castle. And then…

* * *

The mercenaries at Leandro's estate were settling down for the night in a former stable. Cots had been hastily built inside, and someone was already snoring, wrapped in a horse blanket. Another had hung up sweaty footcloths and carefully straightened them. Suddenly, one of the mercenaries burst into the stable, tightening the knot on the belt of his trousers. It was the attendant. "Men, to arms! They're already here!"

"Who's here?" The mercenaries started jumping up. "Who?"

"The king's servants! They arrived on horseback and are going to the manor house! Santiago! Come on, take command!"

The familiar tavern drunkard, Santiago, whom the mercenaries had chosen as their sergeant only an hour ago, grabbed the sword hanging at the head of his cot and shouted, "Follow me!"

The mercenaries jumped up from their beds and rushed after Santiago shouting, "Beat them! Cut the bastards!"

Santiago was the first to run up to the enemy squad. He raised his sword clumsily, with a feminine flourish, as if he were driving chickens from the garden with a twig and hit the helmet of the nearest soldier. The soldier turned around and waved his saber in front of Santiago's face. The sergeant howled, dropped his sword, and clutched his face, the tip of his nose now gone.

The forces of the two detachments were equal in number, but despite all the mercenaries' whistling and shouting to cheer themselves up, they could not equal the soldiers who had been practicing their craft for years. Of course, the duke's mercenaries had achieved the first surprise, and the youngest of Don Daniel's soldiers had backed away. Some even tried to hide in the house near where the fight began, but now, having come to their senses, the king's servants began to advance. Now one mercenary then another, clutching their wounds and howling, fell to the ground. Many ran off at once. One even had the sense to rush back to the stable and cover himself with a blanket there.

Despite the efforts of the soldiers, the most brazen of the mercenaries managed to get into the house. In the main hall of the house, members of Leandro's family and their guests were already getting up from the table, torn from their conversation, alarmed. The saber fight continued there. However, the main conflict had already happened in the first moments. Having come together in the fight, the strongest in spirit drove those who were weaker away. The soldiers of the rightful king were crowding against the mercenaries. Benches, chairs, shelves, mirrors, statues and paintings, and even household utensils, everything that the mercenaries could get their hands on, they threw at Daniel's soldiers in a futile attempt to delay their death for at least a moment. One mercenary grabbed a huge amphora used to fill the oil lamps and threw it at Don Daniel himself, who, now brandishing a halberd, was again fighting in front of his soldiers. The amphora smashed against the wall and oil flooded the floor. Another mercenary, seeing a shovel near the fireplace, scooped up red-hot coals and also threw them at Daniel. The coals fell to the floor, and the oil flared up. The fire instantly engulfed the main hall, the gallery, and rapidly, the entire lower floor.

"Upstairs!" Leandro shouted to his loved ones, seeing that the flames had cut them off from the exit. "Everyone up! To the second floor! Hurry up!" Leandro grabbed Nuno by the shoulders and pushed him towards the stairs and the gallery that circled the rooms on the second floor. Nuno clutched Anacaona's hand and dragged her upstairs with him. The duke hurried after, trying to maintain a dignified posture. Leandro was readily brandishing his great-grandfather's huge two-handed sword, which he had torn from the wall in the main hall. Manuella was pressed against the wall behind Leandro. He felt her breasts against his back, and Leandro suddenly felt a lust for his wife that he had never known before. He shouted, "Manuella! Go to the second floor!"

Manuella did not answer, but grabbed a vase of flowers and smashed it on the head of a soldier who had managed to dive under the invisible line that Leandro was maintaining with his sword. The soldier roared and grabbed his head.

"Manuella!" Leandro sobbed, then the bypass gallery collapsed into the hall with a crash, dropping sparks and leaving fiery traces in the hot air, burying Manuella, Leandro, and several of Daniel's soldiers.

"Get back!" Daniel shouted, retreating toward the opening of the double doors. "Cut, men, those who are in the yard! Catch the fugitives!"

* * *

Nuno raced ahead of everyone because he knew his home better than others. Bursting into the corner room where guests' servants were usually accommodated, he let Anacaona and the duke pass and turned back. He was waiting for his parents to catch up, but they never appeared. Then, he heard the crash of the grand staircase falling into the fire. There was no way up anymore! Nuno had not yet realized his loss, but he did understand that it was impossible to stay here for any length of time. The fire was about to reach this room. Nuno rushed to the window and opened it. There was a balcony under the window which, like the inner gallery, encircled the whole house, but on the outside.

"Anacaona! Your Grace! Look!" and Nuno stretched his hand downward.

The duke surprised himself with the speed at which he jumped over the windowsill. There was a haystack where Nuno was pointing. The duke jumped down first. Spitting out the grass dust, he turned around and stretched out his hands to Anacaona, who froze on the edge of the balcony, "Please, Senhorita!"

Anacaona finally jumped safely onto the hay, and Nuno jumped into the half-collapsed stack after her. A moment later, all three ran towards the darkness of the oak grove, not far from the other side of the house, behind the forge. The house was burning behind the fugitives, Nuno's home, his only home, because there were no others in his life yet. Suddenly, columns of sparks and flames burst out of all the windows of the house at once. There were heart-rending screams; one was clearly female.

When he reached the oak grove, the duke grabbed the trunk of a tree and stopped. Nuno and Anacaona were standing nearby. They were holding hands. Their breathing quickly calmed down – the benefits of youth.

"Nuno," the duke said, trying to speak evenly, "you saw that the top floor of the house collapsed."

"Yes," Nuno answered.

"That means that your parents may no longer be alive." As an old soldier, the duke knew that it was better to say such things right away, so that hope would not drag a man to the bottom when he could not fix anything.

Nuno said nothing. The duke looked at the young man. By the light of the stars and the moon, he saw that Anacaona was holding Nuno's head to her chest and whispering something in her incomprehensible language.

"Nuno, you have to pull yourself together," the duke continued. "The king has announced a hunt for me, but your father, the worthiest of worthy people, gave me assistance. I'll never forget that. If we manage to get out of this mess, you and your future family will be provided for forever, as long as the de Braganza family exists. However, right now you are in great trouble for the same reason. If the king or his servants capture you, you will be executed. The girl who was sheltered by your family will also be executed because Joao II is a vindictive, terrible, and ignorant person unlike his father, Afonso V, may grace be upon him, but I'll help you. I have to believe what this girl is telling me. I suggest you go to Porto da Vila with me. You know it's not far from here. There I have a caravel ready with a captain and sailors loyal to me. On this caravel, we will be able to get to the ship that Anacaona told us about. You can trust me, Nuno, isn't it?"

"Your Grace, our horses should be grazing nearby," Nuno replied at last. He said it in a voice that the duke recognized as the voice of Leandro, a middle-aged, exhausted man. "They are brought here at night to rest away from mosquitoes and midges. They should be at the edge of the forest, next to the pond." Soon the Duke and his companions were sitting on horses freed from their bonds. The boys who were guarding the horses at night had run away to see the burning house. Nuno made bridles from ropes tossed down by the fire and put them on the horses, and soon the riders set off to the west, towards Porto da Vila.

The duke did not tell Nuno that he was now relying entirely on the thousand warriors Anacaona had told them about. Thanks to Don Daniel's attack and the fire, he now realized that he had nothing more and no one else to count on. Of course, Duke Fernando de Braganza's plan was insane, but who could blame the madness of a man who saves his own life and who blindly goes toward a dream?

* * *

It was late in the evening when the fugitives saw the forest of masts towering over the harbor of Porto da Vila. Three sailors were already waiting for them at the pier. The captain of the caravel was walking along the shore, and two sailors were sitting in the skiff. By the tan on their faces, too dark for this time of year, it was clear that they had been on duty here for more than a day.

"What about the caravel?" The duke said briefly in response to the captain's greeting.

"In perfect order," the captain replied. "There is the beauty," and the captain pointed to a large, rare beauty of a caravel, rocking among a lot of small single-masted fishing ships. The caravel, a ship with low sides and superstructures at the bow and stern, showed her side to the shore. The Braganza family flag was flying on the highest mast.

Nuno jumped into the boat first and offered his hand to Anacaona. Sitting in the boat, she grabbed the sides and looked around. There was no rope mechanism in this boat such as she was used to, but on the edges of the sides, there were what resembled slingshots, the use of which she was not familiar with. She would soon learn they were oarlocks. After her, the duke descended into the boat, still not changing his gloomy expression. The captain sat down last, and the sailors pulled at the oars. As soon as the fugitives were brought aboard the caravel, the sailors immediately lifted the anchors, and the caravel departed for the open sea. When the coast was almost out of sight, the duke ordered the crew to turn south.

Anacaona was surprised as she inspected the rigging of the ship and watched the work of the sailors. The sailors from Aztlan did not know about sails. The sailors scurried along the masts, yards, and shrouds with the agility of monkeys, now and then lowering some sails or raising others. Anacaona immediately understood how the wind set the caravel in motion, but how the ship always managed to go forward despite the changing wind remained a mystery to her. Finally, Nuno explained to her that this was due to the skill of the sailors who changed the sails, including the triangular sail on the bow. Cristiano had taught him this when he was a child.

Skillfully handling the sails, they forced the caravel to go forward even with a headwind. When it happened the first time, Anacaona even clapped her hands. She rejoiced both at what at first glance seemed like a miracle, and at the ingenuity, but after looking at Nuno's face, Anacaona's face changed and became more somber. Nuno was looking towards the shore, which was visible from time to time, and his face was sad. Anacaona took Nuno 's hand and said, "Nuno, I'm very sad too. I just forget about it sometimes. After all, I ran away from my father and still don't know if he is ok. I hope he ended up in Tlaluacatli, where we are heading now. If we continue at the same speed as now, we will meet him soon."

Their conversation was interrupted by the duke. He spoke for a long time with the captain in his cabin and came out less gloomy than he was on shore. Approaching the young people, he put his hand on Nuno's shoulder and looked into his eyes.

"I will have to avenge my father and mother," Nuno said.

"I'll help you do it," the duke replied and looked towards the disappearing strip of land. Now the duke had to find out whom exactly Nuno wanted to take revenge on. Would it be the former family friend, Captain Daniel, or the king? This time, he did not bother the young man with questions, nor did he try to convince him that without the king's order, Daniel would not have dared to invade his parents' house. The time will come; he will understand.

* * *

The next morning, with the first rays of the sun, the barrelman, sitting atop the mast in the crow's nest, shouted, "A mountain is right ahead!"

The half-dressed captain immediately jumped out of his cabin. "What mountain, fool?" he shouted to the sailor. "There are no mountains here."

"But I see a mountain, Your Grace!" the sailor said stubbornly, "a red mountain! You can see for yourself."

The captain went to the side of the caravel, grabbed the shrouds, and climbed up. When he reached halfway, he froze and began to peer into the sea. Ahead, in the waters that the captain had traveled up and down from his youth, a mountain of unnaturally regular outlines darkened the horizon. Or was it not a mountain? What was it? The captain rubbed his sleepy eyes and stared again at the incomprehensible sight rising out of the sea.

"The sailor is right," said the duke, who had come on deck. I told you about the big ship. It will be so big that it looks like an island or a mountain. If I understand correctly, it should be a city. A floating city."

Anacaona and Nuno came on deck. "Nuno, you will soon see your girlfriend's ship," the duke said, smiling. "Get up on the bow, and they will bring us a spyglass."

When Anacaona saw the spyglass for the first time, she did not immediately understand what it was. Nuno looked into the tube himself, nodded his head, and handed it to Anacaona. She put the eyepiece to her eye and screamed, "Tlaluacatli! Yes, it is! But why..." Anacaona removed the tube from her eye and then looked into it again. "Why is it either close or far away?"

"It's magic, but it's made by human hands," Nuno said and smiled.

"So, your companion recognized her ship?" The duke asked him.

"Ask her if the cannons from her ship are going to shoot at us," said the captain, who had also climbed to the bow platform. "If they do, we will have nothing to answer with. We don't have cannons."

"Are there cannons there?" de Braganza asked Nuno. "Cannons. Does she understand?"

"No," Nuno was confused. "We didn't talk with her about war and cannons ... But how huge it is!" Nuno said, turning his gaze back to the mountain in the ocean. "My God, it's really a whole city and people live in it!"

The caravel was getting ever closer to the red city. Through the spyglass, it had easily deceived the eye, but now that the vessel loomed nearer and was easily examined, it was impossible to doubt the size of this giant red-orange ship. Her bow and stern were indeed at least three hundred paces apart, and there was a pyramid in the center. It seemed so out of place there that one might have thought that the purpose of the ship was simply to transport this pyramid.

"Therefore, a thousand warriors can also be there," the duke continued to reflect. "And it may also be possible to take them into battle against the king. Yes, but if they don't know what cannons are… What the hell… what if they don't know who the king is…? Fine… They may not have a king, but they must have a god. And any god must have an enemy equal to him. There is no god without enemies. So, we need to make sure that the king is such an enemy in the eyes of these strangers."

* * *

Coatl was standing in his temple room at the top of the pyramid. The walls of this room had small openings lined up in a row, through which sunlight broke in. On the wall hung a large tapestry, dotted with figures of people, near which various plants were painted. These drawings were framed by painted green ornaments. Another frame was drawn inside this frame. The space inside it was crossed out crisscross, and in the center of this figure was an image of an eagle sitting on a cactus. This tapestry was a map of the area beyond where Tlaluacatli had already traveled.

Next to this hung the tonalpohualli calendar, depicted on amatl. On the table, where the priest was standing now, there was a xuihpohualli calendar, an image of a circle divided into sectors. It was a Stone of the Sun, a model of the world, a compass, and a calendar, containing another inscribed circle bristling with triangles and rays. Inside the inscribed radiant circle was another circle, inside which were other figures, including a human face with an open mouth and tongue sticking out. This calendar on the table could rotate, so that, if necessary, it could be aligned with the direction of the Path of Huitzilopochtli.

In the center of this circle, Coatl placed a glass human skull mounted on a stick. Rays falling on the skull through small windows were refracted through the empty eye sockets and illuminated one of the patterns on the circle, depending on the time and place in which Tlaluacatli, the round calendar, and the sun were located. With the help of these devices, Coatl calculated time and also determined the location of Tlaluacatli.

From time to time, Coatl looked out at the sea through the small windows. They were so small that a hand could hardly fit through them. With what the priest saw outside, he additionally checked his calculations. Today, it seemed to him that the glass skull illuminated the wrong figure on the calendar according to the time of day and place under the sun. Coatl looked out to see the shadow cast by the pyramid. Glancing at the sea, the priest was dumbfounded. A boat was approaching Tlaluacatli. On its deck, protruding pillars rose, hung with white canvases emblazoned with red crosses in the middle. Without knowing the exact distance to the boat, it was difficult to determine its size. Still, Coatl realized that it was very large – at least twenty-five paces long and seven wide.

Coatl ran out of his room but remembered that the high priest and tlatoani was not supposed to lose his head under any circumstances. He quickly, but without fuss, descended the secret staircase that led from the room at the top of the pyramid to his house, crossed the bamboo forest, and went to Ocotlan. Soon, Ocotlan was gathering his warriors on the lower pier and checking their equipment.

* * *

The caravel came very close to the floating city with the pyramid in the center. It was obvious to everyone that the size of the caravel compared to the enormous vessel was similar to a sparrow and a cow. "The entrance to Tlaluacatli is below, under the deck," Anacaona explained to Nuno, the captain, and the duke. "Usual boats can go there, but your big boat will not be able to go there," Anacaona said and pointed to the masts of the caravel. "We need to get into a simple boat." A boat was lowered from the caravel. Anacaona sat in the bow of the boat, and Nuno and the Duke sat behind her. Two sailors worked the oars.

The boat navigated under the deck of the floating city. The creaking of the rowlocks and the splashing of water against the oars began to echo. The sailors, who were sitting with their backs to the giant ship, finally looked up and back and gaped. One of them crossed himself.

"Over there!" Anacaona said, pointing to the dock where boats were tied up, drifting on barely noticeable waves. The upper tier of the pier was occupied by armed men. There were several dozens of them. Even in the semi-darkness of the piers hidden beneath the deck, Nuno could see that all these warriors looked more or less like Anacaona. For some reason, they were all the same height, no one towered an inch above the other except one man; he was clearly their leader and was two heads taller than everyone else. Next to him stood another man who did not look like an ordinary warrior. On the head of this man was a huge headdress, which reminded Nuno of the fanned tail of a peacock.

As the Portuguese boat began to near the deck, the giant raised his hand and gave the warriors some kind of sign. At the same time, as if they were performing a round dance figure, they put their spears in front of them.

"Ocotlan!" Anacaona shouted. "These people came in peace."

Ocotlan peered at the girl sitting on the bow of the boat and said something to the priest, Coatl, whose headdress had surprised Nuno so much. Coatl, without taking his eyes off the guests, replied something back to him. Ocotlan raised his hand again and made another gesture. The spears of the warriors returned to their original position.

A Moment from the Past - Escape from Axayacatl

"The priests warned our old man Moctezuma, but how did he behave? He didn't listen to them. That's why our land was cursed. The teteo have punished us," said Axayacatl, weyitlatoani of Tenochtitlan. Tizok and Ahuitzotl, Axayacatl's brothers, whom he had invited to his palace today, listened attentively to him. "Remember how many people died from lack of food in the fields!" Axayacatl continued to raise his voice. "How many animals died first from drought and then from the cold? Texcoco waters first flooded Tenochtitlan and fish swam near Huey Teocalli, and then the water retreated very far, and the plantings in the chinampas dried up. All he had to do was to obey the priests and bring the people of the Mexihkah as a gift to the teteo, and not just simple slaves."

From the windows of the hall, one could see the tops of the pyramids of the great city. Tizok and Ahuitzotl, sitting on the skins spread out on the floor, did not move and, fixing their eyes on Axayacatl's face, listened attentively to him. They knew that it was better not to contradict their younger brother. Maybe he wasn't the cleverest, but the tlatoque of other cities loved him, and the priests talked about his proximity to the teteo. He did no wrong to his brothers; on the contrary, he often consulted with them, as he was now. His brothers just had to listen carefully and do what he said, for woe to him who incurred the wrath of Axayacatl! He was in a rage right now. He was about to grab his favorite translucent, blue obsidian dagger hanging from his belt and pounce. Even possibly on one of his brothers.

"So that's what I'm telling you. The curse of Tlaltecuitli, the teotl of the earth, may touch even me. The priests warned my grandfather that he should not keep this girl alive. She's cursed! She will spread her curse on all of our altepetl! She will bring new disasters to Tenochtitlan!"

"In that case, get rid of her," Tizok suggested. "Atotoztli has long been transformed into a bird flying across the sky and into the sun. No one can stop you."

"I thought the girl was living with Atotoztli," Axayacatl shouted, "but it has turned out that she hid her somewhere else. When Atotoztli went under the fifth earth, I forced her maid to answer my questions, and she told me where the girl was hidden. My jaguars have already rushed there. Believe me, I will give her to the teotl Tlaltecuitli myself when I find her!" With these words, Axayacatl grabbed his knife.

Chimalli had learned he would no longer receive funds for taking care of the girl from a maid from the weyitlatoani's palace. This maid regularly visited their small but cozy house in the city of Tlacopan, which was part of the Triple Alliance. Atotoztli had settled Anacaona and Chimalli in this city, connected to the island of Tenochtitlan by a bridge, in order to keep the girl closer to herself but, at the same time, away from Axayacatl. Anacaona wasn't to know she had a mother; that's what Atotoztli had decided.

The maid showed great courage when she ran to Chimalli and told him about Atotoztli's death. After all, mention of the death of a cihuatlatoani was forbidden outside the palace. The secret was kept in order to prepare for the transition of power from Moctezuma and Atotoztli to the new weyitlatoani. To do this, it was necessary to eliminate a lot of high-ranking officials, judges, and generally unnecessary witnesses who may prevent a smooth transition of power to the new supreme ruler. If they found out about the cihuatlatoani's death, they could escape before they were detained.

The next day, Chimalli and six-year-old Anacaona went to the forest as usual. There they collected fruits for the girl and medicinal herbs for the father's needs. As the little girl helped her father collect the medicinal herbs, she sniffed them and carefully put them in special rag pockets, but Chimalli could not stop thinking about Anacaona's future, whom he loved very much. Of course, he thought, now she would be taken to the palace and after that, would disappear from his life. A girl with the blood of weyitlatoani in her veins should never have lived the hard life of macehualtin.

However, Chimalli had been alarmed by the urgency of the maid. After telling him about Atotoztli's death, she added that Anacaona was in great trouble and immediately ran away. What kind of trouble could it be? And how could he, Chimalli, prevent it? Fortunately, returning home, Chimalli saw the jaguar warriors from afar with their ribbons on their forearms. Some of them were running around the house and asking neighbors questions. Others searched inside the house, occasionally shouting to the warriors who remained outside, and it became clear to Chimalli the kind of trouble his adopted daughter was in. The power in the country was passing into other hands, and Anacaona could interfere. Of course, these assailants could only have been sent to Chimalli's house by Axayacatl himself.

Once, a long time ago when Axayacatl was the tlacochcalcatl under Moctezuma, he introduced a new rule for his army. During one of the military campaigns, Axayacatl decided that his warriors would wear ribbons that depicted the name of the warrior, the city from which he came, and the number of captives he captured. The innovation turned out to be very convenient. First of all, it made it possible to identify the dead. Secondly, the ribbons also helped the otomies, the chiefs of the detachments, give military commands to their subordinates with the help of special gestures.

Over time, all the warriors of Tenochtitlan began to wear such ribbons, and then civil officials began to wear them. It even became fashionable to wear such ribbons. Depending on the position of the owner, the ribbon had a special color, usually scarlet or yellow for warriors, and white for state employees. Later, laws were also issued that punished impostors for fake ribbons or false information on them. Ribbons eventually were worn by all people in Aztlan who were related to public service. Thanks to these ribbons, Chimalli easily identified Axayacatl's jaguars. He always remembered the hatred with which Axayacatl looked at the newborn Anacaona as he cut the umbilical cord connecting daughter to mother with his obsidian knife.

Therefore, as soon as he saw the jaguars in his house, Chimalli immediately grabbed Anacaona by the hand and retreated with her into the shadows. After waiting for the right moment, he led her away from the house. Anacaona stared open-mouthed into his face. In her surprise, she even dropped the orange she was eating, but her father did not let her pick it up. They walked faster and faster, and soon they were away from their home, and then from the city. Chimalli did not yet know where they would go, but he understood that he and his daughter could not stay in Tlacopan now, and it would be impossible to go to Tenochtitlan. They would be looking for them there too. Right now, the safest place for them was the crowded road they were walking on. However,

Anacaona soon began to tire. The girl did not understand why they could not return home. Finally, she whimpered.

Hearing his daughter crying, Chimalli stopped, squatted down, and hugged her, "Daughter, we don't have a home now," he said.

"Why?"

"Because evil people have settled there. They are very dangerous, more dangerous than snakes and crocodiles."

The shrewd Anacaona stopped crying and sighed, "So we'll have to look for another home!"

After a little rest, the father and daughter continued their journey along the road that circled the lake. Two days later they came to the city of Texcoco. The road had tired them out tremendously. During all this time, Chimalli ate only a couple of fruits, and he fed his daughter only once when he managed to kill a blackbird and roast it over a small fire. During the day they were tormented by the blinding sun, and at night Chimalli carried his daughter in his arms.

At the entrance to Texcoco, Chimalli saw a lot of warriors who were clearly preparing for a military campaign, "Where is your tlacochcalcatl?" Chimalli asked them.

The warriors took him and Anacaona to their commander. "What do you want?" he asked, looking suspiciously at Chimalli, then at his daughter.

"Do you need an experienced ticitl?" Chimalli asked in response.

Suddenly, this very formidable-looking man smiled. "Experienced, you say? We have a lot of ticiti, but none are experienced. Axayacatl kept the most skilled ones to himself."

"I'm ready to be a ticitl during your campaign," Chimalli said. "I have been treating people for many years."

"Yes? And where are you going to put her?" The tlacochcalcatl pointed at Anacaona. At the same time, he could no longer refrain and smiled.

"She'll stay with me," Chimalli said. "She has already experienced mortal danger, and the war will be no more terrible for her." Chimalli was telling the absolute truth. He understood that he and Anacaona would not be able to survive on the street or in the jungle. With this company, they would have food, lodging, and protection from the Axayacatl's jaguar warriors who would now be looking for them everywhere, and no one would think to look for a father with a six-year-old daughter among warriors going on a campaign.

This is how Chimalli and Anacaona found themselves at war for the first time, joining a military campaign to the distant lands of Iztli Koyotl.

Chapter 11. Forgery

Brother Pascoal believed that the punishment of humanity for the Tower of Babel would one day end. Through his prayers and studies, he intended to bring the day closer when people all over the world could begin to understand each other again. He believed he could understand any foreigner if he put his mind to it. After all, the apostles, the messengers of Christ, had the gift of understanding all the languages in the world. Brother Pascoal himself had already learned a dozen languages, including the languages of the Marranos and Moriscos. He gained this particular knowledge by helping his father hire sailors for long sea voyages. Only a few Portuguese would agree to sail into uncharted seas. The mercenaries, heretics fleeing from Castile, or prisoners who were sold as slaves in the markets, came to the rescue. However, it was necessary to negotiate with them, teach them how to work on ships, and explain the rules of payment. The most difficult were the taciturn captains who always lied, telling tales about their past successes and trying every possible way to evade responsibility for the hired team.

As a result, he cultivated and multiplied his knowledge, which he extracted himself at the monastery at which he lived. For Pascoal, any word was like a candle between two mirrors, which was repeated from reflection to reflection, each time not noticeably changed, it recurred into infinity. "That's how languages repeat the same word," Pascoal argued, "but each in its own way, because all people are brothers, which means they all have the same language."

In the Lisbon Jeronimos monastery, all this was not yet considered heresy, but no one considered young Pascoal's opinion there. All that was required of him was to perform feats of obedience, pray, observe the rules and the authorities, and not indulge in new fantasies that would embarrass the brethren. Therefore, the abbot had recently imposed a penance on Pascoal and sent him to the white clergy in the church of Leiria to atone for his superstition. "Those whom you love, you will punish," the abbot said with finality and added, "Don't come back until you have learned the languages of birds and wolves." About this possibility, Brother Pascoal had accidentally also let slip. Therefore, Pascoal's father would have to wait a little for his son's help to hire sailors, perhaps only for a season.

Brother Pascoal recalled all this as he was entering the prison. Was this a trap? It all came together very well – his penance, the need for an interpreter conveniently here, away from Lisbon and his father... Maybe they would take him to where the prisoner was supposedly sitting and leave him there as well? He wouldn't be able to tell his father anything.

It was cold and stuffy in the dungeon. There, on a round block, sat a man dressed in only a loincloth. Next to him was a table with a jug on it. There were no other items in the cell. Pascoal looked at the man and realized he was shivering from the cold. Judging by his face and tattoos, he was definitely not European but was lighter skinned than most Africans.

"Who are you?" Pascoal asked him in Arabic.

The prisoner uttered a word, but Pascoal did not understand him.

"Who are you?" he repeated his question in Hebrew.

Pascoal asked his question in all the languages he knew, but the prisoner either pronounced the word he had already said or did not answer at all.

"Well?" Furtado got bored. "What does he say?"

"He says he wants to get warm, Senhor Officer," Pascoal answered. "And he wants to eat. Also, he needs light because the darkness can make him blind."

"He wants to eat? He is a bandit!" Furtado said angrily. "He and his friends killed our soldiers, and probably killed others elsewhere as well, on the high road."

"Really? And I suppose rumors have already spread around the city that this is the Red Ghost?" Pascoal said ambiguously.

"What?"

"Here's what, Senhor Officer, I can't talk to him here because your torch will soon go out, and he and I have to talk with our fingers. In general, I need to be able to consider him properly in order to determine the right language. In addition, he needs to be fed and warmed. Otherwise, he'll die, and we won't learn anything from him. Oh, then you'll get it from the authorities!"

"You are a heretic to protect him!" Furtado shouted. "They were right about you! Eh, you should be put here yourself!"

"I'll be waiting for you to bring this man upstairs," Pascoal said calmly. He really knew how to be arrogant when he wanted to.

"And how dare they keep you in a monastery!?" Furtado called after him.

"They'll also leave you without a pension," Pascoal snapped over his shoulder.

"Should I poison both of them?" Furtado thought. "Have they already been conspiring?"

* * *

Upstairs, Pascoal was given a bright room with a barred window. The prisoner was put right near him. At the request of Pascoal, a large bowl of porridge with meat was brought to the prisoner from the fortress kitchen, and he was given a spoon. The prisoner smiled, turned over the spoon in his hands, put it down, and proceeded to eat with his fingers. Furtado glared at him and then at Pascoal with hatred. His plan was all going to hell with the help of a monk.

"While this bastard is here," Furtado was thinking "he won't allow me the opportunity to poison the prisoner, that's for sure, and he won't give me a chance to do it later either. He'll go straight from here to his people in the church and talk about everything. He'll probably complain to the castellan too. Who knows, maybe this prisoner is really a big deal? He carried so much gold on himself. Naked, but he wore it blatantly."

"Bring here what he had with him," said Pascoal as if he read his thoughts, "He says that he had jewelry." Pascoal had presumed they were there by the pale marks on the arms, shoulders, and chest of the half-naked prisoner.

"No, he literally sees through me like through water, this monk. Eh, my bad luck again!" Furtado thought and turned away.

Soon the prisoner was brought his cape made of light fabric and his gold jewelry.

Meanwhile, Pascoal and the prisoner got acquainted. They did it the way that multilingual people all over the world usually do. "Pascoal," the monk tapped himself on the chest. Then he pointed his finger at the prisoner's chest.

The man smiled and also hit his chest, "Chimalli."

Pascoal called the head of the garrison and demanded paper and quill.

"What is this for?" Furtado asked suspiciously.

"I am going to study his language."

"Why? What is there to study? He's only one, and even then, not for long," Furtado said stubbornly.

"To bring him to our faith." Pascoal looked Furtado right in the eyes. Furtado bit his tongue. Promptly, paper and quill were brought to the room.

It turned out that the prisoner drew very well, in a manner that was strange to Pascoal. He produced angular figures of people, animals, trees, and boats; they were strange, drawn all about the same size. This is how the prisoner proceeded to describe his homeland. Having depicted a seashore with palm trees on the edge, he said, "Aztlan."

Pascoal took the paper from him, drew on the other side of the sheet something like a reflection of this shore, and said, "Portugal."

Chimalli nodded his head briskly. With the help of such drawings, Pascoal continued to learn the new language. Soon he found out that this language was called "Mexihkah," that Chimalli has a "siuakonetl," daughter, and he himself is a master of "xiollini kuauakpa chisiuinakilistli," which Pascoal understood to mean "remove pain."

By the end of the day, they began to understand each other better. Pascoal wrote down "okichtli," man, "siuatl," woman, "pilli," child, "atl," water, "tlan," land, "tlakualli," food, and "kuauitl," tree... Pascoal, with the help of Chimalli, drew sheet after sheet of pictures, repeated new words, and obediently made corrections to their pronunciation. Pascoal also helped by creating gestures and facial expressions. They were so thorough that by the evening of the next day, Pascoal pronounced easy and brief phrases in the new language almost fluently. The attendant standing outside the door was puzzled to hear their laughter, the laughter of two unfortunate people, a prisoner, whom anyone could kill like a dog here, and a youngster, forever deprived of carnal joys.

Pascoal now knew for sure that Chimalli had come to Portugal from a country that he, Pascoal, was not familiar with. Despite the darkness of his skin and hair, Chimalli did not know about Africa or the countries of the Middle East. He didn't know about Europe or Asia either, and when Pascoal shared his knowledge of India with Chimalli, it was firmly established that the prisoner did not come from there either. The fabric from which Chimalli's light clothes were made was also not familiar to anyone in the fortress.

Chimalli also could not possibly be a runaway slave, as was suggested at the very beginning. First of all, he didn't have the hands of a laborer at all. Secondly, Chimalli had a lot of gold jewelry that he knew how to wear with dignity. Finally, he was very adept at drawing and knew how to add, subtract, multiply, and divide. Pascoal easily mastered the different way of writing down numbers which were represented by dots and horizontal lines. Pascoal remembered that he himself wrote down numbers in a similar way early in his childhood before he could read and write.

Chimalli's knowledge was nothing like anything else discovered by any person, even in countries the Portuguese considered savage. He was a man from a completely different world, and this world was developed no less than the world of Europe, but where did he come from? Was it not from heaven itself?

The long conversation between Pascoal and Chimalli ended with Pascoal going to Furtado and addressing him, "Senhor Officer, you are very lucky. You were entrusted with the life of a very important person, and you saved it. This man is a messenger from another world, and this meeting will change our world. Your name will go down in history. Continue to take care of our guest, and I will go to Lisbon immediately. A person will be brought here to present him to the court of scientists, priests, and the highest dignitaries of the state. Perhaps His Majesty the King himself will meet with him."

With these words, Pascoal hugged Furtado and, just in case, used his favorite weapon, ambiguity, "Yes, and you, too, may also have your hand shaken by the head of the royal prison in Lisbon himself." For the first time in thirty years, Furtado felt heat rise in his cheeks and he flushed.

* * *

Daniel's squad stormed into the fortress with the thunder of hooves of exhausted horses. The garrison commander, Lieutenant Furtado, was the first to run up to Daniel,

"Senhor Captain, trouble! The bastard who attacked our soldiers is being taken to Lisbon! And not only that, but they are also making a curiosity out of it, more so than a giraffe! And all of us, they say, are nothing compared to him."

Daniel barely looked at Furtado and did not deign to answer him. He had no time for this boring fool, almost an idiot.

The family of Leandro, a man whom he could consider, if not his friend, then at least Estela's future father-in-law, had died, and Leandro was dead because he, Daniel, could not control the actions of his subordinates and those mercenaries who, it turns out, were waiting for them at the Sinta estate.

How many times did Don Daniel, in front of the mirror, learn a special stately step, wave his hat, make bows, and politely nod his head? How much had he endured the shouts of his daughter, who was eternally indignant at her father's inability to learn stately manners! And now all this has come to an end! And what a scary one!

The daughter's fiancé must have died, although neither Daniel nor the soldiers saw his death with their own eyes, but what they all did see was enough to affirm that Leandro's family was dead. Together with his wife, son, and guest, Duke de Braganza. The laborers who had come running from all over the estate with their pitiful buckets could not even extinguish the embers still smoldering at the site of the fire.

Daniel stumbled into the hallway of his house where his wife was preparing a bath for him and collapsed on the couch. Immediately, Estela's cat silently approached Daniel. After sniffing Daniel, she began to purr and rub against his body. The door of his daughter's room creaked, and Estela came out into the hallway. "Father, you're not yourself today," she said. "I feel something has happened. What? Respond!"

Daniel got up from the couch, straightened up, and suddenly fell on his knees in front of his daughter, "Estela! Estela, I'm sorry!"

"What is it?" Estela shouted. "What has happened?"

"Don Leandro's house burned down," Daniel cried. He raised his hands and hid his face in his palms. "Don Leandro is dead, and his family also died in the fire. I'm sorry, Estela!"

Estela was silent. A thick blue vein was bulging on her neck, and a huge crease appeared on her forehead.

"My soldiers came to his house to capture a dangerous criminal," Daniel continued to mumble, holding his face and swaying from side to side, "but Leandro's servants and mercenaries attacked my soldiers. We had to fight back. The house caught fire, and the second floor collapsed onto the first, and Leandro and his family were there. I did my best not to let all those people interfere with your happiness, Estela. But now it's over. Nuno is no more!"

Estela screamed and sank to the floor.

Carmina came running to her daughter's cry, "What did you do to her? Stop it!" she shouted.

Estela screamed again and began to beat against the hard floor and tear at her hair.

"It's my fault! I told him about the ribbon!" flashed through her mind. "Why did I do it, why? I just wanted to be with Nuno. I just wanted to live there. To live on their estate!"

"Daughter! Daughter!" Carmina and Daniel shouted.

Estela let out another deafening scream and rolled towards the wall. When she reached the precious Chinese vase, however, she stopped and fell silent. Daniel was already running towards her with a cup of water, "Have a drink, Estela…" He put his hand to the back of his daughter's head and raised the cup to her lips, but Estela suddenly pushed his hand away, abruptly stood up, and began to straighten her dress.

"They died, you say, in a fire..." she repeated Daniel's words. "But there are a lot of other people left on the estate. Francisco, the steward, is alive, I hope?"

"What are you talking about, Estela?" Carmine said with worry.

Daniel briefly repeated to his wife what he had just told his daughter.

"What a horror!" Carmine moaned.

"And Francisco… Well, maybe he's all right," Daniel turned to his daughter again.

"And the others are also well, the servants, hands, grooms..." Estela continued.

"I believe so. So what?" Daniel asked. He no longer understood how he should behave or understand his daughter's unexpectedly businesslike statements.

"So, they'll all confirm my engagement to Nuno," Estela snapped.

"What engagement? Which one?" Daniel and Carmina spoke up, interrupting each other. Had their daughter gone mad?

"Which one what? I was always visiting there. I even had my own room there. According to the customs of our Christian people, if a young man and a girl spend the night under the same roof, they are obliged to get married. Don't make a face, Mama. Father, stop gawking at me, I'm not your superintendent."

"Estela..." Daniel whispered,

"Yes! The estate will be mine," Estela confirmed her parents' conjecture.

"But Estela!" Carmina exclaimed, "There was no engagement."

"Oh, Mamma! This stupid custom does not require mandatory witnesses. So, it was because I say so, and you and my father were witnesses. Father, you must take me to the king to finish this matter fast. We will tell him everything, and he will recognize me as Nuno's wife. Then the estate will be mine."

"Estela, that would be a forgery!" Daniel exclaimed.

"And what can you offer me in exchange, father?" Estela shouted. Her eyes began to fill with tears, and her voice trembled. "Marry a lieutenant? And go with him to feed lice in some malarial fortress? Closer to the Moors? Or to the Castilians who continue to sharpen knives against us? And will you give me a dowry? All three of my dresses and a box of seashells? Your own mare, father, who is a year older than me? Your salary for a month in advance? What else? What can you offer me?!"

Estela's beautiful face was transformed by anger. Her eyes were dark and bloodshot. The wrinkle that barely crossed her forehead had turned into a deep cleft, and her mouth was now disfigured by a predatory grin; it seemed that all of Estela's teeth had become fangs. Carmine and Daniel had never seen their daughter so fierce and ugly.

"What?! What?!" Estela continued to shout, clenching her fists.

Carmine, who was moving her lips soundlessly, clasped her fingers and held her hands in front of her chest. They were shaking.

Daniel suddenly realized with horror, that Estela was capable of killing a person, and if she were to lunge at him in her madness with a dagger, he would not be able to defend himself, because even under pain of death, he would not raise his hand against his daughter. "Estela…," he muttered.

"Yes, if you want to know, I slept in the same bed as him! I am no longer a virgin, dear parents."

Daniel managed to catch his wife in time as she fainted because he was already close to her. Carmina immediately came to her senses and, looking at Daniel with horror, began to push him away.

"Nuno asked me to marry him!" Estela continued to lie, "and I agreed. We were going to announce it any day now, but then this brown stray tart appeared at Nuno's house!"

Estela paused and took a deep breath. Carmine looked at Daniel with the eyes of a newborn. Finally, her lips moved, "Daniel… do as she says…"

"And quickly!" Estela shouted. "Otherwise, the Leandro family will have other heirs. You can be sure of that."

Daniel remembered that, at the time of the attack, there was some dark-skinned girl near Nuno. He was also holding her hand when he dragged her upstairs, damn it! He betrayed Estela, and therefore, there was nothing to lament here! They must pay for this dishonor! "I agree," Daniel finally said bowed his head.

* * *

The next day, Daniel and Estela, accompanied by two servants and a maid, went to Lisbon, everyone riding. Daniel didn't need to invent an excuse to leave the fortress. Daniel would have to tell the king in person about the death of such a large figure as Duke de Braganza and the circumstances surrounding his death.

"Don't forget, father, that Leandro's family has always been on the side of the king, just like ours," Estela instructed her father. "Tell the king that you came to Leandro only to capture de Braganza. If, God forbid, the king finds out that Leandro sided with the duke, he will be angry and take his estate for himself. Say that the fight started suddenly, and Leandro did not recognize you, because he thought that his house was being attacked by the very robbers you were catching."

Daniel looked gloomily in front of him and obediently nodded. He had already decided to agree with everything Estela said.

When the tower of St. George's Castle appeared on the horizon, Estela crossed herself and then turned back to her thoughts. She knew that having acquired ownership of the estate of the late Don Leandro, she would easily find a worthy husband. Perhaps even a knight. As for Nuno, well, what could you do if the Lord God himself punished his family? There was always a reason, but now her life was just beginning! A good, interesting, secure life!

Daniel, who was now stealing glances at his daughter, noticed her smile and shuddered.

A Moment from the Past - Coatl's Revenge

There were two cities, one called Tenochtitlan, and the other Texcoco. These cities stood on opposite shores of a lake. At one time, the tlatoani of Texcoco was Nezahualcoyotl. The altepetl and ruling tlatoani Texcoco dynasty were extremely militant, but Nezahualcoyotl was strongly supported by his relatives, and this union was as solid as a block of basalt.

Tlatoani Nezahualcoyotl had many wives, including his main wife, Azkalsochitzin, and a macehualtin named Izali. Coatl, the current priest, judge, and tlatoani of the floating city of Tlaluacatli, was the son of Izali and nearly twenty-five years older than his youngest brother, Nezahualpilli, son of Azkalsochitzin. According to tradition, the youngest son became the ruler of Texcoco following the death of Nezahualcoyotl because it was believed the younger son would be able to rule the altepetl longer.

The two brothers did not get along with each other. They rarely met, although, following the precepts of their father, they were close friends with other members of their huge family. Despite the brothers' dislike for each other, they never reached internecine enmity, and this made their altepetl, the ruling dynasty of the city of Texcoco, and its subordinate lands, the strongest in the Triple Alliance of the cities of Tenochtitlan, Texcoco, and Tlacopan.

Their father, Nezahualcoyotl, had believed until his last breath that the strengthening of Texcoco would one day make this city the capital of the Triple Alliance, although during his lifetime Tenochtitlan was discreetly considered as such. However, there was renewed life to his hope. After all, Tenochtitlan had been losing its former influence in the Triple Alliance over the last score of years. This was primarily due to a series of natural disasters, but also, contrary to a request from Huitzilopochtli, as declared by the priests, Atotoztli, the mother of Axayacatl, the current ruler of Tenochtitlan, had given birth not to a boy who would strengthen their altepetl, but a girl. Over the years, the people of Tenochtitlan murmured. People were dissatisfied with this fate, especially since other residents of the cities of the Triple Alliance were accustomed to pinning their hopes first on the weyitlatoani of Tenochtitlan, then his council, and only then on themselves and their local tlatoani.

In his youth, when Coatl went to the calmecac, a boy named Cuauhtli studied with him. He came from the city of Teotihuacan, and they grew to notably dislike each other and eventually became true enemies. The calmecac's students were severely punished for fighting, but Coatl and Cuauhtli often fought anyway, always finding new reasons, from a careless word to merely a sidelong glance. After Coatl and Cuauhtli finished their studies at the calmecac, they no longer saw each other. Cuauhtli became one of the priests in his city of Teotihuacan and a judge in the teccalli, court, and Coatl held similar positions in Texcoco.

When Coatl was thirty-six years old, he was already beginning to get tired and believed that his life would soon come to an end, but then, an amazing event happened to him. Axayacatl, who had already long been the weyitlatoani of Tenochtitlan, invited prominent men of his state to his palace. The weyitlatoani's need for educated and experienced people was growing because his state was constantly expanding. He intended for them to help him subordinate the inhabitants of newly acquired lands to the Tenochtitlan way of life and force them to adopt the traditions of Aztlan.

This time Axayacatl decided to have some fun. He ordered his cihuacoatl to depict the names of new positions on pieces of amatl, roll them up, and, not knowing which position was on which amatl, he would distribute them to each of the invited guests. That was how it was explained to Coatl. On the night of a full moon, the guests gathered in the main hall of the palace and were placed in several rows. Ceremonial fires burned everywhere in clay bowls. Through the hum of voices filling the hall, Coatl heard the neighbor on his right hiss, "Ah, you are here, son of a macehualtin." Coatl looked at the neighbor to find Cuauhtli leering at him, "Just wait 'til you must wash my feet and drink the water," Cuauhtli continued.

The blood rushed to Coatl's head. He clenched his fists and, just like a decade and a half ago, rushed at the enemy of his childhood, but suddenly a loud exclamation interrupted them, "Tonatiu kuautik!" The greeting was uttered by Axayacatl himself, weyitlatoani of Tenochtitlan, as he entered the hall.

Axayacatl's favorite obsidian translucent blue dagger, glinting in the firelight, hung from his belt. The weather was cool, and his body was covered with a cloak made of a dense luxurious turquoise fabric with black geometric patterns. Axayacatl's head was decorated with a headwrap made of the same fabric, gathered on the side with a lush knot of scarlet ribbon. His feet, shod in sandals with the same scarlet knots, noiselessly stepped on the stone slabs of the floor. In his right hand, the ruler held a staff decorated with tufts of feathers. Gold rings and earrings hung from his nose and ears, and a huge gold plate hung on his chest, decorated along the sides with drawings and precious stones. The plate depicted a pyramid with two temples on top. An eagle flew to the right of the pyramid, holding a snake with its claws, and a large cactus grew to the left. Axayacatl's retinue dressed in a similar way, but the colors of their clothes were much more muted, and the jewelry they wore still made it possible to distinguish their faces.

The great tlatoani ascended to the dais in the center of the hall and addressed his guests, "Oh, most worthy men! You know why you were called here, and I needn't repeat myself. At this time, each of you will receive from me a certificate with the title of your tecuhtli, your appointed position of service. You will not unfold the letters until I order each of you to do so." Axayacatl, without looking back, reached his hand behind, and the attendant put the first scroll into it. The weyitlatoani approached the nearest guest and handed the scroll to him. In this manner, he went around all the rows, and Coatl and Cuauhtli received their scrolls.

Once he had finished distributing the certificates, Axayacatl returned to his dais and looked curiously at the faces of the guests. This was a performance for only one spectator, the great tlatoani. The spectacle he had prepared for himself promised unprecedented excitement. Now he would be able to see, one by one, the expressions of all human feelings as they were experienced.

"And now," Axayacatl proclaimed, "each of you in turn, starting with the one who received his scroll first, will unroll it and read aloud, at the top of his voice, his tecuhtli." Axayacatl tried but couldn't hide his grin.

At that moment, the earth shook, and a rumble resounded. Ornaments, lamps, and dried heads of predators began to fall from the walls. Axayacatl looked at his retinue with horror and was the first to rush toward the exit of the palace. The retinue rushed after him. Only one person, a warrior with terrible scars and nasolabial folds on his face, managed to shout, "To the exit! One at a time! Strictly one by one… one by one… ru-u-u-n!" But the man was already being crushed by the maddened crowd, full of the best men of Aztlan. An earthquake had begun, and each of them knew well what it was.

Someone was rushing at full speed, lifting the hem of his festive robe to his knees, someone was limping but still running, spewing curses in impotent rage, and others were already buried under the weight of falling walls, painted columns, and stones from the ceiling. At the exit from the hall, people trampled each other in a terrible crush, regardless of their faces and ranks. The doomed swore, fought, and cried.

One of the columns fell directly on Cuauhtli, who failed to get away from it as it fell. It crushed only his right leg, but that was enough. The pain was so intense that Cuauhtli immediately realized that his death was imminent; only a miracle could save him. Cuauhtli saw Coatl rush past, but then suddenly froze in place. Coatl's hatred was very strong. Even now, as the walls continued to fall, and there was no one left in the hall, Coatl's whole being was calling him to escape, to save himself, to live, but he stopped near his defeated enemy and looked him in the face.

From out in the city and inside the hall came the terrible screams of citizens who were being buried alive by the earthquake. In some places, people were writhing in agony under the slabs of luxurious carvings. There were many dead. Coatl picked up a piece of stone decoration that crowned one of the columns and with an effort raised it over his head. "No!" Cuauhtli shouted a heart–rending plea. "No need! My father will make you a rich man! I will work for you for the rest of my life! I… I will wash your feet and drink the water!"

Oh, what a moment of sweet revenge it was, which is not granted to every mortal on this earth! Coatl screamed and slammed the stone on the head of Cuauhtli. The man fell silent; His head became a terrible mess of blood, hair, skull fragments, and the colorful ribbons with which Cuauhtli had adorned himself. Cuauhtli's hands relaxed, and he released the scroll he had received from the weyitlatoani.

Coatl knew he had nothing left to lose. His fate would be decided at this moment. The bustle and horror that had engulfed the whole city suddenly ceased to exist around him. He unrolled the scroll he received from Axayacatl and read, "Selection and counting of slaves of the Iztli Koyotl tribe and their delivery to festivals in Aztlan. Training of those who agree to celebrate festivals together with the residents of Aztlan." Coatl grimaced. Even if this earthquake had not happened, he would still have resigned or claimed to be crippled, sick, or crazy. He wanted no more of the dreary everyday life he had experienced in his many years of service.

He picked up the bloody scroll that had fallen out of Cuauhtli's hand, unrolled it, and read, "Tlatoani of Tlaluacatli." Coatl had a vague idea of where the city of Tlaluacatli was located. However, the position of tlatoani meant that there would now be possibilities of promotion and free competition with the tlatoani of other cities. If he could manage to subjugate this unknown city to the influence of his family, he could further strengthen the altepetl of Texcoco. With this credited to him, he could benefit from the division of even higher positions, vacated from time to time due to natural causes. If Coatl, as tlatoani of Tlaluacatli, could also manage to subject other cities to this, he may well become as strong as his brother Nezahualpilli, tlatoani of Texcoco.

The noise of falling walls and the cries of people and animals had already diminished within the palace, and now only the groans of crushed and dying people could be heard. Coatl suddenly heard the treacherous murmur of water rushing up toward the walls of the palace. The water began to permeate the inside, and the flood began to pick up pieces of furniture and move the dead from their places. Their bodies, caught up in the current, moved in the most nightmarish ways.

Coatl climbed up the rubble that remained of the wall of the great hall where the festive ceremony had taken place only a few minutes before. From the top of the crumbling wall, illuminated by the bright light of the moon, he could see streams of water, dirt, and garbage flowing through the streets of the huge, once magnificent, city. Somewhere in the distance, a fire started, and black smoke billowed over the dirty water filled with debris. Coatl was as calm as he had ever been in his life.

"I hope," he thought at that moment, "there will be no water in Tlaluacatli."

Chapter 12. The Caravel

Coatl strode along the deck of the floating city, followed by Nuno, Anacaona, and Duke Fernando de Braganza. Ocotlan and a couple of his warriors brought up the rear. Ocotlan did not like de Braganza from the very beginning, and he did not take his eyes off the duke. The duke and Nuno hardly had time to turn their heads; there was so much to take in. The duke realized that no matter how stable this bamboo ship was, any military carrack could smash it into splinters with a couple of cannon volleys. It was not difficult to imagine what would become of its inhabitants after that, but still, the duke looked at them with interest. All the people looked like Anacaona, which did not surprise him. They were all clean and neatly dressed, and many wore jewelry made of gold, silver, and precious stones. The duke could not help but admit that even people without jewelry looked much better than Portuguese sailors and peasants.

At the same time, the duke, no matter how little experience he had in crafts and agriculture, noticed the tools and techniques of the ship's inhabitants were quite primitive. It was also difficult for him to understand why the ship supported such a large farm that included a large herd of cattle. After all, wouldn't it be much easier to simply load the necessary supplies onto the ship? He also noticed how both working and living quarters were kept perfectly clean here.

The bamboo forest also stunned the ship's guests. Anacaona had difficulty explaining to them why growing a forest was better than a supply of cut bamboo. The well-groomed, neat paths in the forest made a particularly strong impression on them.

The contentment of these people was reflected in their faces. They were swarthy and not always beautiful, but always friendly. Nuno and the duke saw them greeting each other this morning, holding hands, and sometimes even sitting down together in a convenient place. At the sight of the duke in his black armor, they were frightened, but promptly a smile stretched across their lips again.

Nuno noted how much better the local girls looked than their peers from Portuguese villages who, by the age of fifteen, were already beginning to fade, the stamp of worry and eternal fatigue appearing on their faces. These same dark-skinned beauties with unique tattoos on their faces were always neat, smiling, and glowing. They were dressed quite lightly, but Nuno never perceived any lustful glances from men aimed in their direction. They themselves wore only loincloths, and Nuno surreptitiously envied their attire; he would not mind walking like this most of the year.

After looking at all these curiosities, the duke assumed that the inhabitants of the ship had sailed here from Africa, from places that Portuguese sailors had not yet reached. He remembered how he had said in the Cortes in his own city of Evora that spending money on sea voyages meant throwing it away. The duke had assumed that the civilized Portuguese would need little from India or any other, what he considered savage, countries. Their spices were too far away and unnecessary, whether it was essential to sail after them or wander across dry lands. However, those same savages would need a lot from Portugal, so let them come themselves. Most likely, the duke guessed, this is exactly what had happened.

When the Europeans were approaching the house of Coatl, the duke managed to whisper, "Nuno, you will be my interpreter. You will translate everything I tell him, and you will not ask me questions, no questions at all, Nuno! Even if I have to deceive this person, you are only to translate, and in no case dispute my statements. If you want to keep your noble rank and estate, you will do just that."

The more Nuno got to know the duke, the less he liked him, and yet the young man decided that it was better to accept his situation. He decided to comply with the duke's demand but did not answer him. The duke was enraged by Nuno's silence, but he understood that he was in a very precarious situation, and he did not have command now. Until the king was deposed, Duke Fernando de Braganza could only ask, and it wasn't worth putting pressure on Nuno either. The young man had just lost his family and was unlikely to recover quickly from such a blow of fate.

The decorations in the house where they brought the Europeans seemed too modest for the commander of a floating city. Entering his chambers, Coatl sat down on a low wooden bench and motioned for the guests to sit down also. However, the duke could not sit in his armor, so he remained on his feet, and Nuno and Anacaona followed suit. The conversation began, and Nuno began to translate with the help of Anacaona and many of his drawings and notes.

"I am tlatoani of Tlaluacatli," said Coatl.

"He's the leader of this city on the water," Anacaona suggested to Nuno.

"I am the master of the land you came to," said the duke.

"Who are your teteo?" Coatl asked.

"We have only one God. His son lived in Jerusalem, a city to the east, but now he, too, is already in heaven, having suffered for all of us." Nuno replied, after which the duke and Nuno crossed themselves.

Coatl began to guess the Uehkatlan teteo could be anyone living in the sky, but if the metstli tlapalli didn't know them, then they couldn't possibly celebrate the same festivals. There was nowhere else to go — they had reached the place from which the sun always rose. So, Huitzilopochtli is definitely not here, and no one knows anything about him.

"What is the name of your land? Africa or India?" asked the duke.

"Their country is called Aztlan," Nuno answered.

Coatl, hearing the familiar word, nodded.

The duke did not ask the priest for details. He had already decided that these people came from Africa and continued to consider them Africans. "Why did you come to my land?" he asked.

"That reason does not concern you," Coatl replied, "because you don't participate in our festivals, and you, the tlatoani of your land, will have to pay tribute to me and make your land part of my altepetl and the land of Aztlan."

The duke had learned to control himself in the face of mortal danger even in his adolescence, but now, he had to restrain himself from laughing. It turned out to be much more difficult, but the duke coped. He asked, "What kind of tribute do you require?"

Coatl pointed to the duke's armor and sword, "The metal from which that is made." Coatl then pointed his index finger at the corner of the room. The duke looked and realized that there was a pile of weapons the foreigners had managed to collect on the shore: swords, crossbows, and even one arquebus. These weapons were undoubtedly taken from the soldiers of the Leiria garrison, who, according to Leandro's reports, disappeared in recent days.

Coatl looked proudly at the duke again. De Braganza almost laughed again when he realized how highly this half-naked man appreciated an ordinary soldier's weapon. Indeed, Coatl now imagined what envy this quarry would cause from his brother Nezahualpilli and all of Texcoco and Aztlan.

The duke was also calculating. Of course, there would be no question of any tribute, exchange, or trade with these savages, but they would have to be enticed at all costs to attack the castle of St. George and capture the king, and immediately, while the garrison of Lisbon was still besieging the duke's fortress. By that time, the army from Porto should arrive; Fernando still believed this. Then, the savages could be taken out of the city and killed. After that victory, the duke's soldiers would sail here, take all the gold, even that from which the African savages made dishes, and burn this bamboo vessel. There was enough gold here to buy off the entire army of Castile in case it wasn't possible to capture the king right away and real soldiers were needed instead of mercenaries.

"I agree," the duke said. "But you'll have to help me as well."

"How am I supposed to help you, tlatoani metstli tlapalli?"

"Your warriors will help me capture a castle. It is my castle, but now my enemy is sitting in it, an enemy who captured it by force, without any right to do so."

Nuno couldn't translate the word "castle" because Anacaona didn't understand the meaning of that word, so he said "city" instead.

"How many warriors does your enemy have?"

"Fifty," the duke replied, "and if you and your warriors capture the castle, I will perpetually pay tribute to you with such weapons and the metal from which they are made. I have an excess of such metal, and you will not be lacking in it. I will also assign you craftsmen who will teach your artisans how to handle the metal and make these weapons with it."

Coatl did not notice how Ocotlan, who had been in the corner of the room all the time, broke into a wide smile. It was obvious that he liked this offer very much, but Coatl's eyes also lit up, although not a single wrinkle trembled on his face. "If that's the case," he said after a pause, "then I need not talk with you but with the one to whom your city belongs now. After all, he must be stronger than you."

"You are correct, good man," the duke said humbly, "but the current lord of the castle has gone mad. He will not accept any people who want to talk to him and gives orders to kill anyone who approaches the fortress, whomever it may be. He does not want to talk and negotiate with anyone, but you can negotiate with me."

Nuno had not expected to have the skill with which he was now translating the speeches of Coatl and the duke and surprised himself. Anacaona hardly had to help him. Nuno's soul began to fill with excitement and anticipation for revenge. He had no doubt that the duke and the priest were now talking about the fortress of Leiria and about avenging the deaths of his father and mother. When he translated the duke's last words, a snake-like smile flashed on Coatl's lips, but immediately his face became calm again.

"My warriors can defeat fifty men," Coatl said. "I can put ten times fifty warriors in line right now."

"Then," replied the duke, "we must hurry because the enemy has called for help, and soon he will have thirty times fifty warriors."

"Therefore, we will hurry," Coatl replied.

Having agreed, the duke and tlatoani began to discuss the details of the upcoming campaign. When the duke and Coatl had agreed on everything, the priest summoned the cihuacoatl of the Tlaluacatli, Camaxtli. Coatl ordered him to prepare the floating city of Tlaluacatli to follow the duke's big boat, and informed the duke, "When my men are ready for Tlaluacatli to follow your big boat, they will tell you."

However, Nuno was beginning to suspect something was wrong. "Can you explain, Your Grace," he asked the duke, "where such a large army will go?"

"To my castle," de Braganza chuckled and turned away.

This didn't explain anything to Nuno. Why would they aim to take the fortress of Leiria? In any case, it was now clear to him that there was no intention to fight for Sinta. As Anacaona stood next to him, he became even more bewildered and torn. He didn't want to part with Anacaona. He would rather stay with her on this ship, and not return to the duke's caravel. Nuno told Coatl about this. He agreed. Coatl understood that it would be beneficial to have one metstli tlapalli hostage in case this strange tlatoani in black metal ichkahuipilli wanted to escape or deceive Coatl. Besides, this young metstli tlapalli spoke the language of Mexihkah quite well.

Meanwhile, the duke, accompanied by Ocotlan, went to the docks. There he boarded a boat with the sailors, who exchanged their knives for several gold trinkets, and the boat sailed toward the caravel. The duke was tired as hell and he desperately wanted to scratch his back, but his armor prevented him from doing so. Still, de Braganza was glad. He had fooled the leader of these savages. He was about to corner the king and force him to reckon with not only the Cortes but also with the best men of the kingdom. However, the plan of attack and all the details still had to be devised.

"Nuno," Anacaona said when the duke left Coatl's house, "I want you to meet my father."

"Chimalli disappeared with you, Anacaona," Coatl said sharply. "The warriors that were in the boats that went to the shore presumed you were stolen or ran away."

"I haven't seen my father since the warriors and I landed!" Anacaona replied, confused. How did this happen? When Anacaona had seen the warrior's boats leave the shore for the sea, she had assumed her father had sailed with them, but it turned out that he had stayed there, alone! He would surely face trouble from these terrible people with their sharp macuahuitl and spears and their constant readiness to use them! She had become convinced of this at Nuno's house.

"Coatl!" she exclaimed. "Order for me to be taken ashore, too, the next time we go there! If my father is there, I have to find him! We will definitely have wounded if we go to the city of this metstli tlapalli tlatoani, and I can take the place of my father in almost everything! I will treat the wounded! I also even know how to ride those big animals that the metstli tlapalli ride! He taught me," and Anacaona nodded at Nuno.

Coatl thought about it. It had not escaped his attention that Anacaona and this young metstli tlapalli, whom she had brought to Tlaluacatli, showed a fondness for each other. In addition, although she had been on the shore of Uehkatlan for only a short time, the warriors headed there would be completely unfamiliar with the land. Even a little of Anacaona's experience could come in handy. In addition, she already understood a little of the language of metstli tlapalli.

"All right," said Coatl, "but stay together. You will go ashore with the warriors." Anacaona and Nuno smiled, grasped each other's hands, and left the house, heading into the bamboo forest.

* * *

After seeing the duke off, Ocotlan returned to Coatl's house. He was perfectly able to hide his feelings and put any mask on his face, and he usually chose a stone one. "Coatl, it's a trap!" he said in his usual big voice that caused the dishes on the tables to rattle. "Didn't you see the eyes of that metstli tlapalli? Didn't you look into his soul? He didn't come with good intentions. He wants to lure us away and destroy our warriors."

Coatl went to the table and poured two mugs of octli from a jug. He handed one mug to Ocotlan and took another for himself. Coatl drank, put the empty mug on the table, and said, "Calm down, Ocotlan. This metstli tlapalli has no need to conquer us. After all, he didn't know anything about us until he got here."

"But now he knows!" Ocotlan roared.

"He needs something else entirely," Coatl said and looked at the bamboo forest through the window. "We're going to the shore. There, our warriors will land and go to his city where our guest is the legitimate tlatoani. Another tlatoani has captured it and does not want to give it back so we will go there and conquer this city. He needs us to help him become the tlatoani of his city again, but we will do what we do with all the new cities of Aztlan. He and his lands will join my altepetl, and you..."

Coatl paused. Ocotlan listened attentively and politely restraining a belch from the intoxicating drink.

"... and you will become the tlatoani of this city and its land, Ocotlan," Coatl continued, "because as soon as we take the city of this metstli tlapalli, we will kill both him and the one he asks us to fight against, and then we will find out without both of them where they mine their metal."

"I don't believe there are only fifty men guarding his city," Ocotlan said. "We were there with you, Coatl. And in the distance, we saw many other warriors. They walked around the field or rode on their big animals. If there are so many of them out in the field, there should be even more in the city because the city is much more important."

"This metstli tlapalli has no choice, but he has no need to deceive us either," Coatl replied with confidence. "That's why he came to us, and if he said there are fifty warriors there, then there are fifty of them. It's clear, but if we delay, there will be many more of them because help is already coming to them. Don't delay, Ocotlan. Watch how the warriors will prepare for our new military campaign."

* * *

Nuno and Anacaona walked around the floating city, and she showed Nuno things he had not had the opportunity to see before. He was especially struck by the bamboo pipes under the ceilings from which everyone could get as much water as they wanted at any moment. It was so easy! Nuno firmly decided that when he restored his estate, he would definitely arrange the same type of plumbing in it. Passing by the neat garden beds, Nuno noticed large red fruits. He was sure that everything that grew on earth was available in Sinta's gardens, but he had never seen such fruit as this.

"Tomatl," Anacaona said and plucked off a tomato. She simply wiped it on the sleeve of her dress, bit off a piece, and handed Nuno the other half. He took a bite of it and found he liked the flavor. Nuno was surprised that he had never seen a tomato in the markets of Leiria or even Lisbon.

In one of the halls, they saw young people and boys playing ball. Noticing Nuno, the boys froze and looked at him, some with fright, and some with challenging glares. Anacaona laughed and took Nuno's hand. The players came to life again. They came closer to Nuno, examined him, touched his clothes, and, finally, his hands.

"Nuno, play with them," Anacaona said. "It's very simple. See the ring on the wall?" Nuno raised his head and saw the massive circle with a hole in the center, the edge of the circle attached to the wall. "Look!" Anacaona took the ball from one of the boys and forcefully hit the ball on her knee. The ball bounced off the leg, flew through the hole, and fell to the floor. The crowd of players buzzed with delight. "That's how you play ollamalitzli," Anacaona said.

Nuno immediately joined the game. The ball turned out to be light and bouncy. Nuno couldn't figure out what the ball was made of, but he had no need to ask about it now.

One of the players kicked the ball toward Nuno with his hip. He caught the ball with his hands on the fly and easily, as if he had been playing with it all his life, launched it into the circle. The ball went through it without even hitting the edges. Nuno mentally praised himself. But then Anacaona said, "Nuno, you can't take the ball with your hands." Nuno looked at her with surprise. How then could he get the ball through the ring?

Just then, a tall man in a beige cape, belted with a turquoise belt, came into the ballroom. It was Camaxtli, the cihuacoatl of Tlaluacatli, whom Nuno had already seen at Coatl's house.

"Everybody out! Tlaluacatli will be moving soon!" He turned and left without even looking at how the players would behave. They obediently went to the exit. Nuno and Anacaona followed them. Below the deck, where twilight reigned, there was a huge pool into which the players began to jump. Nuno thought that the players had decided to practice swimming, but they began to grab bunches of some kind of tough grass and rub their bodies with them. Nuno realized that they were washing, and at the same time, taking a break from the game. It occurred to him that a ship with such facilities could not possibly be designed for transporting slaves, wars, trade, or any other purposes for which ships were usually built in his homeland. Of course, such facilities could only serve the people who work and rest here, who live in peace and joy!

They continued down the stairs even lower. As Nuno's eyes adjusted to the twilight, he was able to make out the lower part of the ship. Light came in through narrow, long slits in the stern. The ship had two hulls. In fact, it was not one ship, but two connected by a common large deck on which the pyramid stood. At the end of each of the two hulls, a huge wheel with blades was spinning, beating on the water. These wheels were hidden inside the hull, so they could not be seen from the outside.

Anacaona led Nuno to the stern of the hull they were currently on, and Nuno could see what was driving the ship. Dozens, maybe hundreds of people were constantly pulling up a rope that seemed to have no beginning or end; it came from somewhere out of the twilight and left into the dusk. This rope communicated with the mechanism, which then drove one of the wheels. Another team, in the same manner, pulled another rope inside the second hull and forced the second wheel to spin.

It just so happened that while Nuno and Anacaona were watching, a man standing on a platform near the workers shouted something, and the wheel began to rise. As it rose out of the water, the ship began to turn because the other wheel continued to work. Despite the fact that the wheel removed from the water was now hanging in the air, people continued to pull the rope, and the wheel continued to rotate. Anacaona explained the wheel was always kept turning before being lowered into the water because otherwise, it would be impossible to set it into motion. Soon, the wheel that was removed from the water was allowed to sink back into the water. The ship stopped turning and went straight again.

The man standing on the platform was the helmsman. As Anacaona explained, he was following commands that were transmitted to him from the temple room at the top of the pyramid. Anacaona didn't know for sure, but she assumed that these commands were transmitted by the same person who called the ball players out of the hall and into the pool, Camaxtli, he was Coatl's assistant and the second man on the ship.

Nuno saw ropes hanging on the walls inside the hull. These were spares. In the event of a breakage of the working rope, it could be replaced immediately. There were also many women around who were weaving new ropes. Nuno had already seen the fiber from which they were woven; they were made from some vines and plants that wrapped around the bamboo above in the forest.

Beside the rope, constantly in motion, pulled by these people, a row of bamboo trunks about half the height of a man protruded from the floor. They stood at an angle, and under each of the trunks, there was a large ceramic pot with handles. The end of each trunk was covered with long narrow slits, and the other end went down under the stern and into the water. Water entered the trunks and was forced up due to the forward movement of the ship. From time to time, as these pots filled with water, they were taken away by two attendants who threaded poles through the handles and putting them on their shoulders, left, leaving an empty pot behind. Some women then came to the ends of the trunks and put a mixture made up of ground leaves, vines, and some kind of gray powder inside through the slits. The ends were then wrapped with fine nets that held the mixture inside, and the water coming from below passed through this mixture before pouring out of the bamboo trunk and into the pot.

Pots already filled with water were placed nearby, since there was plenty of room under the deck, and they did not interfere with the paddlemen. Different nets with another mixture and a portion of powder were then thrown into the pots with water. Anacaona explained to Nuno that after a few days, the water treated in this way would become drinkable, and the mixture inside the nets turns white and hardens. This mixture, which absorbed sea salt, was then simply thrown into the ocean. After this process, the water was poured into other pots and taken away. Trees and vegetable gardens could be watered with this water, and when mixed with rainwater, animals could also drink it.

After watching the work of the paddlemen, Nuno and Anacaona went back on deck. Only now was Nuno able to see the pyramid up close; he had previously only seen it from the duke's caravel. Seeing the steps, he invited Anacaona to climb, but Anacaona's face twisted in horror, "No, Nuno! You can't! You can't go up there! Only Coatl, Ocotlan, and Camaxtli can enter there."

Nuno took another look at the pyramid. The pyramid was built of large steps covered with drawings. They depicted such terrible scenes that Nuno felt uneasy, and yet they were only drawings, but then Nuno noticed the strange wooden frame at the top of the pyramid. It was standing at the entrance to the room at the peak. Looking closer, Nuno saw that sticks were inserted inside of this frame and human skulls were impaled on them. Nuno looked at Anacaona with horror. She answered with a sad look and said nothing.

Recovering from the shock, Nuno approached the side of the ship. He saw the caravel moving away in the distance, all the sails hoisted. It occurred to Nuno that Duke Fernando de Braganza could be standing at the stern at this moment and looking at them too. Suddenly Nuno realized that he did not want to meet him again, and he didn't want to return to his estate after all he had experienced, either. He did not want to face the filth, malice, and greed, the abominations that he saw every day at his estate and in all the other places where he had to go. Besides, no one was waiting for him there. Yet there was one reason to return.

"We will definitely find your father," Nuno told Anacaona, watching the caravel.

A strip of land appeared ahead as the sun began to set.

A Moment from the Past - Knighthood

Asilah had not yet been conquered when the men began to renovate the main mosque. Everything appeared to have been tossed out of it except the walls where the adornments that still decorated them were one of the few reminders that it had once been a mosque. Outside, the distinguishable minarets still towered overhead. Now, imported or hastily made crucifixes were hung on the walls of the former mosque, and icons were placed in the spaces between windows. Benches were placed between the entrance to the temple and a wooden altar that had been brought along from Lagos. A path was laid out in the passage. By the evening, a priest had consecrated the temple.

On the eve of knighthood for the heir to the throne, Joao prepared for his accolade; he bathed, put on a white shirt, and over it, a scarlet cape. His boots were decorated with gold spurs. All night he stood at the altar with his head down, praying, and tried not to listen to the screams of the soldiers coming from outside. The following afternoon, Joao stood for mass, offered confession, and received communion.

Finally, the initiation began. King Afonso V of Portugal, father of Joao, girded him with a sword, and Father Pedro, who had accompanied the army, put his hands on the young man's shoulders. Joao felt the eyes of those witnessing the ceremony on his back. Among them were the nobles who accompanied the king on the campaign, Don Daniel, who captured the fortress gates, Duke de Braganza, whose detachment was the first to break into the fortress and who saved his life, and Fernao Gomes, a navigator and assistant to the king who had made multiple trips to African shores. Gomes's face was disfigured by a terrible wound, and the torn and stitched cheek continued to bleed.

At the end of the ceremonial speech, Father Pedro removed his hands from Joao's shoulders and solemnly said, "My son, you are now knighted."

Then the king himself spoke. He put an ancient sword on his son's shoulder. It was a sword of Damascus steel with a handle so richly decorated with rubies that it seemed to be made only of these gems and nothing else. Previously, this sword belonged to the Vizier Shadulla, the now-defeated commander of the Muslim army. After paying tribute to his son's bravery and his art of winning victories, the king entreated him to devote his life to protecting his native land from infidels and troublemakers. Finally, the King said, "And trust, my son, only your friends."

"Who are they, our friends?" Joao asked unexpectedly to everyone.

The King looked confused. It did not immediately occur to him that Joao was dead tired from the fight the day before, then the night spent on his feet at the altar, and finally from the excitement associated with his knighting. Afonso nodded at the guests at the ceremony. "Your friends," the king explained, "are those you trust and those who trust you," and with an iron-gloved palm, the king pointed at the guests. However, this hint did not seem to reach the tired Joao.

Joao looked at the sword that had just been presented to him. The rubies on the hilt sparkled in the rays of the sun that invaded through the small windows. He raised the sword above his head and said, "Here, Father, is my friend whom I trust, and let those who will trust it, who will trust everything it does, find me themselves. They will be my friends and friends of Portugal!"

The young Joao had not yet learned how to express himself in such a way that his words were understandable to those around him and not only to him alone. Judging by the faces of the king and the guests, they failed to understand him now. Only one person among those standing at the altar understood him correctly. Haste was imperative! It was going to be necessary to select people and place them in the king's entourage and in the Cortes quickly, because the day Joao was named king, hard times would come for him, for this man.

Chapter 13. Chimalli and the King

"Aren't you late, Senhors?" Joao II said as three navigators entered his office in the tower of the Castle of St. George and began to bow. One of them, Bartolomeu Dias, straightened up and was about to open his mouth and say something when a bell rang.

"You're not too late," the king grinned. "Well, come in and get acquainted."

Bartolomeu, Christopher Columbus and Vasco da Gama came to the table. The King was sitting at the head of it, and at the other end, they noticed a swarthy, half-naked man of about fifty years of age in unusual clothes. His head, arms, and body were decorated with gold chains, earrings, rings, and tattoos. On his face, ears, and nose there were traces left by previous adornments. There was a dish of roast beef in front of the strange-looking man, and he ate it with an appetite.

Two people rose from their seats on the other side of the table – an elderly sailor, with whom Bartolomeu Dias was already familiar, and a young monk in a wool shirt. The sailor's face was disfigured by a terrible scar on his cheek. A blissful smile was playing on the monk's face. "Fernao Gomes," the king introduced the sailor. Gomes politely bowed to the newcomers. The king rang the bell. The servants entered the study. They held trays of dishes and filled jugs in their hands, which they began to put on the table near the plates that had been placed in advance.

"You may be acquainted with this gentleman," the king continued. Dias nodded. "Fernao Gomes is a brave navigator who is currently exploring the African coast. Every year, he travels another hundred leagues to the south and brings back new curiosities, and most importantly, the maps. These maps show native settlements and places where valuables can be mined."

"I am glad to meet such wonderful gentlemen, of whom I have already heard a great deal," Gomes said to the new guests of the king. His speech was unusual and not quite clear. It was distorted by the wound that disfigured his cheek, but it seemed that Gomes was not at all shy about it. "I would like to introduce my son Pascoal to you. Pascoal decided to link his fate with God, and not with long voyages. He is a novice of the Jeronimos Monastery in Lisbon, founded as you know by our great Henry the Navigator, but currently, he is serving in the church of Leiria."

Pascoal's smile stretched across his face and nodded.

"Fortunately, he still tries to help me," Gomes continued. "He already knows a lot of foreign languages. With his help, I am able to talk to foreign sailors, merchants, and scientists that may visit our ports as well as foreigners who work for me here in Portugal or are engaged in long-distance campaigns. The other day, one of these foreigners mysteriously ended up in the hands of soldiers who serve in the fortress of Leiria, and Pascoal brought this wonderful man here," Gomes pointed to the guest in the unusual dress. "His name is Chimalli."

Hearing his name, Chimalli stopped eating and looked curiously at the king's guests.

"What country did he come from?" Vasco da Gama asked.

"That's the thing," Gomes exclaimed, "that we haven't been able to find out yet!"

"Sit down, Senhors, and share our meal," the king addressed the captains. They took their places at the table with bows.

"I have met many foreigners, both on the shores of different countries and at sea," Gomes continued. "I have traveled all over Europe and all the coastal countries that our ships have ever reached. I have talked to travelers who have visited China, India, and some of the hottest desert countries in the world. From these people, I learned what the natives of these countries look like and how they behave. But he," and Gomes pointed to Chimalli, "did not come from these countries. That's the only thing we've been able to ascertain for sure. He came from a country that is still unknown to us. His country is not yet in the ecumene."

All the navigators looked at Chimalli. This time he was clearly abashed. Now Pascoal took the floor, "He appeared in the forest near Leiria, on the high road by the seashore in the middle of the night." he added to his father's story with a smile.

The navigators exchanged glances. "My son, Senhors," Gomes continued, "hints at rumors about the Red Ghost that supposedly prowls the coastal areas, commits murders, and commits other outrages there. Such rumors appear among the people from year to year, and always, as you know, it turns out to be only hearsay. Unless the dark crowd delegates some unfortunate person as the ghost, and then, woe to him."

Fernao noticed how cautiously the navigators were examining Chimalli. The alien's skin really had a copper-red hue, and his dress, crumpled and soiled by all his troubles, still retained a somewhat red color. Fernao laughed, "No, no, Senhors, Chimalli is not a ghost at all. He's a traveler, and Pascoal brought him here from Leiria."

Joao II did not take his eyes off Fernao Gomes, and judging by his face, the king did not like this turn in the narrative very much. He obviously knew about something related to these stupid rumors, but he didn't say it out loud.

"You, Senhors, may ask why our traveler ended up here, in His Majesty's palace. Take a look at his jewelry; its appearance does not deceive you. It is really made of gold and precious stones."

"Of the gold Portugal needs so much today," the king saw fit to add. "Go on, Gomes"

"Thank you, Your Majesty, but this man, Senhors, does not value gold as high as our jewelers and money changers appreciate it. In truth, they are valuable to him only because they do not rust and always shine. However, iron is not known in his homeland, and he says that it would be more valuable than gold because there is an abundance of gold there, but there is no iron at all. Surely you understand what kind of profit such an exchange promises?"

The navigators were silent. The news stunned them. If Fernao had told anyone about this elsewhere, they would have considered him crazy. However, he said all this in the presence of the king, in the presence of a savage hung with gold, and his son who brought this savage.

"His Majesty, the king, agrees with my proposal to equip ships and sail to the homeland of this Chimalli," continued Fernao Gomes. "Of course, those that brave this voyage will be generously rewarded."

"But what direction exactly will these ships go?" Vasco da Gama asked.

"We don't know that yet," the smiling Pascoal said again. "We only know that it's impossible to get there by land. The homeland of this man is beyond the sea on which he sailed."

"Why do you think that?" Vasco da Gama asked.

"When I ask him how he ended up in the forest, he pronounced the word 'atl' in his language, which means water, but there are no lakes or rivers where he ended up, just as there are no places in Portugal that would be inhabited by such a people."

"So, he means the ocean?" Dias suggested.

"I think so," Pascoal nodded.

"Try to ask him from which part of his 'atl' he sailed," the king addressed the navigators, "And Pascoal will try to translate."

"Does he know such words as India, Africa, Europe, or China?" Columbus asked.

"No. Maybe he knows of these lands, but he doesn't know such words," Pascoal replied. "Sometimes he pronounces the word 'Aztlan.' Maybe that's the name of the land from which he came."

"Aztlan..." said Dias, looking incredulously at Pascoal and Chimalli. "Aztlan... And what is north, south, west, east, does he know?"

"Surprisingly, he knows," Pascoal said. "Despite his appearance, he is a very knowledgeable person, but he identifies the cardinal directions differently. First, they bear the names of animals or objects. Second, they are located close to our cardinal directions but do not exactly coincide with them. He draws a circle, but I still don't understand how exactly to discern the landmark within this circle, and without that, it is impossible to understand the connection between their directions and ours."

"I see that he doesn't use utensils and eats with his hands," Columbus said. "It's amazing for a man with such wealth as he has. Oh, yes, pardon me... but his clothes and jewelry are still quite skillfully made. Do they really belong to him?"

"I forgot to mention that he also knows the beginnings of mathematics. As for the clothes, I'll try to ask him now." Pascoal opened the bag he always carried with him and took out a pile of papers covered with drawings, geometric shapes, numbers, and lots of dots and lines. Finding the images of the dress and necklace, he showed them to Chimalli and looked at him questioningly.

"Tekitl," Chimalli answered.

"Tekitl? Neh amo asikamati" *I don't understand you.*

"Kema, tekitl," Chimalli said. He took the gnawed bone from his plate and put it next to Pascoal's plate, and then took a piece of bread from Pascoal and moved it to his own plate. Having done this, he looked directly at Pascoal.

"Trade!" Pascoal guessed. "Tekitl means trade. Teuatl tekitl Aztlan?" *Did you trade it in Aztlan?*

"Kema," Chimalli agreed.

"He says he bought or exchanged this dress in his homeland," Pascoal declared. He immediately took a quill out of his bag and wrote down the new word.

"Now we know that the Aztlan people make the things they need and trade them," Bartolomeu Dias said. "So, our iron can also be exchanged, tekitl for gold."

"Ask him how long he sailed to get to our land from his," Columbus asked.

"Ken ueyak xiya tlan?" *How long did you sail to our land?* Pascoal asked Chimalli.

Chimalli got up and walked over to the dish on which the forks, new to Portugal, were lying. He took five forks to Pascoal and laid them out on the table in a row. Pascoal rummaged through the papers, found a sheet covered with lines and dots, and poked his finger at one of the drawings, "Iluitl?"

"Kema," Chimalli agreed.

"He says twenty–five days," Pascoal translated.

"One fork equals five days?" Columbus was surprised. "Did he have lunch once every five days?"

Pascoal burst into silver laughter, but, glancing at the king, stopped.

"No, Senhor Captain. One line is five. If you are interested, one dot means one. Five dots are replaced with one line. Five lines will be twenty-five. 'Iluitl' means day."

Suddenly Chimalli walked over to the king. The king and everyone sitting jumped up from their seats. Fernao wanted to grab his sword but remembered that he had handed it over to the guards. Without thinking twice, he rushed to Chimalli to stop him.

However, Chimalli only took two peas from the king's plate and then carried them back. He put them next to the forks, looked at Pascoal, and trembled when he saw the reflection of the act on the monk's face.

"Sempoualli chikome iluitl," he pronounced embarrassed.

"Twenty–seven days," Pascoal translated, returning to his senses.

Everyone was silent. The King sat down again and pushed the plate of food away from him.

"Go on," he said to the guests.

"Did he come alone?" Columbus asked. All the Europeans present laughed, but Columbus continued, "You understood me correctly. I want to ask, where is his ship? Where are the other voyagers?"

"I asked him about it before," Pascoal said. "I have not yet learned the language of this stranger very well; it is hard to believe what I have learned from him so far. From what I have understood, he says they live in a city called Tlaluacatli. He says that this city is inhabited by more than a thousand people and is located very close to our shore. When I asked him to draw his city, he drew this," and Pascoal put a strange drawing on the table that depicted two large ships with some kind of pyramidic structure between them. At the same time, the drawing did not show any of the most indispensable parts of a ship such as masts and rigging.

"It still looks like a ship, not a city with houses or town streets," Vasco Da Gama said, looking at the drawing.

"How did they know which way to sail?" Dias asked. "How did they navigate their directions?"

Pascoal rummaged through the papers again. He showed Chimalli one drawing and then another, asking him questions, sometimes drawing, or just crossing something out. Finally, Pascoal raised his head and solemnly said, "He says they were going toward the sunrise."

"Wait!" Columbus said loudly. He walked over to a dish of finger foods, took an egg from it, and showed it to Chimalli.

"Tell him that the egg is the sun, and this table is the sea." Pascoal translated the words of the navigator for Chimalli. Columbus hid his hand with the egg under the table, waited, and then slowly began to raise it. When the egg rose above the table, Columbus looked questioningly at Chimalli.

Chimalli pointed to the egg with his hand and said, "Tonatiu tleko" *Sunrise*.

"Unbelievable! This can't be happening!" exclaimed Columbus.

"Explain yourself," said the king.

"Certainly" Columbus recklessly scooped up some of the dishes. At the same time, a piece of meat fell to the floor which Chimalli looked at with regret. After looking at the others, he decided not to pick it up. Columbus pulled a paper folded several times out of an immense pocket and spread it out on the table. "I've been working on this map for years, and it's not finished yet. Here…" Columbus took one of the forks, and placed its middle in the center of Portugal, crossing the Iberian Peninsula with the handle. The pointed half of the fork went beyond its borders, the teeth pointing to the left of the land, past the coast of Portugal. Columbus took the egg and placed it near the blunt end of the fork that lay in Genoa, Columbus' hometown. "In May," Columbus explained pointing at the egg, "the sun rises around here, and if what he says is true, it means that he sailed from over there," and Columbus covered the expanse of the big ocean with his palm, the direction of the pointing prongs of the fork, and which no navigator had yet dared to sail. Everyone stared at his outstretched hand.

"Over there," Columbus explained, pointing to the window behind the king. From the westward-facing window, one could see the mouth of the Tagus River flowing into the sea. Columbus removed his palm from the map. Below it was a picture of the sea, dotted with groups of points. To the west of Portugal, the Azores were visible on this map.

"You yourself said a few days ago that you wanted to go that direction to get to India," the king said to Columbus.

"Yes, Your Majesty," Columbus nodded.

Fernao Gomes, who had been standing a little to one side all this time, smiled and said, "Your Majesty, I think I can guess who will lead the next voyage in that direction."

The king stood at the window, looked at the caravels headed out of the Tagus toward the sea, paused, then said, "And yet I do not know how much one can trust this savage. To get to our shore on a boat without sails with a thousand people. What kind of ship can this be? Even galleys, rowing vessels, and such have sails! The captains of the carracks, who guard us against attacks by sea, did not report the approach of any large ships toward Portugal, and if this ship is so big, it would have definitely been noticed and reported immediately!"

The King squinted at the fork, which was still pointing west, "Besides," he continued, "we also must not forget the circumstances under which our soldiers caught this crazy old man. In the vicinity of Leiria, several strange incidents have occurred in recent days. One soldier from the mounted patrol was killed, and the second soldier, his partner, disappeared. An attack was made on a military convoy, and its guards also disappeared without a trace. Maybe it's a bunch of crazy people? Isn't our guest, who walks through the forest at night, is covered with gold, and steals food from the king's dish right in front of his eyes, quite possibly crazy? Or maybe this madman just doesn't want to go back to prison? He sits here, eats, and drinks from the royal table, and comes up with one fairy tale after another?"

The navigators looked at each other anxiously. They didn't know about these incidents.

"But if he really got here by sea, then I am primarily concerned about a ship that sailed unnoticed to the shores of Portugal. Of course, I am also worried about bandits in the vicinity of Leiria, who may be killing and kidnapping my soldiers. Yes, and this Red Ghost, from which there is always no rest. We need to figure out if these are separate events, or if they are related." The King paused and stared at the landscape outside the window again. The king's guests were also silent. Brother Pascoal and Chimalli exchanged glances and smiled.

"Give me time to think," the king finally broke the silence. "I'll call on you again. Everyone can go." Through the window, the king saw a horseman riding through the castle gate. Judging by the horse, it was a messenger. One could only hope that he brought good news.

The king's expectations were justified. A messenger brought news: General Afonso was leading his garrison back to Lisbon, and the garrison of the Vila Viçosa Castle had joined the ranks. An army of eight hundred men was approaching Lisbon. Thus, the first fruits of this bloodless conquest were already in his hands, the personal garrison of Duke de Braganza, who had previously defended the castle at Vila Viçosa. The king would send the garrison of de Braganza to the south to help other detachments in the Algarve, and he himself would visit Vila Viçosa in the near future and confiscate everything of value from there.

Chapter 14. Outcome

Duke Fernando de Braganza was sitting in his cabin and thinking about his plan of attack on the residence of the king, the castle of St. George. Nothing could escape his attention or occur unexpectedly. Now was the only opportunity for the duke to enact his scheme. He was a knight, a soldier, a general and knew of military affairs! Of course, he was aware that the African savages, de Braganza continued to believe the strangers were African, would be unable to besiege the castle of St. George. However, the Lord himself had brought His help to the duke, sending the garrison of the castle away and granting him this opportunity. Right now, there were no more than a hundred people inside the castle, only the guards, servants, and a few other military servants of the king. If he attacked them and could get inside, they would not be able to offer serious resistance, but if they managed to close the castle gate, the savages, with their bows and spears, instead of bombards, siege engines, and ladders would not be able to take the castle.

The gate would have to be opened somehow, and then the savages would be able to crush the defenders of the castle with their numbers, and then, once the king fulfilled the conditions that the rebellious duke would present to him, the savages would receive the arsenal of the castle. It wouldn't do them much good. They wouldn't know how to use the crossbows, muskets, or cannons anyway. The duke looked complacently at the prepared scroll, the commitment that the king would sign. The scroll was tied with a white ribbon woven with depictions of bizarre people with animal heads.

The duke had secretly picked the ribbon up at Coatl's house on the ship.

So, thought the duke, first it would be necessary to bring the ship as close as possible to Lisbon in order for the savages to land. It would not work if it was too near the city, because even at night, it would be impossible not to notice such a large ship and an army. Seeing the savages, local people would take them for the Moors and hurry off to the Royal castle to report it. Then, the castle would have time to prepare for the attack. He would need to land far from the city and go running toward the castle.

If Africans appeared in Lisbon by day and made their way to the castle through the city, the citizens, seeing gold jewelry on the savages, would start to trade and barter. News about such profitable exchange would spread quickly to the merchants and money changers. Soon, the crowds would flood the streets and alleys and block the narrow streets of the city, and the Africans would be slowed too much. So, it would be best to move at night along the widest roads and streets, advancing to the castle on the hill quickly.

Here began the most difficult part of the plan. Perhaps the guards would not notice the savages running to the hill among the city houses, but as the Africans began to climb the hill to the castle, the guards at the gates and, moreover, on the walls would be able to spot them at a glance. The guards would not only close the gates, but they would also be fortified with stones, which were always kept at the ready. The sentries would sound the alarm and start shooting, and the whole plan would be ruined. This could not be allowed.

The duke raised his head and looked at the bulkhead of his cabin. He suddenly remembered the fire in the house of Don Leandro, from which they barely escaped. The fire was so terrible that all who could, ran and carried buckets of water and pikes to try to extinguish the blaze. Taking advantage of the commotion, the duke, along with Nuno and Anacaona, managed to escape unnoticed. Through the windows of the cabin at the stern of the caravel, the duke could see the outline of the giant ship as it followed. On the wall above the windows was the de Braganza family coat of arms, and the duke decided, let it be what it will be! There was no turning back for him, he had nothing to lose. There would be no name, no title, no life itself if he were to escape now and leave. The duke suddenly stood up from his chair, "What if..." he thought, the lips of the duke pulling up into a devious smile. He had devised a plan to get into the castle without siege.

* * *

"Great news!" The king exclaimed. He put a half-eaten chicken leg on a platter, grabbed a napkin, crumpled it, and threw it on the table. "Daniel! You managed to get rid of de Braganza and accomplish something that was beyond the power of a whole army! You have shamed General Afonso! That's right! Yes!" At the exclamation, a piece of partially chewed chicken flew out of the king's mouth. The chicken hit Daniel in the face. He took a step back but bumped into Estela's fist as she stood a little behind him.

Daniel swayed, but immediately pulled himself together, "Glad to be of service, Your Majesty!" he answered loudly.

"Ah, what wonderful soldiers are at my service! But what have you got going on there in Leiria? I have heard nothing but chatter about the city all day," continued the king. He suddenly remembered how, before his eyes and under his command, Daniel's squad had stormed the walls of Asilah and was the first to break into the city and open the gates for Duke de Braganza's cavalry detachment. The king turned his mind away from de Braganza; he no longer wanted to mark the beginning of that glorious defeat of the Moors with the duke. "Well! You will be rewarded for this feat!"

"Yes, your Majesty!" said Daniel. Estela sighed. For such a situation, the soldier-father could have found better words.

"Daniel," continued the king, going up to the guests. "The sun is on the wane, and the road to Leiria is long. I offer you hospitality. My secretary will show you to the chambers reserved for my best guests. Lodge there for the night, my good sir, and lady." With the king's first glance at Estela, he decided she would soon share his bed. He would indulge her, and she would be obliged. He said, "I have also considered your daughter's request! She will be a worthy owner of Sinta. Yes, yes! You deserve this estate, dear Estela. I have no doubt about that. In the morning, the secretary will give you my decree on this matter. I recognize you as the widow of the unfortunate Nuno, the sole heir of his parents, who also tragically passed away."

Daniel blushed. When they first entered the study, the king looked first at Estela, and then at him, and he had given his daughter such a look... If anyone else had ever dared to look at his daughter like that, Daniel would have smashed his nose without delay. Daniel glanced at Estela. Damn it! It was up to her now! It was no longer up to her father!

Estela was also making incredible efforts to hold herself together, with great difficulty. Her mind was starting to get muddled, and her soul and body wanted to sing, shout and dance. Everything had turned out exactly as she had planned! However, now she had to appear to show both gratitude to the king for his generosity and hospitality, and grief for the young groom who had tragically gone to heaven. In her mind, she was already imagining huge halls, noble and rich guests, and luxurious feasts — a life in which no one counted money or days.

The king was already openly taking in Estela with his eyes. Tomorrow he would honorably send out the old father to Leiria. However, the daughter would be delayed for another day or two due to sluggishness or the sudden illness of the secretary. This beauty and Joao II would have a nice few days together, then they would part forever. The King was sure of that. He knew that he was not capable of falling in love with a woman for more than two or three days. After that, he had to let them all go, with a generous reward of course, and there was never a case where the parents of these girls failed to greet them with joyful hugs.

After dismissing the guests, the king sat down in a chair in front of the window, put his hands behind his head, and thought. He was happy today. Yes, happy! His sworn enemy, de Braganza, was destroyed. Surprisingly, the unexpected sometimes does exactly what you have been planning for weeks, months, or years! That's how chance brought such good news and this beautiful girl to his castle. He would do a good deed for this family by rewarding both Estela and her father.

Joao II, who did not tolerate wine well, decided to celebrate this day anyway. He poured himself a full goblet and drank it down in one gulp. Immediately he seemed to be lifted up by angels. They carried him to the bed chamber and laid him on the bed. The King had not yet had time to inquire about Estela when he found himself in the arms of a deep sleep. The valet pulled off His Majesty's boots and covered the king with a blanket. He knew the king would sleep until morning, and the king's sleep would be so deep that even a cannon shot would not be able to wake him.

* * *

Camaxtli, cihuacoatl of Tlaluacatli was tired, no, exhausted under the weight of the secret that he had to keep, and he decided to share it with Ocotlan. Camaxtli knew that only Ocotlan would be able to take his secret seriously, or… Camaxtli didn't want to think about the worst, but he didn't want to keep this secret to himself either. He couldn't take it anymore. It was too much to bear.

At the hour when the ixiptlatli was being offered to Tezcatlipoca, as Coatl stood at the top of the pyramid and the crowd danced at its foot, the cihuacoatl, Camaxtli, and the tlacochcalcatl, Ocotlan, were standing in the ollamalitzli room just under the hanging circle and among scattered rubber balls. The warriors were waiting for Ocotlan below deck to go to the shore, and Camaxtli begged the commander to give him a moment of attention, and told him, "Only now, with Coatl and the rest of the people gone for the festival, was I able to get into the tlatoani's house and take this," Camaxtli showed Ocotlan a scroll. "Before you read it, I have to tell you something. When Moctezuma conquered the Totonac tribes, I, one of the most capable students in Teotihuacan, was sent to build this city, Tlaluacatli. Together with me, the best masters of Itza built this city; those experienced in the construction of large boats, and the best stargazers. I helped build all this …" and Camaxtli made a circle around himself with his hands, "together with them."

Ocotlan looked into the eyes of Camaxtli and was silent. They could hear the shouts of the crowd and the music that accompanied the dance of death. "My father,"

Camaxtli continued, "loved the starry sky and knew it well. He knew how to draw it so that, having these paths on amatl at hand, the warriors of the sea could always find the right way in any direction. One day he went to Tenochtitlan, to the weyitlatoani Axayacatl. He showed him the paths with directions, which he had made especially for the Tlaluacatli voyage. Axayacatl's stargazers said that they were the best paths inscribed on amatl that they had ever seen. Axayacatl decided that my father and I were the best suited to manage Tlaluacatli on the Big Water because my father held the best knowledge of where to go, and I knew everything about how Tlaluacatli was built."

"Of course," Ocotlan agreed. "After all, you know better if you built it yourself."

"My father," Camaxtli continued, "could have found the right way on the water even without the paths he had drawn on the amatl, even without the sun, which could go behind the clouds for a long time. The man from the Itza tribes, who also knows how to navigate, helped me learn about it in Tlaluacatli. Axayacatl promised my father that he would make him tlatoani of Tlaluacatli and announce it at a special festive meeting in his palace. At the same time, Axayacatl was going to entrust me with the navigation of Tlaluacatli along the paths that my father had drawn. He told my father, his friend, that he had prepared this and all other appointments for new positions in advance, but when they were distributed, he wanted to check the honesty of some people. I don't know how he was going to check it, but during the ceremony, the curse of Tepeyollotl happened."

"Are you talking about that terrible earthquake?" Ocotlan asked.

"Yes, and during that disaster, my father died, and now look…" Camaxtli stretched out the scroll he was clutching to Ocotlan. Ocotlan opened it and saw on it the signs denoting the position of tlatoani of Tlaluacatli. The scroll was covered with brown spots of dried blood. "This is the scroll that the great tlatoani Axayacatl handed my father," said Camaxtli, "and now Coatl hides it."

"Coatl?" frowned Ocotlan.

"Yes. Blood stains may keep the secret of my father's death, and they may keep the secret of how Coatl became tlatoani of Tlaluacatli, but yet he does not know how to calculate the path of the stars and other heavenly bodies. He is only able to find his way by the sun, and even then, with difficulty."

Ocotlan looked at the scroll again, rolled it up, and turned to Camaxtli. "Put it back where you found it," he said, "and don't tell anyone what you have told me." With these words, Ocotlan left the room. Somewhere above, there was a thud of a body flying down the steps of the pyramid. Finally, it hit the water. The crowd roared with delight.

Camaxtli did not understand Ocotlan's behavior, but his heart felt much lighter.

* * *

A deafening explosion shook the buildings near the port of Lisbon, and then a huge flame erupted on the water. It was a fire on the caravel of Duke de Braganza. The flames were so large that, as it turned out later, a girl blind from birth, in a house that stood on the hill nearly two leagues from the port could see it. In the meantime, the fire that engulfed the ship blinded the residents of nearby houses and illuminated the clouds in the midnight sky. Birds rushed over the river with shouts. Everywhere in the city, there were cries of awakened infants and old women crossed themselves. The port was as bright as on a clear afternoon. Those townspeople that had boats and small ships in the port rushed out to check on their crafts while many other onlookers clamored out of their homes just to watch the fire. There were stampedes on the streets.

"Look at that!" said one of the archers on the south tower to his partner, who was walking along the western wall of the castle. "Someone just went broke. That's not lucky for that poor guy." The partner walked nervously along the wall towards the fire.

The guard of the south gate shouted from below, "Hey, there! What's burning? What blew up?"

The archer leaned over the edge of the tower and shouted back, "Tavino! Roger! Just look at how beautiful it is!"

The guards exchanged glances. It was forbidden to leave their posts on pain of death. However, the sight, judging by the glare that illuminated the clouds and the sky, was such that it would have been like death to miss it. One of them spat with annoyance, opened the door in the gate, and, immediately turning onto the spiral staircase, began to climb the south tower. His partner looked around. There wasn't a soul to be seen. Then he, too, darted through the door, slammed it shut, barely managing to pull his pike up to him, and also began to climb up. Meanwhile, the archers who walked on the other walls of the castle also began to come up to the south wall.

The sight of the fire was truly stunning. It seemed as if a giant flower was opening its petals in the middle of the sea. The flames were rising so high that the ship itself could hardly be seen.

The guards at the north gate were also restless. "Shawan!" One of the guards shouted to the other, "Look!"

"I'm looking. Well, it is just fire. Big deal!"

"Look there!" the partner pointed to the tops of the towers illuminated by the fire. "All the men ran to the south wall. Yeah, they'll get a good look at everything there, and we…"

"They'll be hanged…"

"I told you; everyone ran. They won't hang everyone! Let's go after them!"

Abandoning their post, the guards of the north gate also climbed the wall and ran after the others. Glancing at the courtyard inside the castle, they saw servants and maids, cooks and grooms, coachmen and coopers, in short, all the inhabitants of the castle, running to the south wall."

Suddenly, one of the guards of the north gate named Evangelisto stopped. Shawan was already lost from his sight, merged with the crowd on the south wall. Who the hell stayed at their posts then? Evangelisto had very recently been flogged for drunkenness. The punishment was still fresh in his memory and vividly echoed on his butt. What was he thinking? Would he have to taste punishment again? Evangelisto frowned, took his pike more comfortably, and went back. Other guards were running towards him. The flames of the fire were reflected in their wide-open eyes. Some were so crazy that they pushed Evangelisto, who was interfering with their passage.

When he reached his post at the gate of the north tower, Evangelisto opened the door in the gate and looked out. The fire illuminated the city, the surrounding area, and the slopes of the hill on which the castle stood, but at the gate of the north tower, sheltered from the fire by the hill, the castle, and the tower itself, the glow was not visible. Wherever Evangelisto's eyes turned, there was darkness and not a soul anywhere.

Evangelisto crossed the bridge over the moat. Despite the noise of the fire and the screams that merged into a general hum, he did not hear anything suspicious. Evangelisto's hearing was good. He was able to guess by the sound how many horsemen were approaching the castle and in which direction they were going. By the creak of armor and the clang of weapons, he could also determine the number of troops that were making themselves known. In addition, if unknown people approached the gate, they would first be seen from afar by the guards on the tower, then met by the guards at the gate. Whoever approached the castle knew perfectly well that dozens of eyes were watching at that moment. The guards knew that too. None of them felt lonely, even when the pitch-black darkness descended on the city. No one was afraid, because everyone was holding the best weapons in their hands: pikes, swords, halberds, and crossbows.

Evangelisto walked to the northern slope of the hill and looked down. The flames of the fire flared up fiercely, probably something exploded in the hold, and in the light of this flash, he saw something incredible, and he experienced a horror he had never experienced before. Up the hill, through the streets and roads leading to the castle, an army was rushing at Evangelisto. The warriors did not run, but jumped forward, covering a distance of several fathoms with each jump. These people were half-naked, all their clothes and hats were made up of animal skins, and their helmets had feathers sticking out in different directions. They were already running up to the path that ran under the castle, encircling the entire hill. At the same time, they moved completely noiselessly. The whole army was rushing forward and at the same time, did not make a sound!

Evangelisto clumsily turned back to the bridge. He was rushing to the gate. The door in the gate had to be closed in time by all means! However, his armor and pike prevented it from being done quickly enough. Evangelisto was hit on the back with a monstrous force and, before he could reach the bridge, he was shoved into the moat.

The eagle and jaguar warriors, who had received clear orders from Ocotlan and Tupac, who, in turn, had been instructed by the duke, knew about this door in the gate. Evangelisto, coming out of this door, did not close it, and now the warriors rushed straight to it. Some moments passed, and then the north gate of the castle of St. George, the strongest of all strongholds in Portugal, the abode of the king, his nobles, and officials, were thrown open. The foreign army rushed inside with the speed of a mountain stream. None of them really knew what would be waiting for them there. Some of these eagles and jaguars were timid; they had never seen such huge stone houses in their lives, now illuminated by the flames of the massive fire in the distance.

Then the silence that this army had been protecting for so long was suddenly broken by a heart-rending scream. A sleepy laundress, who did not yet know about the fire, but went out to the yard for another need, screamed at the sight of the eagles and jaguars. The strangers rushed to the unfortunate woman. With one wave of a club with obsidian blades, she fell to the ground dead. But her cry had been heard. The laundress's husband, an old sergeant of the royal guard meant to retire the next week, spewing curses, was hurrying after the distraught guards to disperse the sentries to their posts but heard the scream and rushed back. At the sight of the foreigners, he immediately rushed to the south wall.

"Alarm! Alarm, you rascals!" he shouted. The sergeant didn't have time to run far. He didn't survive his wife by a minute, but the sergeant's alarm had been heard.

"Men, alarm!" A young soldier shouted as he ran along the edge of the southern wall towards a cluster of sentries who had thoughtlessly abandoned their posts. "We've been attacked! To arms!" Meanwhile, the warriors ruthlessly dealt with other inhabitants of the castle. They found them in the courtyard, in servants' dwellings, workshops, guard rooms, and other houses. The warriors, sometimes in threes or sometimes even in tens, rushed at everyone and did not give anyone a single chance to survive.

Soon, arrows began to fly from the walls at the eagles and jaguars. The guards who had come to their senses ran out into the courtyard and engaged in battle there. There were few of them, but they knew the castle well, and now the strangers were falling under the swings of their swords. Here and there they began to retreat. Finally, the commander of a small detachment left behind by the departed garrison ran out of the barracks. Without looking, he fired a crossbow into the darkness in front of him, dropped that, and drew his sword. "Attack!" he shouted to the sleepy soldiers in the barracks who were already grabbing weapons.

A terrible life-and-death battle ensued in the courtyard. Arrows fired by the newcomers' bows hit the Portuguese armor now and then without harming them.

However, the warriors, using their special shoes, were able to jump up and forward, each time successfully hitting soldiers who were petrified at the sight of such a miracle. These strangers were learning literally on the fly. They no longer fired at the armor, nor did they hit the soldiers with their terrible clubs. No, they aimed at necks and faces, and their blows were crushing. Portuguese soldiers fell one by one on the cobblestones that paved the courtyard. Blood was already flowing down it in streams.

Coatl, Ocotlan, Duke de Braganza, Nuno, and Anacaona were among those who broke into the castle through the north gate and were the last to enter. "Close the gate immediately!" The duke shouted. "Nuno! What are you standing still for?! Help!" Without waiting for an answer from the dumbfounded Nuno, the duke himself grabbed the gate. The other door was immediately closed by some vigilant jaguar. With the help of Nuno, the duke showed Tupac, who arrived just in time, how the gate could be locked. Then he ordered the gates to be filled up from the inside with the stones, boulders, and logs that were stored right at hand. By order of the duke, Tupac sent detachments of his warriors to another gate, ordering them to do the same with that one.

Soon, the bodies of almost all the last defenders of the castle lay in the courtyard. Guards armed with bows still continued to shoot at the strangers from the walls, but there were already only a few of them left. Some of the sentries who had gone down to the courtyard got involved in the battle and died there. Five jaguars, who noticed where the sentries were coming from, opened the door of the tower and rushed up to the walls. Soon the last defenders of the castle were falling from the walls lifeless.

The warriors, gradually lowering their weapons, began to look around. Some averted their eyes from the castle tower and walls, and then looked at them again, unable to believe what they were seeing. They had seen pyramids in their homeland, but still, the gigantic structures here, which served as a haven for the tlatoani of the local metstli tlapalli, were greatly superior to their pyramids.

Coatl, too, was beginning to realize that even the hundreds of handpicked eagles and jaguars he had brought here would be too small an army to hold this huge city or even the palace itself. So, it was necessary to quickly do what they came here for and return to Tlaluacatli. Soon the other squad would come here, the one the metstli tlapalli in black ichkahuipilli had spoken about before, and there would be many more warriors in this detachment than the already defeated defenders of this city.

At that time, Coatl did not yet know how true his guesses were. Indeed, a garrison under the command of General Afonso was already nearing the city. The huge detachment of the general was tired from the trek from Evora to Lisbon, and his soldiers were continuing on with the last of their strength, but there were hundreds of them, so they could still take on an enemy at a moment's notice. However, none of them, including Afonso, knew that the castle had been captured.

* * *

Today, Duke Fernando de Braganza had been incredibly lucky. The guards guarding the entrance to the tower of the royal residence, hearing the heart-rending screams of those fighting with the warriors, had rushed to the aid of their brothers-in-arms, and now the way to the king's chambers was open. All that was necessary was to climb to the top of the tower where the king was, and now, the duke was making exactly this ascent. The duke knew St. George's

Castle very well. He had visited many times, had gone through all the corridors and stairs in his time, spent days there at meetings with kings and his nobles, and nights at feasts.

Following the duke, at the head of a detachment of eagles and jaguars, Coatl and Ocotlan burst into the open doors of the royal residence. Nuno was running after them, holding Anacaona's hand. They raced up, almost overtaking the duke. They were all in a hurry because they realized that they themselves were now in danger and therefore, must return to Tlaluacatli as soon as possible.

On the stairs of one of the intermediate floors, the way was blocked by two guards who had remained faithful to their duty and stayed to protect the king in the upper reaches of the tower. With their pikes in front of them, they rushed at the strangers, but the warriors, as they had done more than once that night, used a completely unexpected technique; they jumped up to the high ceilings and fell on them from above. Their attack brought success. The lifeless bodies of the guards remained lying on the floor, and the duke and his companions continued their way – first along the corridor, and then up the stairs.

The duke was no longer young, and the armor, which he had not taken off, created additional difficulty for him. Yet now he felt neither the weight of years nor the weight of the armor. He ran and ran forward, panting with joyful certainty. Now his dream would come true! The king would be brought to submission of the Cortes or be destroyed! Once he reached the bedchamber door, the duke did not stop. Knowing that this door opened inward, he threw his whole body at it. The door swung open. After running in a few more steps, the duke found himself in the center of the luxurious royal chambers. Coatl and Ocotlan followed the duke, as well as Nuno and Anacaona. The room was dark and quiet. The spacious bedroom was only illuminated by the flashes of the distant fire. Nuno returned to the entrance of the bedroom and brought in a torch that burned steadily.

* * *

Daniel woke up to a clamor, which he immediately recognized as the sounds of a fierce battle. Strange exclamations, which even Moors did not make, accompanied the noise, and it certainly wasn't Portuguese soldiers who were shouting; Daniel knew their battle cries well. Daniel jumped out of bed and rushed to the window. A fire was burning somewhere far away. Below, in the courtyard of the castle, the battle was raging. The guards of the castle were fighting off a lot of people whom Daniel recognized with horror – the tribesmen of the very prisoner who had recently been captured by his soldiers on the shore of the Big Turtle.

Estela ran out of the next room. Like Daniel, she was wearing a nightgown, "Father, what's going on there?"

As if in response to Estela, the trampling of sabatons and the cursing of guards running down the corridor were heard outside the door. The sound continued down the stairs toward the first floor.

"What's going on?!" Estela raised her voice.

"I don't know yet," Daniel exclaimed, "but either this guard doesn't know how to fight, or their commanders have already been killed."

"Who are they fighting with?"

"I don't know!" Daniel shouted louder. "I don't understand what is happening. Even if the castle were attacked by Moors or rebels, their army could not have approached unnoticed. Even as they arrived, they would have begun a siege of the castle first, but there has been no siege, that's clear, and there's a big fire somewhere. It seems to be in the direction of the river."

Someone ran past Daniel's door in the opposite direction. Judging by the creaking and rattling, there were several people, one in armor and others wearing a lot of small jewelry. Daniel hugged his daughter and sat down with her. The noise receded towards the stairs, which began at the end of the corridor and led up. Daniel opened the door a crack and looked out into the corridor.

"Father, don't go there!" Estela, usually obstinate and self–willed, pleaded. "If the castle was attacked, then…"

The guardroom the guards had abandoned was not far away. Daniel rushed there and saw open cabinets with weapons. Daniel grabbed two muskets and a sword and returned to Estela. At that moment, there was a crash from above. Daniel would have been glad not to trust his instincts, but he already knew the reason for the noise, someone had broken into the king's bedroom. Judging by the way Estela screamed, she understood it too.

Was the King in danger? Daniel walked over to the lamp flickering on a table in the corner of the room and examined the muskets. They were loaded. "Estela!" he said sternly. "Pick up a musket. You may have to fire it."

Estela resolutely took the musket in her hands. "Raise the muzzle to the ceiling," Daniel said, and Estela raised her musket. "Look…" Daniel pulled back the trigger "Your musket is armed. All you have to do is point the musket at the enemy and pull here…" Daniel put his finger on the trigger, "but God forbid you to pull on it earlier. Do you hear?"

"Yes, Father."

"Take your finger away. Like that. Put it in this place only when you have to shoot. Now let's go." Daniel cautiously looked out of the room into the corridor. There was no one there. Meanwhile, incomprehensible noises were coming from the king's bedroom.

Estela suddenly remembered how recently she and Nuno were riding to the Big Turtle Hill on the coast, and Nuno was telling her that his father wanted him to learn how to shoot. Then, Estela had secretly laughed at him. How could she have imagined that she herself would need this skill so soon?

Daniel stood where he was, listening to the noises in the royal bedroom and in the courtyard. He thought painfully. What should they do? Their rooms were in the middle of a corridor between two staircases. If they went out into the corridor, they would not be able to hide, since the corridor was long and narrow. Even if they managed to hit the enemy with the muskets, it still would not mean salvation. Other intruders could have followed, but who the hell were they?

Daniel returned to the room, went to the window, and looked out into the courtyard, too high. To jump out of here would result in crashing on the cobblestones, or at least breaking legs. It would not be possible to escape in this way anyway. Daniel remembered the creaking of the gate, which he heard as soon as he woke up. The gates were closed. There was no way out of the castle. Had the castle been captured by the very rebels mentioned in the King's message? In the very message that sent Daniel to Leandro's house to capture Duke de Braganza? So, could these men be the duke's accomplices? If so, then he and Estela, the captain who killed the duke at the Sinta estate and his daughter, would not be left alive by the rebels. What else could they do? For Estela's sake, Daniel should hide in the rooms reserved for him and his daughter, sit there quietly, and pray, but duty commanded Daniel to go to the king's defense. Daniel was reminded of this again by the sounds coming from above. He must come to the defense of Joao II! The whole city should know about the battle in the castle by now! Help must be hurrying to the castle!

* * *

The king woke up as someone grabbed him by the front of his shirt and pressed him against the wall. In the semi-darkness, the king could not see anything, and the wine he had drunk the day before continued to spin his head and muddle his mind. The king rubbed his eyes and shook his head. He was finally able to somewhat make out the people who were surrounding him now. They were half-naked swarthy men, dressed in capes made of feathers and animal skins. In their hands, they held strange-looking clubs, with some glittering plates on the edges. One of them was taller than the others by two heads, and his chest, covered with tattoos, was like a barrel. Next to him stood the other half-naked man in a headdress decorated with feathers that resembled the tail of a peacock. Closest to the king was a man in black armor, painted with gold, that gleamed in the light of the torch.

"You thought you'd play your father?" he asked. The king immediately recognized him.

"De Braganza..." he muttered.

"You're finally in my hands! Oh, how many times I have dreamed of this meeting! You sent men to find me, didn't you? Well, here I am, in front of you! Aren't you happy to see me, Joao? Or are you? I'm asking you, coxcomb!" With these words, the duke shook the king once more. The King began to guess that this was not a dream.

"Captain Daniel killed you," the king said slowly.

Hearing the king's answer, Nuno shuddered. So, the duke was right. His parents were killed by order of the king. Nuno felt his hands itching. Now he wanted to take this bastard out of the duke's hands and start beating him against the wall himself, knocking him to the floor, and finishing him off completely!

Ocotlan looked at Coatl. The priest caught the look and responded with a smile. Everything was going as planned. One tlatoani was going to kill the other, but it should have ended sooner. Otherwise, who knows how many more metstli tlapalli were en route to this huge stone house.

The duke grabbed the king by the collar and led him out onto the balcony. "Look over there!" he shouted, pointing to the mouth of the Tagus River. The short May night was coming to an end. In the predawn twilight, the king, looking across the water, could not miss the giant ship moving straight toward the port. The ship was so huge that the houses near the port seemed like dice next to it. The king had never seen anything like it. It occurred to him that everything that was happening to him could still be a dream. He pinched himself, but the ship didn't disappear. Moreover, in the courtyard of the castle, the king could see a lot of savages, whose attire consisted of tufts of feathers, animal skins, and gold chains. In their hands, they held primitive pikes, clubs, and bows.

"Do you know how many cannons there are on that ship?" The duke shouted, pointing again at the giant ship with an incomprehensible pyramid in the middle.

Nuno was surprised. What kind of cannons could there be on the ship?

"Look, look well!" The duke continued to shout, pointing towards the river. "I have only to give the order, and this ship will blow the whole of Lisbon to pieces with just one volley, with a single shot from all the cannons, and all that will be left of your castle is a pile of sand. You won't survive either because you'll end up in hell!" The duke treated him, the king, with such rudeness that Joao still believed that everything happening to him was a nightmare. No one had ever allowed themselves to talk to him like that, much less grab him by his clothes.

Ocotlan and Coatl exchanged glances again. Yes, they had to get back as soon as possible. Many warriors had already managed to get hold of the metstli tlapalli's weapons made of the unknown precious metal during the battle. It remained only to outfit each warrior with one, and to do this, it would be necessary to take all the other iron macuahuitl and their strange bows attached to sticks from this big stone house.

"What do you want from me, de Braganza?" – the king muttered.

"Yes, now you are talking! You must sign this! The duke pulled out a scroll tied with a white ribbon from the depths of his armor and shook it in front of the king's face. Coatl immediately recognized this ribbon, which he had been looking for and could not find before he went ashore. What a scoundrel this metstli tlapalli was! He stole this ribbon from him, from a tlatoani, to whom he was supposed to pay tribute!

"What is it?" the king asked.

The duke released the king, unfolded the scroll, and held it up to Joao's face. "This is the law of the Cortes. The law that will transfer the power of the king to the Cortes of Portugal. The law for the introduction of a real parliamentary republic in the country! You will sign this law, and from now on you will ask the Cortes for consent for every step you take if it concerns the affairs of the state. Is that clear?"

The king was silent and looked with horror at de Braganza's face.

"I'm asking. Do you understand? Or should I throw you off the balcony? In that case, I will sign this paper myself and will tell everyone that the signature is yours. Then, according to the new law, we will choose a new king for Portugal who is more accommodating."

The king did not answer and only looked from the paper in the duke's hand to his companions, then to the giant ship equipped with a thousand cannons and the savages behind the duke. Either the king's dream had turned into a terrible reality, or, on the contrary, reality had transformed into a terrible dream.

The duke thought, "Now the king will do what he is ordered to do. He will sign this law, or the King of Portugal will have to be killed." Suddenly, the duke noticed, the king's lips parted with a smile that was painfully familiar to him. That hereditary smile that the duke had also seen on the lips of Afonso V at those moments when the late king had made fatal decisions. What could it mean? The duke began to consider that somehow, he had possibly made a big mistake.

* * *

Young Ocotlan rushed straight from the coastal bushes into the narrow bed of a fast river and immediately surfaced on the other bank. The force of his dive was such that the river never had the chance to carry him downstream. After getting ashore, Ocotlan went deeper into the jungle and then slowed down a little. His pursuers had to catch up with him, although half of them were already floating down the river, immobilized by poisoned darts.

After running away from the river for a decent distance, Ocotlan finally stopped. The dozen warriors running after him also stopped in surprise. The enemies pointed spears at him. "Be-Na-Za!" Ocotlan shouted as he raised his arm bent at the elbow with his fingers spread out to chest level. Only the Zapotec people greeted each other like that. Then Ocotlan tore off his wet cape and turned his bare thigh to the pursuers. A brand was burned on it, the image of Cociyo, the teotl of rain and lightning. The warriors who had caught up with Ocotlan exchanged glances. There was fright in their eyes. Only members of the tlatoani family had such markings on their bodies.

"I am Ocotlan, of the altepetl of the city of Cuilapan," Ocotlan said. "I am helping our people in this war. Never, you hear, never will we be defeated, because it's me telling my father where and when the Aztlan warriors are going to march. That's why we always beat them, or we manage to get away from them. Look around! You've already lost half of your friends."

The warriors looked around. Only now did they notice that half of their squad had disappeared. "Your friends will become slaves. They won't be killed, and then I will help them escape and return to their mothers and wives. We must take care of each other because the people of Aztlan have many warriors. We also need to have many warriors if we don't want to become part of Aztlan, pay tribute to them, or kill our people every twenty days at their damn festivals!"

The warriors lowered their spears. Some of them were missing one ear. This meant that they had already been captured by Aztlan's people before. "I saw you on the pyramid of Cuilapan," one of the warriors said. "I remember you and your mark. We're leaving. May Cociyo help you." He turned around and walked towards the river. The other warriors followed him. Ocotlan watched his fellow tribesmen go, covered himself with his loincloth again, and walked in the other direction.

* * *

Coatl squinted at Nuno and Anacaona and whispered, "Ocotlan, it's time to finish with these tlatoque." It was an order. At that moment, Ocotlan was supposed to run up to the duke and the king, who were standing on the balcony, and throw them over. If they survived, Ocotlan would have to finish them on the ground. It would be necessary to finish off everyone because it would be dangerous to capture these foreign tlatoque and their people. Who knew what might come into their heads if they were all left together inside this big stone house?

That was the plan of the cunning Coatl, but Ocotlan had other intentions.

As long as Ocotlan could remember, and there were so many times his family had told him the stories, his people had always fought with Aztlan. He had found himself in Tlaluacatli by accident. His intention was to visit the lands of the Totonac tribes in order to meet the altepetls of the conquered cities and tell them that the Zapotec tribes did not submit to Aztlan and to continue to fight that insatiable monster. He wanted to tell the Totonac people they could run to the Zapotecs and join the fight. When Ocotlan received an invitation from Coatl, tlatoani of Tlaluacatli, and agreed to serve there, he did not yet know that Tlaluacatli was not a city, but a large bamboo boat. So, Ocotlan turned out to be a captive of Tlaluacatli, a floating city into the unknown. He dared not refuse the opportunity Coatl had given him; it would be beneath his dignity, and besides, it could arouse suspicion in his enemies.

However, recently, when Ocotlan found the weapon of the first captive from Uehkatlan, the distant land, he realized that he had no reason to regret what had happened, because with such a weapon, if it should end up in the hands of the Zapotecs, they would not only be able to continue the fight against Aztlan, but to win and achieve peace! Camaxtli's story had now been added to this discovery.

Coatl had become tlatoani of Tlaluacatli malevolently which meant he had betrayed the weyitlatoani of Tenochtitlan. Therefore, when he, Ocotlan, finally deposed Coatl, he himself would become the tlatoani of Tlaluacatli, and in the eyes of the weyitlatoani of Tenochtitlan, he would become a hero who overturned an illegal tlatoani, liar, and killer. This already opened up new opportunities for promotion in the main city of a huge country, where he could be even better informed about the military plans of the weyitlatoani Axayacatl.

For the past several days, Ocotlan had been concerned about how to find and capture more metstli tlapalli who knew how to mine the unknown metal and make their weapons so he could transport them to Tlaluacatli. As for Tlaluacatli's return to the homeland, there was no need to worry about that. Tlaluacatli would be in the safe hands of Camaxtli. When the duke himself had offered them weapons as well as an excuse to drag Coatl to the unknown shore of metstli tlapalli, Ocotlan had thanked Huitzilopochtli profoundly for all these gifts.

At the moment when Coatl gave the order to kill the two tlatoani disputants, Ocotlan was prepared to hit the priest with a deadly blow with obsidian claws that were inserted into the glove on his hand, but just as he was about to attack, thunder rang out.

Anacaona screamed in fear and squeezed her eyes shut, and then the deafening thunder rang out again and again. In surprise, Ocotlan crouched down and covered his head with his hands folded over his jaguar fang helmet. Coatl's body fell next to Ocotlan. The priest's head had become a mess of hair, feathers, and blood. Another body fell down behind Ocotlan. Ocotlan raised his head and saw that the duke was looking at the other tlatoani, with the man's shirt still grasped in his fist, with such eyes as if he were looking through the other's head at the wall. Life was draining from the duke's eyes. Ocotlan noticed the opponent's shirt was now covered in blood. Suddenly the body of the duke, clad in his armor, swayed, and fell with a metallic crash, pinning the king. A stream of blood gushed from the throat of the murdered man.

Even the king's servants, who helped him ready for bed did not know about the secret that the monarch went to bed with every night. At one time, the Pope had given his father a gift, a manual mechanism that was invented by some brilliant craftsman from the Tuscan city of Vinci. Firearms of that time were outfitted with a smoldering wick and a manual mechanism activated by pressing a trigger. However, when the trigger was released on this invention, there was a piece of flint at the end of the cocked spring. This flint struck steel which created a spark that ignited the gunpowder. A shot rang out. This mechanism was only the size of a palm, and it was convenient to hide. It was a novelty that few people in Portugal knew about, or maybe no one at all, except King Afonso.

Before his death, King Afonso gave this manual mechanism to his son and taught him how to use it. Since then, Joao always went to bed, hanging this little mechanism from his elbow under his sleeve. He felt that sooner or later this weapon would be useful to him. Things had become very restless since his father had gone to God, and Joao himself had begun to feud with the nobles. Now, as the duke was strangling him, the king already had this mechanism in his hand ready, and only one thought kept him from shooting: what would the other insurgents gathered in his bedroom do to him after that?

Joao shifted his gaze from the giant ship to the south tower where three savages stood in clothes that made them look like huge birds, their figures illuminated by the bonfires burning in the courtyard. Joao wanted to shout at himself, "Hurry up! Make up your mind!" He looked at the duke again. How the king wanted to snatch that stupid scroll out of the duke's hand and shove it in his mouth! Did he really think that the King of Portugal, who had covered himself with glory on the battlefield, would now be afraid of this elderly idiot, especially at such cost? Joao looked at the other people in his bedroom. His gaze stopped at the doorway.

"Well, why are you turning your head, mongrel? What did I say that you didn't understand?" The duke growled, and Joao saw the barrels of two muskets appear in the doorway of his bedroom. Someone had come up the stairs and was now aiming at the people inside the bedroom. Two figures in nightshirts appeared behind the trunks. It was Daniel and Estela. They moved quietly; no one saw them because everyone was watching the duke and the king, who was to be thrown over the balcony or beg for mercy.

The King met Daniel's eyes. Of course, the Lord God himself, through the Pope and this lucky chance, would save the King of Portugal. Only now Daniel and his daughter were able to see those who were in the room. Daniel pointed Estela at a large, muscular savage, and he took aim at the man's neighbor with the luxurious feathered headdress.

"Great!" thought the king. "I'll shoot the duke, and they'll finish these two."

It was at this moment that the duke noticed that smile on the king's face. "This is how I will deal with your Cortes!" said the king, pulling the trigger. A shot rang out. The bullet entered the duke's head from below, through the throat.

* * *

After the meeting with the king, Pasqual and Chimalli stayed at the castle. The king had decided to keep Chimalli with him for the time being. He could be useful at the next meeting with the navigators. There was no point in putting him in prison; he had already shown himself to be a good-natured, easy-going, and reasonable person. Therefore, the king simply assigned Pascoal to Chimalli, who did not have to be asked twice. Both were given an entire barracks for the night which had been empty since the day the garrison left for the castle of Vila Viçosa in Evora.

In the middle of the night, Chimalli got up, sat down on a bedroll spread across a wooden bed, and thought. He was thirsty. Pascoal also stood up. Guessing about Chimalli's thirst, he handed him a jug of water, which was right on the table, and then pointed to the courtyard, where he could go relieve himself. It was dark in the barracks. A weak wind stirred the thick curtain on the window, allowing the light of the bonfires burning in the courtyard to penetrate into the room. Pascoal returned to his bed and was about to go back to sleep, but suddenly screams and the ringing of swords came from the courtyard.

Pascoal sat down again, put his feet on the floor, and thought. He was still poorly acquainted with the usual course of life in fortresses and castles. At this hour, his brethren, who inhabited the monastery, of course, were already leaving their rooms for their matins, but would the castle also hold exercises so early? Or else...

Then the door burst open and a man with a torch rushed into the barracks. Several more rushed in after him. All these half-naked people had capes, and their heads were protected by helmets made of animal skulls. Pascoal immediately realized from their attire that they were Chimalli's tribesmen.

"Tupac!" Chimalli exclaimed. He rushed to meet the warrior, and they embraced each other. Another warrior rushed to Pascoal, raising a club with plates shining on its end as he ran.

"Amo!" *No!* Chimalli shouted, "Kokaa amo yeuatl! Yeh kuauakpa ikniutli" *Don't hurt him! This is our friend!* The warrior lowered his club and looked back at Chimalli.

"Neh ikniutli!" *I'm your friend!* Pascoal confirmed, pressing his palms to his chest. He found the strength to smile.

The warriors looked in amazement at the strange metstli tlapalli who spoke their language. The precocious Pascoal had already figured everything out. These were the people that were fighting with the guards in the courtyard.

They must have entered the castle by stealth. Chimalli and the warrior who had broken into the barracks first, Pascoal noticing a tuft of hair tightly tied with a scarlet ribbon on his head, knew each other well. This warrior was saying something quickly to Chimalli, answering questions thrown at him. Pascoal managed to make out only three words in the warrior's speech, guessing they were names: Ocotlan, Coatl, and Anacaona. With this last name, Chimalli burst into tears and hugged the warrior who smiled and patted the old man on the back.

Leaving Chimalli and Pascoal, the warriors headed deep into the barracks, which, as Pascoal already knew, turned into a long corridor with numerous branches. "We need to find your tlatoani and mine," Chimalli told Pascoal. "My tlatoani will take me back to Tlaluacatli."

* * *

The long horseback ride had tired General Afonso so much that he was cursing that day and hour when he had sworn to his father he would become a military man, and the young soldiers, both mounted and on foot, who followed the general by hundreds, were also exhausted. However, when the stars in the dark blue sky were covered by the black silhouette of the tower, and St. George's Castle was no more than half a league away, the mood of the soldiers began to change. Many, encouraging themselves with curses, walked faster. Some, on the contrary, went limp. The shouts of the sergeants became more frequent and louder. The general only sighed and did not take his eyes off the cherished goal.

Suddenly he saw a flash in a window of the tower. Then came the muffled sound of a gunshot. What the hell? The general was wary. Then there was a second shot, a flash, then the sound. And a third! A third shot!

"Cavalry, follow me at a trot!" The general shouted. "Infantry, run! Keep up!"

"Run! Keep up!" The sergeants shouted behind him.

Some minutes had passed, and General Afonso's army was finally running towards the castle along the last and steepest stretch of road. The General was relieved to see that the gates were closed, but immediately realized that something was wrong!

There was a chilling noticeable absence of guards, whose silhouettes were usually visible on the wall and towers. The general's anxiety was reinforced by his adjutant, Diego, "Your Grace, do you smell burning?"

"Burning?" The general asked. His sense of smell had begun to fail him many years ago, but there was nothing surprising about a burning smell because bonfires were always lit in the castle at night.

"That's right! A pungent burning smell! It is not the castle bonfires; I can assure you! It's... it's coming from the port, I swear! There's smoke coming from there!"

"Okay, we will figure it out!" the general muttered. He was already approaching the gate. There were none of the guards who were supposed to be on duty outside at the entrance. "What's going on ..." the general began to think, but then an arrow hit the general's steel armor shell. Without hurting him, it jumped away. The General turned around. His squad was showered with arrows shot from the walls.

"Put your helmets on!" he shouted. "Spread out!" The commanders of the hundreds were already running up to the general. "Infantry squads! Secure the towers. Wait for attacks from both outside and inside the castle. Squads of archers! Secure the castle and wait for attacks. Cavalry, retreat to the Praça do Comércio and wait for my command there. Execute!"

"Rush to orders!" the commanders shouted at all voices, returning to their squads.

"Your Grace," Diego asked in amazement, "what is happening? Are we now besieging the king's castle after taking the castle of de Braganza with both our and Braganza's garrisons?"

"Don't you see? the castle has been captured!"

"By whom, excuse me, captured?"

"Those who shot at us from the wall captured the castle, fool!"

* * *

The charge fired from the musket threw Nuno against the wall, and the young man slid down by Anacaona's feet. The torch, which he had been holding in his hand, fell onto the carpet next to him. Anacaona, still stunned by the roar of the shot, rushed to Nuno and saw a terrible wound on his back. He was bleeding. Anacaona, who had been on more than one military campaign with her father, had never seen such terrible and large wounds. It could not have been inflicted by an arrow, spear, or even a macuahuitl with their deadly obsidian blades. Only a jaguar's paw could have delivered such a terrible and deep blow.

Anacaona guessed that this wound was related to the thunder she had heard. Turning to the source of the sound, she saw two people in long gray dresses. In their hands, they held some kind of long sticks, similar to the atlatl, the devices the warriors used to throw spears and darts to increase their firing power, but these people held them in a very different way than ordinary spearmen. Faint smoke hung in the air. What was it? What did they hit Nuno with? Didn't they hit him with something? Anacaona's nose smelled something new to her. It was a smell not found in nature. It didn't have the power that was in natural odors. In her imagination, this smell appeared dark gray, and the not-so-pretty image was riddled with sharp spikes.

"Nuno!" Anacaona turned to Nuno again. She pressed her fingers to the young man's neck and made sure that his heart was still pounding. After examining the large wound on his back, Anacaona immediately realized that no matter what had hit Nuno, he had to be bandaged to stop the blood. Suddenly, a vivid image of another new smell that she had felt in the forest the morning when she first found herself on Uehkatlan popped up in her mind. Fancy multicolored patterns painted with bright palettes of colors began to play in her imagination again, but one color, from the new palette, stood out notably in this bizarre pattern. She understood what could help Nuno heal his huge wound. She wasn't able to figure it out right away since she hadn't encountered these smells in the Aztlan jungle. Of course, how could she not know, because this was not a plant, but the bark of a tree that was not commonly found in the jungle where Anacaona grew up, but it was practically everywhere here on Uehkatlan. If she rubbed off this bark and mixed it with other medicinal herbs, then this wound would heal quickly!

Meanwhile, Ocotlan, deafened by the roar in the bedroom, slowly came to his senses. He had already realized that all his plans had gone to pieces. The man in the black metal ichkahuipilli, who had promised to give him the weapons, was dead. Another was struggling and squirming under him. It was the tlatoani the dead man had grabbed by the clothes and tried to strangle. Without thinking twice, Ocotlan rushed over, pulled the struggling man out from under the dead man, and pressed him against the wall, just as the murdered man had done. Unlike de Braganza, Ocotlan wanted nothing more than to strangle this tlatoani of this big stone house. And this time the king could not shoot. The mechanism was loaded with only one bullet, just like Daniel and Estela's muskets.

"Stop!" Daniel shouted. A moment ago, he was still looking at his daughter's petrified face, but Ocotlan's fuss over the bodies of the duke and the king brought him back to reality. After all, he had ordered Estela to shoot at the giant savage! Why did she shoot Nuno? "Stop now!" Daniel shouted again, looking at Ocotlan. Daniel dropped the useless musket and grabbed his sword with his right hand.

The king, whom Ocotlan was pressing against the wall with one hand, was wheezing but still trying to unclench the steel fingers of this giant. Ocotlan's other hand, in a glove equipped with obsidian blades, was raised above the king's head. However, now he had to choose whom to hit first, the tlatoani or this old man in funny clothes who held his steel macuahuitl in his hand.

"You bastard! Let His Majesty go!" Daniel shouted. He did not dare to strike the savage with a sword. Who knew if the savage might really kill the king with the last of his strength in response?

Ocotlan was not afraid of either man. However, he was tormented by the question of what killed Coatl and the young metstli tlapalli who already understood their language. What were those loud noises that had rendered him slightly deaf? Were they connected with the fact that both the young man and Coatl were now lying on the floor? But this was some kind of wonderful weapon if it was a weapon! Yes, yes! And Ocotlan and his people would need such weapons! Who could translate his demands into the language of metstli tlapalli, if the young man were to die?

Ocotlan saw several eagles running across the courtyard, breaking into the towers that led up to the castle walls as they were fitting arrows to their bows. Behind the wall, from the side of the city, a lot of soldiers in light metal ichkahuipilli were also rushing toward the tower while others sat on their big animals. Neither Ocotlan nor his warriors were afraid of these animals anymore. They had already met them more than once while running through the streets to this huge stone house on the hill, and they knew that these animals could be frightened by simply clapping hands in front of their muzzles, but there were a lot of these people riding animals, a myriad of them. Without a fight, it would not be possible to leave the city and get to Tlaluacatli. Ocotlan understood what kind of power these soldiers represented, and he was afraid of their weapons.

"I swear to the Virgin Mary, if you don't let the king go, I'll send you to the hell you came from right now!" Daniel shouted. He approached the balcony where Ocotlan held Joao II. Ocotlan turned around and Daniel swung his sword in front of the giant's nose, and suddenly Ocotlan realized what their salvation would be. As long as the weyitlatoani of Uehkatlan was in the hands of Ocotlan and his warriors, neither the people surrounding the castle nor this old man with a steel macuahuitl would dare to harm them.

Ocotlan opened his hand. The half-strangled king sank to the floor of the balcony and began to gulp air greedily.

"It's all your fault!" Estela shouted. She had only now come to her senses after what she did.

Anacaona turned around. Her face was distorted by a grimace of hatred. Anacaona recognized this girl who had come to Nuno's house and showed her the ribbon Tupac had lost. Anacaona realized she was the one who had just hurt Nuno.

"If you hadn't come to us, no one would have died here!" Estela screamed again. She threw her strange stick at Anacaona. Anacaona ducked. The stick flew over her head and hit the wall. "Damn you!" Estela hissed. She rushed at Anacaona, but Anacaona was quicker and easily dodged her hands. The games Anacaona had played since childhood were now helping her out. Estela slammed into the wall with her whole body and screamed, but immediately turned around and rushed at Anacaona again. This time, Estela got hit in the face, but she still managed to grab Anacaona's hair in her fists. Both girls fell to the floor, rolled out onto the stairs, and landed right at the feet of Chimalli and Tupac, who, together with the jaguars, were running up to the fray.

The jaguars tore Estela away from Anacaona and shoved her away, threatening her with their pikes. Other warriors rushed to Daniel and Joao and tied them up with harvested vines.

Anacaona and Chimalli hugged and cried. Chimalli took Anacaona's face in his hands and said the most tender words he was capable of. After she stopped crying, Anacaona took Chimalli by the hand, led him to Nuno, and pointed to the unconscious young man. Chimalli saw pain and grief in the girl's eyes. Chimalli understood everything.

* * *

"Your Grace," shouted Diego, "look!" General Afonso, who was fiercely inspecting his soldiers lined up in a chain on the way to the city, turned around.

The south gate of St. George's Castle was wide open. A crowd of half-naked dark-skinned people, richly decorated with feathers and capes made of animal skins, came through them. The crowd bristled with pikes and strange weapons resembling clubs. In the center of the crowd was a man in a nightgown. These savages pointed spears and nocked arrows at him. A knife was also held at the throat of the man. General Afonso was horrified to recognize King Joao II of Portugal as this prisoner. The group that led him was surrounded by a chain of other warriors whose heads were covered with helmets made of jaguar skulls.

"Lower your weapons!" Afonso commanded. "Everyone stand still! Let's let them pass." The soldiers lowered their swords, pikes, and crossbows. When the king was escorted past them, they bowed, then raised their heads and followed the procession with frightened glances. The townspeople who had managed to run to the castle behaved the same way.

The King saw Afonso and caught his eye. "They came on a ship with a thousand cannons!" the king shouted. "Their ship is in port on the Tagus! Let them through! Don't stop them from getting out of here!"

"Diego!" Afonso commanded. "Order our people to go ahead of them. Have them warn everyone they meet not to get involved in the fight. As long as the king is in their hands, we are powerless against them."

The crowd continued to march onward. Soon, the line of warriors of Aztlan entered the city center. Shouts and howls were heard as the townspeople recognized their king, in only his nightgown, in the center of the crowd descending to the port. No one could understand what was happening to him. It was clear the king was not walking of his own free will because a knife was held at his throat. Some of the townspeople recognized the savages who led the king as servants of hell. That was how they were depicted on the icons in the churches. Were they really devils, and were they taking the king away from them? Was this not the end of the world?!

Acting on impulse, many citizens threw everything they had at hand from the upper floors and roofs into the line of dark-skinned warriors: chairs, benches, flowerpots, tubs, and kitchen utensils. The bravest even poured the contents of night vessels on the strangers. From time to time the savages answered them with well-aimed shots from bows, after which the death cries of the unfortunate joined the noise of the procession, but the aliens did not allow themselves to be intimidated either. They let out war cries and shouts of victory, which were immediately echoed by all of the warriors.

When the warriors approached the Praça do Comércio, an elderly commoner ran out of the last alley and crashed into their crowd. She was armed with a sword taken from somewhere, but in the morning twilight, the savages failed to notice her weapon. Making her way to the king, she pushed aside the crowd of half-naked warriors with her body. Confused in their surprise, they gave way to her. Finally, the warriors tried to grab the woman by the arms, and she raised her sword over her head and struck the nearest warrior with it. He collapsed, bleeding profusely, and the blows of dozens of terrible clubs immediately fell on the woman. The body of the brave townswoman disappeared among the stream of feathers, skins, and animal skulls.

Finally, the crowd reached the center of Praça do Comércio located at the port where the garrison cavalry was stationed. The square was the gem of the city – spacious and fenced on three sides by two-story white houses with red-tiled roofs. These houses stood close to each other, forming walls. The first floors were occupied by shopping stalls, decorated with a series of low arches for access. The fourth, undeveloped side of the square harmoniously turned into a pier.

The cavalrymen hugged the necks of their horses, stood silently, and gritted their teeth. They had been ordered not to attack the warriors. Many of them, for fear of succumbing to temptation, hid their horses in the passages and now looked gloomily out of the arches. Aztlan's warriors, realizing their impunity, took weapons away from a few of the king's soldiers. One of the cavalrymen broke his crossbow in front of the warriors in order to keep it out of their hands and promptly paid for it with his life.

A whole fleet of boats was waiting for the warriors at the pier. The first several dozen boarded boats and went to their ship, which was at the mouth of the Tagus. At night, when landing on the shore, the boats had sailed several times from the ship to the shore, delivering new detachments of warriors, but now, no one waited for the return of the boats. The warriors began to seize the boats and small vessels of the townspeople.

The shouts, whistles, and hooting of the savages announced them to the port and its surroundings. Some of the fishermen and seafaring merchants, who did not want to part with their goods, tried to recapture their boats and longboats from the strangers, but they were all destined to fall in the unequal battle. The luckiest sailors were just thrown into the water.

The King was taken away in the last boat. It was rowed to the ship surrounded by a dozen other boats filled with warriors in bird feathers and Portuguese captives. The eyes of Joao, who was sitting in the boat, and General Afonso, who remained on the shore, met.

* * *

Nuno came to his senses and opened his eyes. Above him was a bright blue clear sky. A gusty wind, saturated with the smells of the sea, beat on the young man's face. Nuno's back hurt so much that he groaned. He tried to get up, but the pain was unbearable. Nuno lay down again. Where was he?

Overcoming the pain, Nuno turned his head and saw the pyramid. He was on the Tlaluacatli ship. Nuno looked along the base of the pyramid and saw that warriors were lying at the stern. There were so many of them, and they all seemed to be moaning. The bodies of the warriors were covered with bloody scabs. Among the injured warriors, there were people who offered them water and food, but almost all refused to eat. The faces of the unfortunate warriors were speckled with black spots. From time to time, people walking between the warriors picked up another lifeless body and threw it overboard. Those lying there had been struck by some unknown disease.

Nuno turned his head the other way. Anacaona was next to him. Nuno did not recognize her immediately because her face and hands, the entire surface of her body, were covered with black spots. These spots even concealed the tattoos on Anacaona's face. Her eyes were closed, but she was breathing. Nuno tried to get up again and again but could not do it. He looked at his side and saw that Anacaona was squeezing his hand. She must have grasped it before she fell into oblivion. Anacaona had been with Nuno every minute since he was shot in the back and lost consciousness at St. George's Castle. Nuno squeezed Anacaona's hand and she opened her eyes. A faint smile appeared on the girl's face. "Now you are my slave, Nuno!" she whispered. "I captured you."

"Tonatiu kuautik," Nuno replied. He started to laugh, but immediately stopped and coughed, the pain in his back immediately spreading throughout his body. Then a shadow fell across his face, and Nuno saw a young man in a brown monk's robe in front of him. He had blond hair and blue eyes.

"I don't believe my eyes!" The young man said with a smile. "Maybe I could become a good doctor, and then I could take out all sorts of pieces of iron and lead from people." With these words, the young man showed Nuno a large round bullet and laughed. Then he looked somewhere to the side and shouted in the foreign language that Nuno already understood, "Chimalli, he's alive! Examine him and bring the new ointment that Anacaona made. The wound heals very quickly."

Then the young man turned back to Nuno, "My name is Pascoal. I'll help you. Don't dare to die here. Our journey is just beginning!"

Historical Notes

After Axayacatl, the Aztec empire was ruled by both of his older brothers in turn. This time is considered the golden age of the heyday of the empire. The Zapotec civilization withstood a continuous struggle with the Aztec Empire and was conquered only by the conquistadors half a century later. The accuracy of the Mayan and Aztec calendars still causes admiration and controversy among historians and astronomers.

Duke Fernando II de Braganza was executed by order of Joao II on June 20, 1483, in the Vila Viçosa castle of the city of Evora. His title and possessions were confiscated, and the family fled to Castile. After the death of Joao II, his family returned to their homeland. Until now, the Braganza dynasty is the most famous in Portugal.

Joao II ruled until 1495 and died at the age of forty without leaving an heir. With his support, a large number of voyages were made, which many centuries later will be called the Age of Discovery.

Bartolomeu Dias was the first European to circumnavigate Africa and reach the Indian Ocean in 1488. Ten years later, in 1498, his countryman Vasco da Gama will make the first sea crossing from Europe to India in the world. Vasco da Gama's flagship on his third trip to India will be the Santa Catarina carrack, already built at Portuguese shipyards in India.

Joao II will refuse to support Christopher Columbus's voyage to the West, who will soon after move from Portugal to Castile. There Christopher Columbus enlisted the support of Queen Isabella I and discovered America in 1492 under the flag of Castile. Ironically, on the way from the newly discovered lands back to Castile, his first stop will be the port of Lisbon, where he will meet Joao II again and personally tell him that he had reached India.

The fact that this is not India, but America, humanity will find out 10 years later, in 1502, when another great navigator from Florence, Amerigo Vespucci, with the help of Columbus' maps and on Portuguese ships, will study the east coast of modern South America and prove that this is not India, but a new continent. Twenty years after that, the Aztec Empire will cease to exist.

Keywords

Altepetl (pl. altepeme) – an ethno–territorial unit in a state ruled by its own dynasty. As a rule, altepetl was a city-state or a land plot as part of a larger state entity. Altepetl had to pay tax to the state of which he was a member and obey its laws. He could also deliver goods to the single market without paying a duty, and trade in all cities that were part of the common state.

Amatl – paper.

Atlatl (pl atlatls) – a spear-thrower.

Amotlaxtlauas – the name of the Caribbean islands in the book.

Aztlan – in the book, the name of a region corresponds to today's understanding of the Aztec Empire.

Calmecac (pl calmecacs) – a school for the upper class. The sciences that were studied in it differed from the telpochcallin, since calmecac provided knowledge on the management of certain branches of the state.

Chinampa (pl chinampas) – man-made floating gardens.

Cihuacoatl – the weyitlatoani's chief assistant. In the book is the assistant of any tlatoani.

Cihuatlatoani – a female official weyitlatoani, tlatoani or cihuacoatl.

Cuauhocelotl – the title of a warrior who captured four captives in battle.

Estli ahkopechtli – the name of the altar in the book which
translates as "blood table."

Festival – in the book is a religious celebration of the
Mexihkah tribes, accompanied by human sacrifices.

The Fire Festival (Fire Ceremony) – a festival in honor of
Xuihpohualli.

Huey Teocalli – a huge religious complex that included
pyramids, statues, and other structures in the center of
Tenochtitlan; It is no longer in existence.

Huitzilopochtli – one of the main divine mythical creatures
of the peoples of Mesoamerica.

Ichkahuipilli – armor made of fabric and impregnated with a
special solution. They were able to withstand the impact
of the macuahuitl and atlatl. Depending on the rank of
the warrior, they had a different cut and color. Some
armor covered the torso and legs to the knees.
Ichkahuipilli resembled European quilting, and in
strength was not inferior to chain mail.

Itza – in the book, representatives of the Maya civilization,
which by the time of the events described had ceased to
exist as a centralized state.

Ixiptlatli (pl ixiptlatli) – a person chosen for the ritual
ceremony of the festival in honor of Tezcatlipoca.

Iztli Koyotl – in the book, the tribes who lived north of
Aztlan in the territory of today's USA. Perhaps they had a
single leadership.

Macehualli (pl Macehualtin) – a commoner.

Macuahuitl (pl Maccuahuimeh) – a weapon resembling a club or sword with several rows of blades or spikes made of obsidian.

Metstli (pl Metstin) – the moon.

Metstli tlapalli – the color of the moon. In the book, Aztecs use this nickname to refer to Europeans.

Mexihkah (Mexica) – 1) the tribes that formed the Aztec Empire; what the peoples called themselves at that time. 2) In the book, the language of the Mexihkah tribes, which today is known as Nahuatl.

Nahuatl – the language of the Mesoamerican people (Aztecs) and many other peoples who inhabited Mesoamerica. It is not known for certain what the representatives of the Mexihkah (Mexica) peoples called themselves and their language at that time, so in the book they call it Mexihkah, and not Nahuatl. Today, no more than two million people speak this language.

Nahui Ollin – a religious symbol denoting the cyclical nature of phenomena.

Ollamalitzli – a rubber ball game. The players were divided into two teams, whose task was to throw the ball into a suspended ring. The rules of the game did not allow hitting the ball with palms and feet.

Otomies – a high military rank that allows a warrior to command detachments of professional warriors such as the eagles and jaguars.

The Path – in the book, sometimes, it is a map drawn on amatl.

Patolli – a game for four participants, the winnings which
often consisted of the total contribution of all players.
On the field of this game, they threw beans (similar to
dice), moved the pieces, and the sum of the dots on the
beans indicated the number of moves. The player who
managed to collect all his pieces on a certain field first
was recognized as the winner. The game was a
combination of luck and strategy, according to which the
player himself chose which pieces to walk.

Pilli (pl pipiltin) – a nobleman or representative of the upper
class; this was usually the name given to high officials and
large landowners.

Pochtecatl (pl pochteca) – merchants and artisans. Usually,
they formed family enterprises, in which all family
members who performed certain duties worked together.
Men of this class moved goods from city to city, and their
wives helped to produce and sell these goods.

Quetzalcoatl – one of the main deities in the mythology of
the peoples of Mesoamerica.

Shorn ones – the highest military rank comparable to the
rank of general in the armies of Europe at that time.

Telpochcalli (pl telpochcallin) – a free school or center for
people of the low and middle classes, as education was
mandatory for all children.

Tenochtitlan – the city and capital of the Mexihkah tribes and
one of the three main cities of the Triple Alliance which
formed the Aztec Empire.

Teotl (pl teteo) - a Nahuatl term for sacredness or divinity
that is sometimes translated as "god." For the Aztecs teotl

was the metaphysical omnipresence upon which their religious philosophy was based.

Tepeyollotl – one of the main deities in the mythology of the peoples of Mesoamerica.

Texcoco – 1) a city, one of the three main cities of the Mexihkah tribes, which was part of the Triple Alliance; 2) a lake in the central area of Mesoamerica, around which the statehood of the Mexihkah tribes was formed. Currently, the lake does not exist, Mexico City is located in its place.

Tezcatlipoca – one of the main deities in the mythology of the peoples of Mesoamerica.

Ticitl (pl Ticiti) – a healer or a medic using both traditional and non–traditional methods of treatment.

Tlacochcalcatl – the chief military commander under weyitlatoani or tlatoani.

Tlacopan – one of the three main cities of the Mexihkah tribes, which was part of the Triple Alliance.

Tlaltecuitli – one of the main deities in the mythology of the peoples of Mesoamerica.

Tlaluacatli – the name of the Aztec ship-town in the book. The ship has the status of a town with its inherent administrative entities, functions, and positions. Therefore, the Aztecs call it a town, and the Europeans call it a ship.

Tlamani – the title of a warrior who captured one captive in battle.

Tlatoani (pl tlatoque) – the ruler of a region, city, or town.

Tonalpohualli – 1) is the ritual calendar of the peoples of
Mexihkah tribes; 2) is one year cycle of this calendar,
consisting of 260 days.

Tonatiu kuautik – a greeting in the book, which is
pronounced by one person and does not need a return
greeting. Usually, along with the greeting, the hand rises
to chest level with splayed fingers, indicating the sun.

Totonac – tribes who lived to the east of the Mexihkah tribes.
They lived on the coast of the Gulf of Mexico, as well as
on the lands of the ancient Olmec civilization.

Toxcatl – the name of the fifth month in the Xuihpohualli,
the eighteen–month calendar of the Mexihkah tribes.

Tozoztontli – the third month in the Xuihpohualli, the
eighteen-month calendar of the Mexihkah tribes. The
festival of the same name was held this month.

Triple Alliance – The cities of Tenochtitlan, Texcoco, and
Tlacopan, which formed the Aztec Empire

Tzompantli (pl tzompantlis) – a wooden stand or niche in the
wall, which was intended to display human skulls.

Uehkatlan – in the book "distant land" designates the landing
place of the Aztecs in Europe.

The Path of Huitzilopochtli – in the book denotes the East,
the side of the world where the Sun rises.

Weyitlatoani (weyi tlatoani; pl weyitlatoque) –the main ruler
of the state, in the book – the main ruler of Aztlan.

Winal – a twenty–day period, which was one month in the
calendar of the Maya tribes.

Xuihpohualli – the solar calendar of the Mexihkah, in which
there were 360 days and which once in 52 years coincided
with the ritual calendar of Tonalpohualli, in which there
were 260 days. This day was called the Fire Festival or
Fire Ceremony. In the book, it is also a compass for
determining paths.

Back Matter

Yuriy Chizhov - Literature language helper
Sherry Marshall - Proofreader and editor
Tatiana Kniazeva - Book cover art designer

https://www.facebook.com/redcityontheocean

www.ingramcontent.com/pod-product-compliance
Lightning Source LLC
Chambersburg PA
CBHW072052190726
48294CB00005B/1476